The Swaddling
Search for the Healing Cloth

P. H. Bray

malcolm down
PUBLISHING

First published 2024 by Malcolm Down Publishing Ltd

www.malcolmdown.co.uk
28 27 26 25 24 7 6 5 4 3 2 1

British Library Cataloguing in Publication Data
A catalogue record for this book is available from the British Library.

ISBN 978-1-915046-73-4
Cover design by Esther Kotecha

Art direction by Sarah Grace
Printed in the UK

Dedicated to

My beautiful grandchildren

To Gill

Enjoy the book

Phil ♥

[signature]

12/9/24

The First Gospel of the
INFANCY of JESUS CHRIST

~~~

The following accounts are found in the book of Joseph the High-Priest, called by some Caiaphas: …

CHAPTER III

And it came to pass, when the Lord Jesus was born at Bethlehem, a city of Judea in the time of Herod the King; the Magi (wise men) came from the East to Jerusalem, according to the prophecy of Zoroaster, and brought with them offerings: namely, gold, frankincense, and myrrh, and worshipped him, and offered to him their gifts. v2 Then the Lady Mary took one of his *Swaddling clothes* in which the infant was wrapped and gave it to them instead of a blessing, which they received from her as a most noble present…

Chapter One

Melody's decision to go was instant. The latest evidence pointed to it. She had to go. Her few close friends thought it reckless. But for Melody, the question on her mind was not if, but how. The complicated logistics of travelling into a hostile country and putting a team together was daunting. Since being a teenager, she had tried to ignore the visions that plagued her. But eventually, she resigned herself to finding *it*. She wanted to believe the visions, or episodes, as she often called them, would stop when she found it. It was an immense challenge and would probably take a year to plan. But if she was right, she would unearth an artefact that had laid dormant for two centuries, one so unique it had the mystical power to heal. But in the back of her mind, she was fully aware of how dangerous Iran was, especially for a British woman.

She was still considering the magnitude of the task when another one of her visions began. She staggered from the bathroom and headed for the safety of her bed as dizziness and a sense of despair overwhelmed her, clawing at her and pulling her down. So many times she had experienced this. Then the loss of sight would come and the darkness would envelop her, making her unaware she had even collapsed. Then, a beautiful peace fell on her like a warm comfort blanket…

Once again, Melody found herself in Bethlehem. The sky was cloudless, and the stars sparkled. Beneath it, a familiar scene played out. A scene she had witnessed in her visions so many times over the years, but this time it felt different. Everything looked the same and yet this time she wanted to stay, to explore. She was standing outside a small, white, flat-roofed house, its simple wooden door open, beckoning her in. As she moved inside, her eyes adjusted to the dim interior as she stooped to enter the back room. The babble of conversation became clearer. One voice was recognisable. It was Mary, her simple white tunic and apron contrasting with the expensive and elegant attire of the Magi. The fragrance from the oil lamp, along with frankincense and myrrh, filled the air. Woody and aromatic. She watched as Mary again presented the swaddling to the Magi. Her words were soft and comforting, drawing Melody in.

'Instead of a blessing,' she said, with a slight bow of her head, 'I present you with this gift.'

Melody wanted to stay, to linger a little longer. One of the Magi turned towards her, but the vision was fading. *Let me stay, don't stop, I want…*

Melody woke with a start. She glanced at the alarm clock; it was four o'clock, dawn had not yet broken.

Chapter Two

~~~

One student sitting in the front row wore a grey ill-fitting cardigan with leather patches on the elbows. He was waiting, poised, his notes neatly written in his Filofax notebook. He was prepared for the question-and-answer section, relishing the opportunity to challenge the tutor's interpretation. He had written her full name rather than 'Dr Thornton' and had underlined Melody. At the bottom of the page was a pencil sketch he had drawn of her.

'Does anyone have a burning question?' Melody asked.

He was the first to raise his arm. 'Dr Thornton, you named the seminar "The Supernatural and Myths in Science" and used Catherine Emmerich as an example.'

'Yes, she is one of several I used.'

'Surely someone of your standing cannot seriously believe that a nun who lived her entire life in Germany had visions that led to the unearthing of a house belonging to the Virgin Mary in Ephesus?' he asked, his face a picture of piety.

'Yes, I am. That is the point of this lecture. Did you not read the notes from my last lecture? To scoff at the supernatural and say it has no place in archaeology simply denies the evidence, especially in this case. Read "Mary's House" by Donald Carroll and the extraordinary story behind the discovery. They found the house where, in her later years, the Virgin Mary lived and died. They found it using only her visions.

Next question, please.'

'How do you counter the fact the Vatican has never officially recognised it as a miracle?' The same student was almost off his seat.

She avoided looking directly at him this time. 'Pope Pius XII initially declared the house a Holy Place. Pope John XXIII later made the declaration permanent, and Pope Benedict XVI visited the house in 2006 and treated it as a shrine.' She paused, desperately looking around for someone else to ask a question. She could feel it descending into an argument.

'Look, I am not here to tell you what to think about this particular discovery. I am simply asking you to keep an open mind. Treat the supernatural as a tool, like you would Ground-Penetrating Radar. Open your minds to any and every avenue of revelation.' She held up her arms. 'Thank you all for attending. For further reading, I suggest "The Complete Visions of Anne Catherine Emmerich" as recorded in the journals of Clemens Brentano and William Wesene. They're in my notes.'

As the students were leaving, one man who had been watching at the back of the room approached her. He was older than the students, clean-shaven and smiling. 'Hi Melody, well done today. They were a cynical bunch.'

'Hi Farrokh, I can understand their scepticism. Anyway, I'm glad you could come,' she said, kissing him on both cheeks. 'It's nice to see you and also to have a friendly face in the lecture hall. How are you?'

'I'm fine, but intrigued by why you wanted to see me. It sounded urgent.'

'I heard you were going back home. I was hoping you would stay in the UK.'

'It's time I went back. All my family are there, and the Government has offered me a post.'

'I wanted to ask a favour of you.'

'Certainly, if I can.'

'I need a sponsor from a national to visit Iran.'

'Visit Iran. Are you mad?'

'I know it's a big ask–'

'Mel, many Iranians live in fear of the Government there, even those working for them, no, *especially* those working in government departments.' He looked bemused, as though she had asked him to visit a war zone. 'Why on earth would you risk that?' He paused, his mind racing. 'Please tell me this isn't about the swaddling. You're not planning something crazy like a dig, surely?'

'I am determined to go Farrokh, and I'd rather do it through official channels.'

'Melody, please promise me you would never attempt to enter Iran illegally.'

'I have to go; I know it's there. Please, will you sponsor me? You are the only Iranian I know, with any credibility.'

He sighed. 'Mel, I can't believe you're asking me to do this, especially with sanctions in place. Look how long it took them to release Nazanin Zaghari-Ratcliffe on fake spying charges.' He took another moment, stroking his hairless chin and shaking his head.

'You must be crazy to consider it. Think about it, they sponsor Hamas?'

Melody said nothing but only looked up at him with pleading eyes.

He eventually sighed and said, 'I will, but reluctantly. And only because I'm concerned you may attempt to smuggle yourself in,' he raised an eyebrow, 'I also think it is highly unlikely they will give you a visa. The US and the UK are the main sponsors of the sanctions. And of course, you will also need a letter of recommendation from someone important, like an MP.'

'I'm going to ask Brodie,' Melody said, smiling as if it were a foregone conclusion.

'Good luck with that.'

Chapter Three

~

She was waiting in the anteroom outside the study of Associate Professor Broderick Kearney. He was a tutorial fellow of the School of Archaeology, specialising in the Persian Empire, at Magdalen College, Oxford. The smell of wood polish reminded her of a quip a fellow student made that the college seemed to be made almost entirely of stone and polished wood.

The large oak-panelled door opened and he stepped into the waiting room, wearing a tweed jacket and paisley cravat, his highly polished church shoes clicking on the block parquet flooring.

'Good morning, Dr Thornton,' he said, smiling and holding out his arms to greet her.

'Good to see you again, Brodie,' she said, standing. 'And less of the doctor's title.' She kissed him lightly on the cheek.

'Sorry Melody, I couldn't help it, but the title suits you. Come on through, I've ordered coffee for us.'

She followed him into his imposing study, noting it had not changed since she was last there. A high ornate ceiling, leaded windows, and an oak-panelled library. He gestured for her to sit whilst he settled into his worn vintage chair. 'You're looking well, Melody. How's your search for the swaddling going?'

'Straight to the point, as always, Brodie. It would be nice to chat for once. I might be here just to renew acquaintances,' she said, stroking her strawberry blonde ponytail.

There was a knock at the door. His secretary entered with a tray containing coffee and biscuits and left without speaking.

'It would flatter me if you were here just to chat,' he said, pouring coffee for them both. 'However, you have recently written two articles on relics, intimating accounts found in the book of Joseph, regarding the swaddling may have some legitimacy. You're hoping I will validate it.'

The Professor looked up from the cups and raised his eyebrows.

Melody tilted her head and shrugged.

'Milk and sugar?'

Melody relaxed, pleased she would not have to give a long update. 'Black, please,' she said, whilst leaning forward to pick up the fine china cup with her immaculately manicured hand. 'You're quite the detective.'

'What I can't figure out with you is what came first. Was it the religious connection or your interest in archaeology?'

'My grandmother, though I called her Mañana, was my greatest influence,' Melody looked down into her cup, knowing that Brodie was probably thinking about her parents too; her mother died when she was young and her dad had little interest in church. Shaking herself off, she locked back on Brodie and continued.

'She had a real and simple faith and would read stories from a children's Bible she'd bought me. The Nativity story was my favourite. I always had a warm fuzzy feeling when it said, "You shall find the infant wrapped in swaddling clothes and laid in a manger." It was such a lovely picture.' Melody closed her eyes and smiled. 'It was years later, when I was fifteen on a school trip to Egypt, that I became fascinated by archaeology. Now can we move on to why I'm here?'

He nodded and smoothed back his hair, flecks of grey showing through. 'Go on…'

She fumbled in her briefcase. 'I need a visa to visit Iran,' she said. Matter-of-factly, as though she had asked to visit America. She eventually

13

produced a map of Northern Iran and the Caspian Sea, unfolded it and smoothed it out on the table.

Brodie did not react. Instead, he leaned forward and picked up the map, noticing several small circles around the southern tip of the Caspian Sea. His face became serious as he spoke.

'Melody, the Middle East is an unstable region, particularly now. Iran is a dangerous country to be snooping around in. Heaven knows what they would make of a rich Oxford-educated daughter of a retired British Army Colonel. They could arrest you as a spy. We have so little influence there; we may never see you again.' He paused. 'Incidentally, does your father know of this?'

'I don't need my father's permission, Brodie. I'm almost thirty years old. I'm not a child and he's still not got over the disappointment of me not being a boy. Besides, the Caspian Sea is virtually a holiday destination for some.' Her shoulders sank. 'I need a letter of recommendation from a world-class college with a superb reputation in archaeology and a personage with high international esteem, preferably a professor.'

'Melody,' he began, 'The only sign the swaddling existed or indeed was ever presented to the Magi is in the discredited "First Gospel of the Infancy of Jesus". I cannot think of one respected theologian that gives any credence to these gnostic writings.'

'That doesn't mean they are wholly without merit. Besides, it's not just the writings.'

This time Brodie's shoulders sank. 'Look, all you have is a story, probably manufactured by a second-century Christian sect, supposedly written by the High-Priest Caiaphas and purporting to be a gospel. Which incidentally was rejected as heretical fiction. Luther even doubted James and Hebrews for emphasising "works" with faith, so he put them in the back of his Bible with Jude and Revelation and considered them uncertain.' He held up his hands.

'I see,' she said, frowning. 'Is this about the reputation of the college or about your reputation and only wanting to back a certainty or an odds-on favourite? Worried about what people will say about your reputation if I were to fail?'

'That's unfair, Melody, and you know it. I've stuck my neck out countless times. Who supported you when the college wanted to remove funding altogether for your research?'

'You've made your position clear, though I was hoping for a warmer response. Help me build a case–'

'Admit it,' he said, 'there isn't a preponderance of evidence, and what you have is unclear and unconvincing. Look, from what I know, the Gnostic Gospels saw no connection between Jesus and the nation of Israel or the acts of God in the Old Testament. Why have you remained so obsessed about the existence of the swaddling?'

'Obsessed! Listen to yourself. Even your language is negative. Think about it, in every nativity story you've ever heard, read or been part of as a child, you would have heard these words – "Wrapped him in swaddling cloths and laid him in a manger". There is no relic greater than this one. My quest, no, it's more than a quest. My *destiny* is to discover it.'

'Destiny?'

'Higher than that, perhaps more than destiny. I believe I have been chosen.' There was a pause; she continued to glare at him as she began collecting her maps, then stopped and looked up. 'Wasn't it Keats who said, "The two most important days in your life are the day you are born, and the day you find out why?" This is the reason, Brodie. This is why I was born.' She sighed, not letting a self-damning thought about her arrogance hold her back. 'I doubt you would understand, even if I told you.'

'Try me. I want to help, I do. Stay, please?'

Melody composed herself and stared hard at him. *He better mean it.* She put the maps back on the table.

'The story from the book of Joseph, which I read at fifteen, intrigued me because the Virgin Mary gave a piece of the swaddling cloth to the Magi. But then, I imagined I was holding it, draped over my hands, still warm. Then I heard Mary speaking to me. I didn't understand the language, but her words were soft and comforting. It's the reason I learned Hebrew and Persian.'

'Where were you at the time?'

'Boarding school. On the day I first read the "lost gospel" story, I had a strange experience.'

'What do you mean?'

'Later that evening, I had my first vision,' she said, swallowing and watching Brodie's eyebrows rise. 'A sense of utter despair gripped me. It was overwhelming. It seemed to claw at me, pulling me down. My eyes clouded over. I could barely breathe. Then a total loss of sight, leaving only darkness. I panicked. I thought I had gone blind. But then a peace overcame me, a serenity the like of which I had never experienced, and such joy welled up inside me.'

'How long did it last?'

'It felt like an age, and yet it was probably only a few minutes. Scenes began flashing in my mind. Most of the pictures made little sense, like clips from an old film, fuzzy and shaky, though the location was clearly the Middle East and in ancient times. Eventually, one scene unfolded crystal clear. A woman nursing a child reached down and opened a wooden box. She removed a strip of cloth and gave it to one man kneeling opposite saying, "Bimcom bracha, ani magishah lecha et hamatanah hazo".'

'Instead of a blessing, I present you with this gift,' Brodie said, translating from Hebrew.

'Yes. And it was the same voice – soft and comforting. Then it faded away. Oh, how I wanted to stay in that moment.'

'I see,' he said, sitting forward in his chair. 'Then what happened?'

'Unfortunately, a House Mistress began shaking me and asking if I was alright. A classmate had found me and thought I was having a fit.'

'And you believe Mary was the woman in your vision?'

'Yes! I know it sounds crazy, but I believe it was Mary and the gift was the swaddling?'

'Have you had any further experiences?'

'Yes, I've lost count now. There have been so many and all of them concern the swaddling, Mary and the Magi. Over several years, the visions have become clearer, longer and episodic, like watching a box set, sequentially.'

'Have you spoken to anyone about this?'

'You're the first person I've told, apart from the school doctor and my grandmother. Not even my father knows. I didn't want people to think I was going mad.' She paused for a moment. 'Recently, though, there's been a development. A transformation in the visions. It's difficult to explain. I'm no longer watching a film. I'm well...' Melody searched his face, looking for a flicker of empathy.

'You're what?'

'I'm transported into it. Look, I know it's hard to believe, but I am there with them.

Like, instead of watching a film, I am on the set. I'm an invisible onlooker,' she said, shaking her head, 'they sometimes walk through me, as though I were a ghost.'

Brodie was now taking notes. 'What period do they cover?'

Melody straightened her posture. *He seems to have softened his position. I need to fire both barrels now.* 'Chronologically, the visions have been as far back as Mary's betrothal to Joseph and as far forward as the Magi receiving the swaddling,' she smiled with the relief it was finally being shared.

'What did your doctor say, if you don't mind me asking?'

'He wanted to refer me to a psychiatrist or at least a psychotherapist and gave me medication to "relax me", she made air quotes with her fingers. 'But then I read about Catherine Emmerich and her visions in the book, Mary's House. It was such a release to know a nun from the sixteenth century had similar experiences. That was the moment I knew I wasn't mad.'

Brodie was nodding. 'I know the story has its critics, but I researched her work many years ago. I believe her stigmata was the clearest sign of her existential union with Mary. Are you also making a journal of your experiences?'

'Several so far.' She paused. 'I feel better for having told you. I can't explain why I have the visions, and mostly I wish they would stop, but I don't think they will until I discover the swaddling. It's the reason I have to continue the search. I won't give up Brodie, I have to go on.' She paused again. 'I don't expect many will understand, but I have to find the swaddling somehow. If you feel you cannot help, I'll ask my MP.'

'I see,' Brodie said, sitting back, pursing his lips and exhaling; he suddenly stood and paced the room. 'A discovery of this magnitude would certainly be significant, not only in terms of your reputation but also for the college.' He paused, deep in thought. 'It's not so much an evidential problem and now I understand better what's been driving you, I would say it's more of a practical one.' He took the map and smoothed it out.

'The Caspian Sea has so many borders: Russia, Azerbaijan and Turkmenistan, and to the south is Iran. I would regard none of these countries as stable or with high enough regards for women.' By now, he was pointing at the circles on the map. 'Why there Mel? What's the connection with the swaddling or the Magi? What are you not telling me?'

Melody realised this could be her one chance to win over any lingering scepticism. She took a deep breath. 'Do you remember Augustus Schmidt, the German Professor?'

'I met him once when I attended a fundraising event they invited me to at Yale,' he said, sitting down. 'He seemed a decent fellow.'

'His specialism is in the connections between archaeology and the Bible.' She paused and he nodded his acquiescence. 'Five years ago, Cardinal Poggi sought permission from the Pope to grant him exceptional access to the secret Vatican archives.'

Melody sat upright in her chair. 'Here's the interesting bit – on one of those days, he came across some non-catalogued manuscripts. In it was a letter from The Magi, Melchior to his wife, Paadini.'

'Did it confirm the account in the Lost Gospel?' he asked, nodding.

'Yes and crucially, Melchior wrote the letter after the visit of the three Magi to Bethlehem. He told her about the presentation of the swaddling to them by Mary and how later they discovered it had extraordinary powers to heal, possibly giving eternal life, and so, after considering the consequences of it getting into the wrong hands, they decided "to lay it up among their treasures".'

Brodie cut in, 'I presume in an area south of the Caspian Sea?'

'Previous searches have been around Bushehr on the Persian Gulf.' She moved back to the map. 'This letter spoke of the Valley of Ascendency being near Behshahr, on the South-Eastern coast of the Caspian Sea in Iran.' She paused. 'Brodie, I've been looking in the wrong place.'

Brodie digested this recent information. 'Unfortunately, though, it's only a hundred and fifty miles from Tehran, and to get a transit visa you would not only need a sponsor living in Iran, but tickets, hotel reservations and the production of a day-by-day itinerary.'

'I think I can manage all of that. Farrokh Mokri has agreed to be my sponsor.'

Brodie stood up again, pacing the room. 'Can I speak frankly, Mel?'

Oh, dear, is he excited or about to pull the rug? 'You know I still value your opinion.'

'Muslims in Iran will cover a wide spectrum of views in terms of the depth of their faith. There is a universally held view by most of them that poking around looking for Judeo-Christian artefacts is offensive and could possibly be interpreted by the State as blasphemy.'

He returned to his seat. 'Surrounding Iran are hostile or volatile countries. There is no straightforward way in or out, and the UK has little or no diplomatic relations. If anything were to go wrong, I doubt we could get you out. On the flip side, should you be successful? It would be an international game-changer?' He stroked back his hair as he paused again.

Melody could hear birdsong in the quad outside.

'If, after considering this, you still decide you want to go, then I will write in support, but I have a proviso which is non-negotiable. I know someone in anti-surveillance who can equip you better for this task. You must sign up for a course.'

'Agreed.' Melody said, exhaling.

Chapter Four

~~

Melody left the London Underground at Covent Garden and made her way to The Strand. She was looking for the office of 'Cherished Anti-Surveillance' at Savoy Hill. Her appointment was with Stuart Toulson, a so-called 'expert' in personal security and anti-surveillance techniques. It annoyed her she couldn't find her mobile phone; she thought she had it when she left home but couldn't find it on the train. *Maybe I left it at home, or perhaps in the taxi.* Ringing it from King's Cross Station, in case someone had found it, proved futile. It eventually went to voicemail.

Her expectation was a seedy office in some back street but she had to admit the reception waiting area for the private detective agency was impressive. The Art deco furniture looked as if it might have been by Eileen Gray.

A ceramic vase by Clarice Cliff sat in a glass case, and two paintings by the Polish artist Tamara de Lempick hung on either side. The efficient-looking receptionist broke into her thoughts. 'Mr Toulson will be down in a few minutes, Miss Thornton. Can I get you something to drink?'

'No, thank you,' she said, picking up the company's brochure. It targeted CEOs working in the oil industry in Africa and South America. She was not sure this was suitable for her or even necessary, but Brodie had insisted.

The lift door glided open almost silently, and a smartly dressed man stepped out and Melody stood to greet him.

'Good morning, Miss Thornton, I'm sorry to have kept you waiting.'

He talked whilst shaking her hand. 'Please call me Stuart. Do you mind if I call you Melody, surnames are so formal, don't you agree? I always feel I need to know my clients well if I am to keep them safe. Please follow me.'

Melody realised she had not spoken and they were already in the lift. Although in his early forties, he looked in good shape, tall and muscular. He spoke softly but quickly, and with such authority, his voice almost hypnotic.

They left the lift on the third floor and walked a short distance down a beautifully carpeted hallway with more impressive art hanging from the walls and the scent of lotus blossom in the air. They entered his large modern furnished office, and he gestured for her to sit on one of two low-backed, colourful designer armchairs.

'I understand you plan to travel in the Middle East, Melody and you wish to keep the reason for your visit a secret. Though secret is such a loaded word, don't you think? I prefer esoteric, it sounds more mysterious.' He was smiling, but his frankness had caught her off guard. She was about to speak when there was a knock at the door and a young man who seemed vaguely familiar entered with a small brown paper bag and a notepad. He handed it to Stuart without speaking and left; Stuart glanced at the items before placing them on his desk.

'Mr Toulson, I appreciate your time, but I think Brodie overstates the danger and I'm not a child. I am confident I can look after myself. I don't need anti-surveillance training.'

'Brodie said you may say something like that. Now, what I am about to tell you will have one of two effects. You will either storm out of the office indignant and we will never meet again - but only two per cent of people do this. Though actually, I hate statistics. They seem to prove whatever you want; don't you agree? Mark Twain put it perfectly when he said, "there are lies, damn lies and statistics". He leaned his head to one side. 'Alternatively, you will sign up for a three-day introductory course.' He walked over to his desk, glanced again at the notepad, and then continued.

'You rose at 0545 hours this morning and took a black cab to your local train station, where you purchased a return ticket for the 0710 to Kings Cross and a copy of the Daily Telegraph. As you were finding your seat, you bumped into a young man in the aisle who, unknown to you, stole your mobile phone. At Kings Cross, you made a call to your mobile from a public phone box, hoping someone had found it, but no one answered. You then visited Starbucks on the concourse and purchased a grande skinny latte before taking the tube to Covent Garden on the Piccadilly line.'

He opened the brown bag and handed over her iPhone. 'We have not interfered with it or added a tracker, nor have we collected any data from it, although my colleague could have carried out these simple tasks on the train before returning it to you without your knowledge.'

Melody took the phone, speechless.

'Now, the question for you is simple. Are you indignant or are you intrigued? Or to put another way, will you storm or will you stay?'

Chapter Five

~~~

The visa application clerk at the Iranian Embassy in London made a last check through his report and placed the papers in a folder. He swallowed hard, then made the short walk down the corridor and knocked on the commander's door, taking a deep breath before entering the anteroom. The secretary waved him through.

The commander was ending a conversation on the phone; he gestured for him to sit.

'Is that the Thornton file?' he said, putting the phone down.

'Yes, Commander,' he said, handing it over.

'Your initial conclusion?'

'Nothing alarming or of much interest to us.'

'Tell me about the people involved, then?' he asked whilst scanning through the basic application pages.

'Is there something in particular you're looking for, Commander?'

'I'm looking to see if you've done your job properly. Well?'

'Er, the applicant's father is James Joseph William Thornton. He's an investment banker and partner at Sturbridge, Thornton & Howe in the City of London. The family made its fortune in the confectionery business until his grandfather sold the business to a multinational. Well respected in the city, and has even carried out several unpaid advisory roles for the Government, in the Department for Business.'

'Is he still active with the Government?'

'No, Commander. That was with the previous administration, but he is a long-standing donor to the Conservative Party. What may be of some interest is having received a first in economics at Oxford, he followed in his grandfather's footsteps and went straight to Sandhurst Military Academy for officer training. He passed out with the "sword of honour" before joining the Black Watch, 3rd Battalion, Royal Regiment of Scotland, rising to the rank of colonel–'

'So, was he serving in the British Army at the time of the siege of our embassy in 1980?,' the Commander asked, showing a sudden interest.

'Yes, I suppose he was, Commander.'

'I see. I regard that as interesting. Don't you?'

'I assumed because he was in a Scottish Regiment, he–'

'What other theatres of operations was he involved in?'

'The Falklands in 1982.'

'And then?'

'He retired and joined the City firm of Sturbridge & Howe; later, he became a partner.'

'I want more detail regarding his time in the Army. Was he ever involved with the SAS or did he ever advise the Government on defence matters? I want to know if he had any connection, however small, with our embassy siege. Do you understand?'

'Yes, Sir.'

'Was he seconded to NATO at any point in his career?'

'I'm sorry Sir, I don't have that information,' he said, desperate to leave.

'Really? You haven't researched that?' He paused again. 'The letter of support?'

'Ah yes, Associate Professor Broderick Kearney, Tutorial Fellow of the School of Archaeology. His area of expertise is the Persian Empire, at Magdalen College, Oxford. He was her mentor during her university years and is also a friend of the family. He was at Eton with Melody's father.'

'If he specialises in the Persian Empire, he must have visited many of the countries that were part of the Empire, including Israel, Iraq, Egypt and least of all, Iran. I want to know which ones and how many times. Has he any contacts in Israel?' There was a long, silent pause. 'You said there was nothing alarming or of any interest to us. Do you stand by that?'

'No, Sir. I seem to have missed the connection.'

'I see.' He folded his arms and leaned back in his chair. 'What about the applicant's sponsor? Do you know anything of them?'

'Dr Farrokh Mokri is researching territorial waters in the Gulf on behalf of our government. He knows the applicant from his time at Oxford University, where they became friends and have kept in touch. No romantic involvement and no political involvement and he's certainly not on our radar. He now lives with his parents and two sisters in Tehran,' he said, undoing the top button of his shirt.

'Put a watch on them. Let's build up a profile. They could be useful.' The commander stood and spoke as he walked over to the window. How calm and unhurried the scene overlooking Hyde Park was. Nannies in their grey uniforms pushing babies in trollies, like a throwback to the 1950s; joggers, a few picnickers and keep-fit groups. 'And what of the applicant herself?'

'Dr Melody Charlotte Thornton. Her grandmother was Persian. When the Shah was overthrown, she fled from Iran with her husband, a diplomat, and both were Christians. Her mother died in a riding accident when she was a child. Her father did not re-marry. She attended Roedean boarding school at eleven, where she discovered a penchant for archaeology on a field trip to Egypt. Educated at Magdalen College, Oxford, she gained a double first, then a Doctorate in Archaeology and Anthropology. She now lectures on the subject; she is clever and well regarded by her peers having written several papers.'

'Rich and spoilt English girl,' the commander said whilst still looking out onto Hyde Park. 'I need more information regarding the reason for her visit. Why would she visit Iran? Are there any distant members of

26

her family still there? She can afford to go anywhere in the world. Why choose Iran? That's the question I need answering. There's something not quite as it seems here, and I sense an opportunity.' He turned to face the clerk. 'You're new here. Do you enjoy your posting to London?'

'Yes, Commander. My family has settled in well,' he said, stiffening.

'Then if you wish to remain here and not return to the Mother Country, I suggest a more thorough examination of any future applications before you submit a report to me. Next time, I expect a professional drilling down through the details. The kindest thing I can say about this report is it's amateurish. I am disappointed with you. Now, go.'

'Yes, Sir. I shall begin work on it now.' He nodded and made to leave.

'Approve her application,' he said, walking to his desk and picking up the phone.

Chapter Six

~~~

Nikolai Levanevsky lay quietly in his hospital bed. His arm ached where the cannula entered; with each drop of morphine, he sensed his life was slipping away. He looked longingly out of the large French windows. It was a grey day; the clouds scudded across the sky; the tree-lined shore of the Black Sea was deserted. Even the forested slopes of the mountains seemed cold and lifeless and yet, he would give anything to hunt there again, feel the breeze on his face, and smell the pine and damp undergrowth.

'Good morning, Mr Levanevsky. How are you this morning?'

It was one of the six nurses who attended him twenty-four hours a day. This, though, was his favourite. Probably because she grew up in the same town he had lived in.

'I feel like my life is fading away, Sasha.'

'Don't talk like that. Your friend Anatoly said you would keep fighting. You're a bruiser, he told me, who will fight to the end.'

'He was my friend. I was fond of him. We were remarkably close, but I hardly see him now. Not since he had a "religious experience". He was my counterbalance. I was pushy and single-minded. That's right, a bruiser. But Anatoly was a thinker, a numbers man. "The devil is in the detail", he would say, and he was usually right.'

'Did you grow up together?'

'Goodness no. My father was an engineer at the Moscow Tractor factory. He earned a small but living wage. We were poor but well-fed, an austere childhood... communal apartments.'

He was already tiring, his words being delivered in bite-size pieces, his breathing laboured. 'Only one room and that was a living room, dining room and bedroom for the entire family.'

'Wow. I thought my apartment was small with two bedrooms.'

'We shared the kitchen and bathroom on each floor. A fat, sweaty man was always in the kitchen cooking Cabbage Borscht... he stunk of cigarettes and stale vodka. Hated him, over-friendly.' He was trying hard to stay focused. 'Did I mention sharing rooms? The government called it "the new collective vision of the future". Forcing people to live in communes is what I called it. They took advantage of my dad... he was a good and kind man; I swore then – never again.'

'And Anatoly?'

'Privileged... academic Catholic family... Father called them the Intelligentsia. We met at university.'

He felt his eyes closing. He was falling into that familiar place between waking and sleeping, remembering an incident from childhood...

'Take off your shoes and put your school bag away. Your father wants to tell you something, Nikolai,' his mother said, trying to kiss him as he passed.

His dad was sitting in his favourite well-worn chair, grinning. Nikolai plonked himself down on the threadbare carpet next to him. 'They have elected me to be branch secretary of the Works Communist Party, and as a result, we will move to a three-bedroomed apartment with its own kitchen and bathroom so no more smelly neighbours.' His father said, laughing and ruffling Nikolai's hair.

It was an early lesson for Nikolai. Life was not about how hard you worked in Russia, but more about your position in the communist party that counted.

At fifteen, Nikolai joined the communist youth movement and befriended the local commissar. His advice was like gold nuggets. 'Nikolai, you are loyal and enthusiastic. You will go far in the communist party, providing you obey this one simple rule: only say in private what you would be happy to say in public. In the party, they are the same thing; remember the KGB watches and listens to everyone, including its leaders.'

Sasha's voice brought him back to semi-consciousness. 'You must tell me more about it on my next shift, your rise from rags to riches. I have to go now,' she said, placing the clipboard on the end of his bed. 'I'll see you tomorrow.'

Lying in his bed recounting his life again, it seemed like an old movie on a repeat loop – "rags to riches" Sasha had called it. Now his mind drifted back over his time at Moscow University, rags to riches... an early interview with the Vice-Chancellor...

'What makes you think you'll be suitable for the position of editor? After all, the university bulletin is political,' he had asked him.

'I have written several articles for the local communist press and even had a couple of letters printed in our official party newspaper, Pravda. Also, my father is the branch secretary of his works communist party and I learned a lot from him regarding the new collective way of living,' Nikolai said, 'The University Bulletin has a wide readership on the campus and is an ideal opportunity to counter some growing disquiet about our leaders.'

'There are many who think of you as a little too ambitious, and some even consider you ruthless.'

Savouring the opportunity to answer, he sat more upright. 'Speaking the truth often collects enemies, comrade. From your own steadfast leadership, you know being radical is not always popular.'

'Indeed, it isn't, Nikolai. I shall make my recommendation to the committee,' he said, winking.

Back in the dingy accommodation he shared, he considered the consequences of this plum appointment when Anatoly arrived.

'Well, how did it go? Did you get the post?' Anatoly asked.

'The VC is going to recommend me.' Nikolai said.

'I'm still not sure why you want the job, no pay, and you despise most of the university leadership.'

'You need to think strategically, Anatoly. Good looks and intellect won't make you successful. This will be a springboard into the party hierarchy. You must be on the inside to progress your career and change the system.'

'Change, yes, but for what purpose?'

'You want to change it for ideological reasons. I want to change it because this system keeps people like me poor. I want to be rich and powerful and that will not happen under the present regime and system. You cannot change it from the outside. Stick with me, Anatoly. I'm going on the inside and it will be a bumpy ride.'

Chapter Seven

~~

They called the three-day course 'Basic Security and Anti Surveillance Techniques.' Based, according to the preface, on the US Department of State, Diplomacy in Action Briefing.

Sospitas Retreat was an exclusive Manor House tucked away in the Hertfordshire countryside. They did not advertise, and they did not refer to themselves as a hotel and judging by the vetting process at the gatehouse, Melody realised they took security seriously. These were not ordinary security guards. They looked as though they would be more at home in the SAS or a Commando Unit.

'Your passport please, Miss. Then stand on the white line for the image recognition camera,' one of the guards said, not giving a hint of a smile.

She felt a nervous excitement as she drove down the mile-long drive. Lined with poplar trees and surrounded by beautifully manicured grounds, it led to a rather imposing Baroque-style mansion. *Maybe Brodie was right. I've bitten off more than I can chew. Perhaps I should pull out now... No, stop it, you can do this. No – you have to do this.*

She stopped outside the reception, where another well-built young man stepped forward and opened her car door. 'If you make your way into the reception, ma'am, I'll park your car and have your luggage sent up.'

As she took in the grandeur, she considered how it could be a health spa for the wealthy. Even the fountain owed much of its design to the Trevi Fountain in Rome.

Inside, the opulence continued with a mixture of French and Italian paintings and furniture, which gave way occasionally to the Rococo style. As she studied two paintings, a voice she instantly recognised interrupted her.

'Caravaggio or Cortona?' he said. 'Both are approaching emotive dynamism with different styles, don't you think? Though I suspect you prefer Cortona.'

'Then you would be wrong, Stuart,' she said, lying. 'Caravaggio combined a realistic observation of the human state, both physical and emotional, with a dramatic use of lighting, and had a formative influence on the Baroque school of painting, don't you agree?' she said, teasing him. She thought he looked hurt, but then he smiled and took her hand, lightly shaking it.

'You must lie more convincingly than that, Melody, if you are to enter the world of deception. Though deception is such an emotive word, don't you think? I prefer subterfuge. It sounds somehow as though it's legal and allowed, personally-'

'Excuse me, Mr Toulson,' a smartly dressed woman with coiffured hair said as she appeared holding out a plastic key card. She then addressed Melody. 'Allow me to show you to your room, Miss Thornton. This way, we have taken your luggage up. Please follow me.'

Melody turned to Stuart as she moved away. 'You must tell me how you knew I was lying,' she said, opening her eyes wide.

'Later,' he said, 'however, what's more intriguing is why you did.'

She unpacked and left her room to explore the grounds. At one point, she lost sight of the Manor House and began to retrace her steps. She heard gunfire. It was faint, and in the distance, but she couldn't make out the direction of its source.

Later, she showered and dressed for dinner. She was hungry and made her way to the dining room, where the rather portly maître d' greeted her. 'Mr Toulson has reserved a table and would like you to join him, providing that's acceptable?'

'With pleasure,' Melody replied, perhaps a little too cheerily.

The maître d' bowed slightly. 'Allow me to show you to your table.'

It was at the far side of the restaurant, nestled beside large, imposing French windows overlooking the gardens. Stuart Toulson rose as soon as he noticed her and placed the report he was reading on the chair next to him, out of view.

'Melody,' he said, taking her hand lightly again. 'So glad you agreed to join me. Eating alone is such a sad affair, don't you think?'

'I don't expect you to dine alone often, but I'm delighted you invited me.'

The sommelier arrived and looked at Stuart.

'Château Mouton Rothschild 2003,' Stuart said, before returning his attention to Melody. 'They have a fine wine cellar here, or would you prefer something else?' he asked, smiling.

'No, though I wondered if you might choose the Château Lafleur Pomerol 97,' she said smugly.

'It's impressive, but too much black raspberries, kirsch and prunes. Also, it's forward, full-bodied and sexy – it's not for me,' he said without a trace of irony. The head waiter took their food order and left.

Melody began probing him. 'I expected you to be back in London by now.'

'I like to spend some time here. It's good for morale and I like to press the flesh with some of our clients.' He lowered his voice and leaned forward. 'The chap over to your left is the finance minister of an African Country. He lives in fear of being kidnapped, absolutely paranoid. He spends more time here than I do.' As the sommelier poured the wine, he sat back and smiled. 'I hope the Château Lafite is to your taste. It's my only weakness, though I prefer to say it's my predilection.'

Melody sipped the wine, rolled it around in her mouth, and swallowed. 'It reveals an extraordinary richness, opulence, purity, intensity and viscosity.'

'Now I know you're toying with me,' he said. 'Tell me, how are you finding the course so far?'

'I was hoping you would tell me.' She nodded at his papers on the table. 'I assume the report you were reading was my profile?'

'I'm pleased to see your observation levels have improved since London.' He smiled, holding the base of his wine glass. 'As for the report, if I revealed its contents, I'd have to kill you.'

'Then you must tell me how you knew I was lying about Caravaggio; I'm intrigued.'

'Ah yes, the lie. I'll tell you how if you tell me why.'

'Deal,' she said as her starter of confit of salt cod, octopus and green zebra tomatoes arrived.

'There are many ways to detect a lie.' He took a sip of wine before continuing. 'I use facial expressions, mostly. Your micro-expression was one of emotional distress, characterised by the eyebrows being drawn upwards towards the middle of the forehead, causing short lines to appear across it. You also touched your nose; people often touch the nose more when lying. This is perhaps because of a rush of adrenaline to the capillaries in the nose, causing the nose to itch.'

'This is fascinating,' Melody said, 'itchy noses are a giveaway?'

'I also noticed you placed your hand near your mouth, a lying person is more likely to place the hands near the mouth, almost as if to cover the lies coming forth and if the mouth appears tense and the lips pursed, this can also show distress. Besides this, your father has a small chateau in France where you spent a great deal of time when you were young and therefore, I would expect you to favour French artists over Italian.' He had barely looked up whilst he had explained his lie-detecting technique. Now, though, he put down his knife and fork beside his sea bass and locked his gaze on her. 'Now you tell me why?'

'That was exceptionally good. You must make a great ransom negotiator,' she said, avoiding eye contact.

'I try to avoid getting my hands dirty now. I leave advocacy for our intermediaries; they're more detached and experts in analysing the tactical behaviour of kidnappers during hostage negotiation situations. They also endeavour to develop an empirical understanding of the factors that can determine the outcome of a kidnapping for ransom. Will we get a safe return or bring them back in a body bag?'

'I didn't like you knowing me so well,' she spluttered. 'I couldn't be mysterious; you took it away. I felt exposed, almost naked.'

Now Melody looked directly at him. Her frank answer completely disarmed him. There was a pause. His mouth was open, and he was about to reply when the maître d' arrived at the table holding a silver salver with a folded note; he offered it to Stuart. He read it, showing no emotion, and nodded at the bearer, who left immediately.

Stuart stood. 'My apologies Melody, it appears the likely outcome of a situation is worse than we first predicted. I must leave. Please finish your meal. I'll be in touch soon.' He picked up his report to leave, but paused and said, 'Can I say I find you entirely mysterious?' He then turned and left, joining two other concerned-looking men at the dining room entrance.

Melody wondered if this was his way of apologising, whilst speculating about the circumstances that had taken Stuart away so suddenly. She also chastised herself for being so open with him about her motive for lying and pondered whether he would see it as a sign of weakness. *I need to toughen up – get myself fully equipped – and stop flirting.*

Chapter Eight

~~

The message on the writing bureau was an invitation to meet her trainer at 07:30. Following a light breakfast, she arrived in the lobby and a man stepped forward to greet her, dressed in military fatigues with a sharp crew cut and highly polished boots.

'Good morning, ma'am,' he said. 'My name is Ryland Carlisle, and they have assigned me to be your trainer. Would you follow me, please?'

'Do you do all the training?'

'No ma'am. For several years, I was part of a close protection team, responsible for the safety of the executives of multinational oil companies, mainly in Africa and South America. My primary role was to prevent kidnapping.'

'How common is kidnapping? I only seem to see a couple of high-profile cases each year.'

'Last year there were twelve hundred kidnappings for ransom in Mexico alone. The top three countries for kidnappings are Venezuela, the Philippines and Mexico, with an average ransom demand of over one million dollars.' He spoke as he led her into a small, well-lit windowless room. 'It's big business and hideous. Not all of them turn out well. Some come back in body bags, and some we don't see again. I don't want to alarm you, but if you ask me a question, I will brief you accurately, even if it upsets you. That is our rule. There's no baby talk here.'

She followed him through a door boasting a brass sign: The Briefing Room. He immediately gestured for her to sit at a desk.

'What's the schedule for today, then?' she asked.

'Every project is different with contrasting arenas of operation, transportation, duration, objectives, potential threats, assets available and the skill level of the target – that's you. Today we will build up a profile and then, from the intel you provide, a scenario planner will produce a training strategy and a risk assessment of the mission.' He handed her a pen drive. 'Fill in this questionnaire – honestly. If you don't tell us everything, we cannot fully equip you. The more info we have, the better prepared you will be.'

'Are you ex-army?'

'Prior to becoming an operative in Africa for Cherished Anti Surveillance, I served in the Armed Forces for nine years. I also spent time on assignments in the Middle East and South America. I am not prepared to reveal more.'

'I see.'

'It should take you until lunch to complete the questionnaire. Afterwards, while the strategy is being prepared and tested by the suits upstairs, we can make a start on this.' He handed her a booklet entitled 'Personal Security at Home and Abroad'; she immediately opened it and read the contents page:

- Surveillance
- Residential Security
- Personal Security whilst Travelling
- Personal Security in Hotels
- Carjacking

'Well, I'd better get started then. Oh, is Stuart Toulson still around?' she asked, trying to sound nonchalant.

'I doubt that. He spends most of his time in London and only visits here occasionally. I've only ever known him to meet and greet presidents of corporations or countries.' With that reply, he nodded and left.

Melody opened her laptop, plugged in the pen drive, and began scanning the pages. The questionnaire was more detailed than she expected. She had hoped to spend some time walking around the grounds and studying the art treasures that littered the interior, but she reluctantly returned to the questionnaire, feeling like a grumpy teenager forced to do homework.

It asked for the usual personal details one might expect, but quickly wanted incredibly detailed information on what they called 'The Mission'. It felt more like applying for a role in *Mission Impossible*, but considering the trouble and effort both Brodie and Stuart had gone to, she powered through.

She told the story as she had done to Brodie, but without mentioning the visions, constantly wondering if they would understand. Next, it asked her who else was aware, or would eventually be, of her mission, but the area she struggled with was describing who else would have an interest in the outcome. There were three categories: people, organisations and governments. She decided to leave it blank.

She cheered herself up by thinking about lunch. The menu sounded fabulous. They had the Michelin two-star chef, Niall Le Blanc, which didn't surprise her; everything about the place was high end. Two items caught her attention on the menu. Sautéed gourmand of lobster and a chocolate fondue with slithers of pear and fresh strawberries.

After lunch, Ryland was waiting for her in the brightly lit, windowless briefing room. They had arranged a pot of coffee and biscuits on a table to one side and a projector screen hung above it. Other walls had whiteboards and flip charts attached. Ryland greeted her by asking if she enjoyed her lunch. Was he probing or was she becoming paranoid?

'It was lovely, thank you. Pity Stuart had to leave so suddenly.' Now she was probing.

'Yes, I thought I heard the helicopter take off. If it's alright with you, I would like to start with your personal security. Did you read the booklet I gave you earlier?'

Melody was nodding, though still slightly fazed from the read.

'Good, because tomorrow we will test you in real-life scenarios and we have a long afternoon and evening ahead.' He switched on the overhead and three headings appeared.

- Surveillance Avoidance
- Personal Security whilst Travelling
- Personal Security in Hotels

'After a quick glance at your mission, I have selected three areas where I feel you are most at risk. We'll start with surveillance, kidnapping and how to avoid it.'

'At dinner, I was talking to Stuart about negotiating with kidnappers. He said he didn't like to get his hands dirty now, but I thought he would be good at that sort of thing.'

'Mr Toulson is probably one of the best, if not *the* best negotiator in the world, but it has to be someone pretty important to call on him now. There are too many and each one is time-consuming. To be honest, since Mexico, I don't think he's done any.'

'What happened in Mexico?'

'It was two eleven-year-old girls. One was the daughter of a diplomat Mr Toulson had been at university with. He was also her godfather. Apparently, he doted on her. You must realise we don't protect UK diplomats. That's the responsibility of the Foreign Office.'

'What happened?'

'On that fateful day, Mr Toulson's goddaughter, Courtney, broke protocol and left the school grounds without permission. Unfortunately, her driver was late because of a freak accident. Courtney joined her friend outside the school gates to see her new puppy, a present for her birthday.'

'Were you protecting the other girl?'

'No, she had an armed chauffeur. Her father was only a middle-ranking executive with a bank in Mexico City. She was the kidnap target. However, when the kidnappers arrived, and in the heat of the moment, they could not tell the two girls apart; they looked similar, both were blonde and in school uniform, so they snatched them both.' He paused and ran his hand through his hair while shaking his head.

'Did you get them back?'

'Mr Toulson led the negotiating team. Everything went well, and we arranged an exchange in a remote area in Sonora, Northern Mexico. At a river crossing near Félix Gómez, fairly flat land but enough shrubbery to conceal our snipers.'

'Why snipers?'

'Automatic gunfire risks injuring the kidnapped victim. We had six snipers and a snatch team. Just as the swap was about to take place, one kidnapper discharged his weapon.'

'Was it a setup?'

'No, we think he did it by accident. But then all hell broke loose. Everybody was firing, especially the trigger-happy Feds. That's the Federal Mexican Police. They had insisted on being there. We tried to stop them from firing, but they wouldn't listen. Automatic weapons, shotguns and even sidearms. The air was thick with ammo. Our snipers took out the men holding the girls and we moved in to snatch them. Unfortunately, Courtney took a bullet in the neck from a ricochet, and even though we had a paramedic team with us in the helicopter, she died on the way to the hospital in Stuart's arms. They had to pry her from him at the A&E department. Never seen a man sob so much. We all ended up tearful. Fortunately, the other girl lived.'

Melody was speechless for what seemed like an age. 'You were there?'

'Yes, ma'am, I led the snatch team. Got to know Mr Toulson real well during the six-month op.'

'Six months? That's a long time, isn't it?'

'Shortest one I've ever known. They usually take between eighteen months to two years. Everyone knew Mr Toulson put the money up – the British Government won't pay ransom money and the bank were sniffy about it.'

'What happened to the kidnappers? Did they escape?'

'No one got away and there were no prisoners.'

Chapter Nine

~~

Melody dined early and alone that evening. The restaurant seemed strangely quiet. There was little laughter and people seemed to talk in almost a whisper. *Stuart was right. Eating alone is such a sad affair.* The food was excellent, but she stoically avoided the wine. Ryland had insisted on an early start the following day.

The maître d' approached. 'Can I get you anything else, madam?'

'Thank you, no, the meal was delicious.' As she made to stand, he moved silkily behind to pull the chair back, noticing a slight unsteadiness in her stance.

'Are you alright ma'am?' he asked.

'Yes, I'll be fine. It's been a long day,' she said, leaving. She hurried as best she could to get to her room, using the wall in the corridor as a guide. She could feel another episode starting. Her vision was already blurring as she fumbled for the key card. Once in her room, she headed for the bedroom, throwing herself on the bed. Breathing was difficult as her sight disappeared and darkness enveloped her. Then the peace and such serenity…

She was crouched down in a valley, splashing water from the mountain stream onto her face. The cold water refreshed and cooled her. She was filling her canteen when she heard the noise. She froze. It was faint, but she could hear a drone, the familiar high-pitched buzzing sound. Squinting, she scanned the valley, her hand protecting her eyes from the sun's glare. Sheer granite cliffs on one side, and on the other, a gently sloping pasture gave way to sparse woodland. With the drone equipped with heat-seeking cameras, there would be nowhere to hide. *It's growing louder. It's catching up.* She ran.

The thick vegetation forced her to run in the shallow stream. Days of trekking were telling. She was sweating now and her legs ached. The splashing water helped to cool her, but the slippery stones slowed her down. *I can't outrun it. Is this how it ends?*

She felt the downdraft before she heard the wingbeats of the swan. Flying at head height and only two metres away. It looked so large as it slowed to her pace and turned its graceful neck towards her. The long steady beats of its wings were rhythmic, almost hypnotic. Its jet-black eyes stared into hers. Deep, calm, peaceful. Then, complete silence. No splashing sounds, no drone engine. Even the wingbeats were silent and even her running felt like slow motion.

The swan held her gaze. She felt drawn in; it flew ahead of her but glanced back every few seconds as it pulled away, turning through a gap in the undergrowth towards the cliff face. Without thinking, she left the stream and followed, staying on the winding path that narrowed and closed behind her. The twigs and branches flicked her face as she ran, rivulets of blood merging with the sweat. The swan was out of sight, leaving her following the track, running alone and exhausted. She slowed, then came to an abrupt halt, stumbling as she entered the clearing.

Standing there taller than ever, the swan stood facing her. The eyes blinked repeatedly. Melody was going to speak, but a transformation began. Taller and taller, the swan was now twelve feet tall. Yet still, the metamorphosis continued, until it became an angel, pointing to a deep cleft in the rock face.

Melody staggered into the cleft, turned and sank to her knees. Her hearing returned. She heard the drone as it flew past, its sinister red lasers scanning the valley floor. The angel appeared at the entrance and looked deep into Melody's eyes. Then came a flash of intense light...

Chapter Ten

~~

The following morning, Melody met Ryland for breakfast at six o'clock. Today he was in civvies – that's civilian clothes to army folk. He handed her a small package, travel tickets and the itinerary for the day.

The list was in chronological order, starting with a flight from London Luton to Glasgow, Scotland, and ending with a train journey from Glasgow Central to London Euston. The task, or mission as they called it, was to deliver a package to the offices of Grant Killington – Private Investigators on West George St., Glasgow.

'This is the way this exercise works,' he began, as if he were explaining a treasure hunt to a youth group.

'First, imagine you are being followed by someone who does not know your mission, only that you will leave from Luton Airport. Your aim is to lose that person, ensuring you do not lead them to Grant Killington. Second, I want you to identify the person following you back to London and be able to give a detailed description of them.'

Ryland ended the briefing by explaining. 'I will follow you at a discreet distance. I am merely an observer and will not speak to you once we leave here. Do you have any questions?'

'I feel strangely nervous even though it's only an exercise.' And, Melody realised, could determine whether she could go to Iran.

'That's good. Being nervous will increase your awareness. Are you ready to leave?'

'Yes.'

A car was waiting with yet another well-built young man in the driving seat. Melody sat in the back. The moment her seat belt clicked, the Mercedes raced off down the drive and swept past the gatehouse, the guard nodding him through.

The driver spoke now. 'I'll let you know if we're being tailed, Miss. What time is your flight?'

'It's scheduled for 10.30 a.m.,' she said, relaxing into the seat.

At the airport, she made her way to the retail area and, after ensuring she was not being followed, bought a red headscarf, sunglasses and a jute bag. Then headed for the coffee bar opposite the check-in. *Leave the check-in as late as possible. It makes it difficult for a tag to buy a ticket in time.*

Whilst she was drinking her latte, a middle-aged man made his way into the bar area.

'They're making the last call for Glasgow, love,' he said in a northern accent to the woman he was with. Melody then fished the flight ticket out of her bag and hurried to the queue.

She passed through security and once seated on the aeroplane, Melody relaxed. She was confident they had not followed her and again realised she had not seen Ryland.

They were in the air for just over an hour before they touched down in Glasgow. Grey clouds scudded across the sky, making it overcast, the cold sunlight only breaking through occasionally.

She took a black cab and waited until she was seated and out of earshot to give the driver instructions. She looked behind to see if another taxi followed them as they weaved through the busy traffic onto the eastbound M8 motorway.

As they crossed the Kingston Bridge, the elevated position gave Melody her first glimpse of the city. She looked east down the River Clyde, its bridges like exposed veins, providing the lifeblood. To the west stood a disused crane, a cold monument to its proud shipbuilding heritage. Waterfront apartments, cinema complexes and coffee bars now peppered the embankments. They swept off the motorway, speeding down a slip road and onto Argyle Street. In the distance, she could see the glass pyramid of St. Enoch's Shopping Centre.

Passing under Glasgow Central Train Station, she scouted out the area for her return journey. It looked busy. *Busy areas make it easier to lose a tail, but harder to spot one.*

Melody paid the taxi fare from the meter reading; she couldn't understand what the driver was saying. His Glaswegian accent was heavy with the speech delivered like a machine gun.

Her next destination was the shopping centre, and once inside, she found the ladies' toilets. She took off her jacket and stuffed it into the jute bag along with her handbag, then she put on the red headscarf and sunglasses and looked at herself in the mirror.

Changing something even slightly can make them miss you for long enough so you can get away.

Melody spotted an elderly lady who, whilst drying her hands, had been watching her quizzically. She approached her; she was old enough to be her grandmother and might make a perfect foil.

'Excuse me,' she said with an exaggerated tone of anxiety. 'My ex-husband is having me followed. Would you mind if I link arms with you as we leave? It may throw them off. I'm heading for the subway.'

'We cannae have that wee hen. We'll no have your man follow us,' she said whilst holding up and waving her walking stick. 'I'll tak ye to the subway, hen.'

With that, she linked Melody's arm, and they set off through the mall and headed for the subway. All the while the woman chatted away and Melody listened intently, loving her strong accent and unfamiliar words. After thanking the old woman profusely, Melody boarded the inner circuit underground train for one-stop to Buchanan Street.

She left the subway and headed south for a couple of blocks before turning right into West George Street. Melody loved how the planners had designed Glasgow – a grid system. *It's like New York, but without the skyscrapers.*

Soon she was standing outside an elegant building with a brass plate fixed squarely on the limestone facade, declaring Grant Killington, Private Investigators, 3rd Floor.

Melody glanced around and once sure she was not being followed, she stepped inside, removed her headscarf and made her way to the lift. She pressed the button for the fourth floor. As the lift opened, she stepped out and walked down one flight of stairs to the reception of Grant Killington on the third floor.

'My name is Melody Thornton, and I have a package to deliver,' she said, handing over the small jiffy bag to a serious-looking receptionist, who peered over her glasses and smiled whilst punching an extension number into the exchange.

'Morag, I have the parcel for Mr Grant from Sospitas. Are there any instructions for the carrier?' There was a slight pause. 'Thank you, Miss Thornton,' she said, putting down the phone. 'There are no instructions for you. Have a nice day.'

Melody felt slightly deflated as she turned and headed for the stairs. She was looking for a taxi when she glimpsed a man on the opposite pavement darting into a side street. What shocked her was she was certain this was the balding man from the airport.

She turned left and hurriedly headed down the pedestrianised area to its junction with Pitt Street and hailed a taxi for the station.

* * *

Glasgow Central was like stepping back in time. It wouldn't have surprised her to see the Hogwarts Express there. She headed for platform three on the station concourse, where the Edinburgh train was leaving in fifteen minutes. Sitting on a bench, close to the platform entrance, she switched her phone to camera mode and practiced nonchalantly taking pictures of commuters whilst pretending to be in a deep conversation. At 16:34, having taken approximately twenty pictures, she moved over to platform two for the train to London Euston.

Again, sitting on the first bench close to the entrance, she scanned the photos, trying to store them in her memory. *I need to pass this test with honours or they'll pull the plug and I'll be back to square one. I may not get another opportunity to visit Iran. The relationship between the UK and Iran seems to be worsening.*

Ten minutes later, she had a eureka moment; a man carrying a grey Crombie coat walked through the gates and headed towards the front of the train. Melody scanned the photos again. Sure enough, it was him. The trilby had gone, and he was no longer wearing his overcoat, but it was him. She relaxed a little; she was now confident she had identified her tag.

Four and a half hours later, the train pulled into Euston Station. Melody called Ryland on her mobile as she stepped onto the platform. He answered instantly.

'Hello, welcome back. How did you think your mission went?' he asked, with only the minimum of formalities.

'I think it went well most of the time, but I'm sure it…' Melody stopped speaking, the man she had seen at the airport coffee lounge and had glimpsed in Glasgow was walking towards her, holding a mobile phone to his ear.

'Cat got your tongue, Miss Thornton?' he said, before putting the phone in his pocket.

Even now, at close quarters and listening to his voice, she could only just make out it was Ryland. He removed his black-rimmed spectacles, an elaborate wig that made him look partially bald and a small moustache.

'Now describe the person who followed you from Glasgow.'

Melody tapped on her phone and confidently showed Ryland the photo. 'Is this him?'

'It is indeed. Well done. We will discuss the operation on the way back to Sospitas. Mr Toulson has put his helicopter at our disposal from the London Heliport; he said to tell you it's compensation for leaving you alone at dinner.'

'How exciting. Is it the Heliport was once owned by Harrods?' Melody asked, unable to conceal her delight.

'Yes, apparently it belonged to them. Mr Toulson's car is waiting outside to take us there.'

'Is Stuart here?' She struggled to stay professional.

'No, he isn't, and I'm not at liberty to say where he is.'

Chapter Eleven

~

Anatoly had shown concern about Nikolai's health for weeks before eventually persuading him to see a doctor. Nikolai insisted on Anatoly being there, as he didn't want to upset his family.

By the time they completed the blood tests and ultrasound scan results, he was already looking jaundiced. Even the whites of his eyes were yellowing. He remembered feeling numb as the doctor explained to Nikolai that unfortunately, with liver cancer, the liver rarely causes noticeable symptoms until it has reached an advanced stage. The doctor continued with his diagnosis, but Nikolai wasn't listening.

The prognosis devastated Anatoly, and he spent months researching the disease and consulting the world's top cancer specialists. Ultimately, he had to recognise the reality of the situation; they were only offering palliative care. Nikolai was dying.

* * *

Anatoly remembered the first time he met Nikolai at Moscow University. He was like a firefly, always on the move, and he lit up any room he entered. Anatoly was less visible, a number cruncher, but there was a shared sense of destiny, a conviction. One day, they would make a mark on the world.

For Anatoly, it was mostly about changing the political system, moving away from the corrupt, inefficient and discredited 'command economy' into a Westernised free market. Nikolai shared the same beliefs, but only as a 'means to an end'; he wanted, even craved, power and wealth. Now they had it, it seemed so vacuous.

To prepare for his visit to see Nikolai at the hospital, Anatoly was looking through his library for a book he wanted to take. He noticed one was not in the correct place and lifted it out to catalogue later. As he placed it on the table, a postcard fell to the floor.

He imagined it had been a bookmark, but the writing was his own and looked like it was his from his time at university. It was a quote from a man whose life he had admired whilst studying in Moscow: Mahatma Gandhi, the pre-eminent leader of Indian Nationalism in British-ruled India. As he read the words, they seemed to taunt him; it was a quote describing the seven deadly sins so succinctly.

Wealth without work.
Pleasure without conscience.
Science without humanity.
Knowledge without character.
Politics without principle.
Commerce without morality.
Worship without sacrifice.

The words shouted at him. They summed up what his life had become; it was an epiphanic moment. He sank into an old leather chair and re-read the words several times. Two of the lines intrigued him most – politics without principle and commerce without morality.

He decided, there and then, he wanted to change the way he lived. Just as suddenly, he realised that having decided, he felt better than he had for years. The cloud that had hung over him cleared and he found he had clarity in his thinking.

Anatoly knew exactly what he needed to do. It was so clear. Nothing must prevent him. He had a new mission.

Chapter Twelve

~~

Anatoly Artamonovsky had become Nikolai's PA following his appointment to oversee the development of the Western Siberian Oil Extraction Enterprise 'Yuganskneftegaz', in Oblast.

They shared the same political philosophy, although they had distinct personalities. Anatoly was cautious and thoughtful, the perfect foil to Nikolai's bold and sometimes impetuous behaviour.

As a result, they trusted one another implicitly. They both amassed a fortune along with a large stake in the oil and gas company. Anatoly had ten per cent and Nikolai seventy-five. Wealth beyond their wildest dreams.

Uncommonly, in Russia, Anatoly's family were devout Catholics – often in conflict with the State, which described the church as a non-Russian allegiance.

His uncle, Mikhail Artamonovsky, had been a highly respected professor of science and archaeology at Leningrad University.

He and his wife had only one child, a girl called Alana. Although Anatoly did not ask why she was often wheelchair bound, he later discovered she suffered from muscular dystrophy. But she was a feisty girl who seldom let the disability affect her, and he enjoyed spending time with her. Alana was clever and fun to be with. She would often have a new card trick to perform and Anatoly could never fathom out how she did it.

It was his uncle's interests in religion and archaeology Anatoly remembered most about him. He loved visiting him. The cottage was full of books. Even the staircase had small piles of them on each step, and his study had the heady smell of pipe tobacco. Each Christmas, when he was a young boy, he would listen intently, along with Alana in front of the log burning fire, as his uncle told the Nativity story. On one such occasion, Anatoly became fascinated by the Three Wise Men and questioned him about them.

'Who were they? Where did they come from?'

'Anatoly, you have an enquiring mind. Many people called the Three Wise Men the Magi. It's where we get our word magic from and I'm going to show you something few people know.'

He would look secretive and mysterious as he pulled an incredibly old copy of a book from his library while stroking his long white beard. The faded leather cover was cracked and worn.

'They call this book the "Lost Gospel of Joseph". An Englishman called Henry Sike first translated and published this gospel in 1697. It was owned by the Gnostics, a secretive sect of Christians in the second century. You won't find it in the Bible, though.'

It fascinated Anatoly – its name suggested that somehow his uncle had found a lost book. After all, he was an archaeologist.

'Joseph, also called Caiaphas the High-Priest,' his uncle began, 'recorded this about the Magi.'

And it came to pass when the Lord Jesus was born at Bethlehem, a city of Judea in the time of Herod the King; the Magi (wise men) came from the East to Jerusalem, according to the prophecy of Zoroaster, and brought with them offerings: namely, gold, frankincense, and myrrh, and worshipped him, and offered to him their gifts. Then the Lady Mary took one of his swaddling clothes in which the infant was wrapped and gave it to them instead of a blessing, which they received from her as a most noble present. And at the same time there appeared to them an angel in the form of that star which had before been their guide in their journey; the light of which they followed until they returned to their own country. Then they took the swaddling, and with the greatest respect laid it up among their treasures.

After reading it, his uncle leaned forward as if he were sharing a secret. 'Legend has it the swaddling had healing powers, and the Magi hid it to stop it from being misused by King Herod. Whoever finds it, though, will have the greatest treasure of all – the power to heal the sick. Some called it "The Healing Cloth."'

Anatoly was spellbound. It was no surprise that when his uncle died, he bequeathed the book, along with several others about the Magi, to Anatoly.

As the years rolled by and adult scepticism replaced childhood imagination, Anatoly had decided that the account recorded in the 'Lost Gospel of Joseph' was probably fake, made up and written by a discredited gnostic sect, completely inconsistent with Catholic teaching and therefore, unreliable.

Despite this, however, he told the story every Christmas to his children when they were young. And secretly, there was an element of the testimony that intrigued him, along with a nagging question – what if it were true? *Imagine that.*

Chapter Thirteen

~~~

Melody made her way to meet Ryland in the library. It had been too noisy to talk properly in the helicopter.

He was waiting for her when she arrived. He had positioned himself at the far end of the library in one of two comfortable leather wingback chairs next to the windows. The small coffee table in between had several files and a notebook Ryland was flicking through. He rose to greet her, gesturing for her to sit along with a few pleasantries before he turned to serious matters.

'How do you think the exercise went?'

'Mostly, I enjoyed it. However, I found it difficult to stay focused and became suspicious of everyone I saw. How did you consider my performance?'

'I would say it was a mixed bag. You made some rookie mistakes, but overall, you rose to the challenge. Can I take you through it chronologically?'

'Yes, please, I'm intrigued.'

'First, on the way to the airport, the driver asked you what time your flight was, and although you didn't know him, you informed him your flight was leaving at 10:30. You could have given him a vague answer, something like, "Don't worry, if I miss this one, I'll take a later one." Instead, you gave a precise time and, unfortunately for you, there was only one flight at 10:30.'

Melody was nodding. 'Of course, now you mention it, it seems so obvious.'

'Later, whilst you were waiting in the coffee bar, I entered wearing a simple disguise and mentioned they were making a last call for Glasgow, at which point you immediately looked for your ticket, which confirmed this was indeed your flight. Tell me what you were looking for as the taxi left Glasgow Airport?'

'I was looking to see if another taxi had followed but, unfortunately, three or four left at the same time and I couldn't keep track of them.'

'That was your third mistake. You were being followed by a motorcyclist. Do not assume they will use the same mode of transport, often they will not. They may not even fly with you and simply phone ahead for an accomplice to take up the tail. However, your detour through the pedestrianised shopping area was brilliant. By the time he had found somewhere to park, he had lost you and you made it to Grant Killington undiscovered, apart from me, who knew the mission parameters.'

'What did you think of my technique for discovering your tag at Glasgow Station?' she asked, straightening and puffing herself up.

'It was good, but the tag realised he'd been spotted and could have handed over the job to an accomplice if there were more assets on the ground. You may need to be a little more subtle in your methods but, overall, you performed well on this task.'

He smiled whilst reaching for one of the thick folders beneath his notepad. 'I asked you to fill in a questionnaire. I passed the intel you provided over to one of our scenario planners.' He produced a training programme and a risk assessment. Ryland looked at her with what Melody called 'his serious face.' 'Perhaps if we look at the Mission Risk Assessment, it may inform your future decisions.'

Future decisions? Where's this going?

Melody was trying to read it upside down. The first page had the Sospitas logo with confidential stamped across it, but it also held the words Operation Christmas Fairy in bold.

'Christmas Fairy?' exclaimed Melody, creasing her forehead.

Ryland responded, beaming. 'The boffins upstairs take great delight in using imaginative codenames. It's their only opportunity to be creative. They have picked up on the Nativity story and the three Magi. However, what they are good at is drilling down through a mission plan and finding all the risks.'

Ryland sat back. 'To be frank with you, Miss Thornton, we would only use a seasoned operative on a task of this magnitude, and they recommend you walk away from it.'

Melody was speechless; it never occurred to her hiring someone else would be an option. She opened her mouth to speak, but nothing came out.

Ryland continued. 'They have drawn up a comprehensive list of stakeholders. Any country, organisation or individual that may have a stake in what you are looking for. I don't recall ever seeing one as long as this. It encapsulates all the states in the Middle East, including Israel, several European countries and the USA. In terms of organisations, they include the Worldwide Anglican and Catholic Churches, in particular the Vatican, most right-wing churches across the Midwest Bible belt, the Jewish community, Radical Islamists and a handful of Orthodox Churches. Oh, and most of the major museums.'

Ryland slowly turned the page. 'Regarding individuals, well, almost anyone with enough money would be on the market, which would include many of the despots in Africa and South America. The list seems to go on and on.' Ryland looked up from the file. 'Miss Thornton, you'd have more enemies than Hitler had.'

'They are assuming all those people know what I'm searching for. So far, only a handful of people know.' She had lost her playful smile and sat upright in her chair. Ryland flicked past ten pages, making Melody wonder what the preface had to say. 'Is that file for me?'

'Yes, I have a copy here for you, but we like to talk it through first.

At the end of our briefing, you can take your copy away to read at your leisure. However, it must not leave Sospitas for reasons that will become obvious.'

'This is way over the top. Hardly anyone knows.' She was pointing her index finger at the file with a stabbing action.

'Regarding whom may already know, you have stated you have already told an English professor and an Iranian national. The planners also assume you have carried out some research on the internet, possibly using Iranian websites. It may have caught the attention of GCHQ, the NSA in America, and it's well known in security circles that Israel has at least two false Iranian websites to capture information on those showing an interest in Iran. In conclusion, the world and his wife may already know.'

'I won't change my mind, Ryland. I've invested too much time and effort over the years to give up now. Regardless of what happens here today, I will carry on.' She said, moving to stand.

'That's what Mr Toulson said your response would be and, therefore, I propose we look at the revised training plan.' He paused slightly to pull out another file. 'You have already carried out what the planners call a "Dropbox" session to highlight your strengths and weaknesses, and with that information, along with the risk assessment, they have changed the training strategy.'

'That sounds more like it. Look, Ryland,' she said, calming down, 'I'll do whatever training it takes. I need to be... what do you call it, mission-ready?'

'First, you need to be more aware of the information you are needlessly giving away, and the planners have recommended an advanced Dropbox scenario to upgrade your surveillance skills. In addition, they suggest taking a self-defence course and firearms training.'

Ryland continued slowly through the list, showing there was still a lot to learn. 'Miss Thornton, they have also included orienteering, along with navigational skills for diverse and unfamiliar terrain whilst moving at speed, survival skills in both tropical climates and at sea, along with advanced first aid and trauma treatment.'

'If that's what takes, sign me up. I haven't fired a weapon apart from a shotgun during clay pigeon shootings, but whatever it takes and please, call me Melody?'

'No, ma'am, I'm sorry, but it's company protocol. It prevents us from becoming emotionally attached to a client and makes it difficult for us to give impartial advice. You can start on some self-defence after lunch and later this evening you can try out our firing range.'

'Can I take the file to read over lunch?'

'Certainly, but it mustn't leave the site.'

* * *

Over the following months, they gave Melody two further advanced Dropbox exercises. She passed the final one with flying colours. She also excelled at firearms, earning a distinction and her self-defence improved enormously. Ryland gave the go-ahead, on the proviso that she agreed to more navigational skills and trauma treatment training. She not only did so, but asked for further orienteering practice.

She was almost there.

Chapter Fourteen

~~~

It had taken the intervention of the most senior Catholic Bishop in Russia, and the promise of a substantial donation for Anatoly to be granted a meeting at the Vatican.

Cardinal Raffaele Poggi was taking tea when his assistant, the bishop, arrived to prep him for his meeting.

'Your Eminence, you would be wise to mind your council with this Russian Oligarch. There are question marks regarding the way he accumulated such wealth so quickly. The accusations include bribery and false accounting and money laundering,' the bishop said, handing him a background report. 'Many refer to it as "dirty money".'

'Unlike the clean money deposited in our Banco Ambrosiano account, being looked after by Roberto Calvi?' Cardinal Poggi said with a wry smile.

'These are different times, Your Eminence. This Holy See has a more jaundiced view of capitalism.'

'I'm sorry. I was teasing you, Bishop. However, I am intrigued by the subject in question. Let's give him the benefit of the doubt for now and thank you for your report. I expect it will be to your usual high standard.'

The bishop bowed and left.

'This meeting with Mr Artamonovsky, remind me, where is it to be?' he asked his private secretary.

'The Vatican Gardens, Your Eminence. They are forecasting a bright sunny day with just a hint of a breeze. I thought on such a lovely day as this you would enjoy some fresh air.'

'Excellent,' he said, opening the report with a hint of anticipation.

* * *

Anatoly was feeling mellow. He was at ease with himself. His earlier experience reading the quote from Mahatma Gandhi had rebalanced his life. He now had a new purpose, a mission in life. Normally, he would have carried out an enormous amount of research before such an important meeting, but not this time. He had asked his researchers only for headline stories and accounts. He wanted to enjoy his visit.

Cardinal Raffaele Poggi looked like everyone's favourite grandfather – kindly, with a slight smile and crystal-clear eyes. The vivid red skull cap sat perfectly on his neatly trimmed silver-grey hair and, probably because it was a warm day, he wore a white cassock with amaranth red piping and thirty-three red buttons, like cake decorations, which ran the length of his tunic. Each one represented a year of Christ's life. He was sitting on a stone bench under the shade of a Lebanese cedar; the fragrance of nearby jasmine from China filled the air.

'Ah, Mr Artamonovsky, welcome. Are you enjoying the gardens?' the Cardinal asked.

'I could spend a week here. It is so beautiful. Is it true, Your Eminence, Saint Helena spread the site of the Vatican Gardens with earth brought from Golgotha?'

'So, they say, but alas, you only see the gardens. Imagine what it must be like to be a gardener here and feel the soil daily. I think they have the best job in the Vatican, aside from the Holy See, of course. What memory will you take away with you?'

'The beautiful sculptures and I even discovered an olive tree donated by the Israeli Government. The symbolism struck me.'

Once they'd exhausted the usual introductions and pleasantries, the Cardinal became more direct. 'What is the reason for your interest in the Magi and how may I be able to assist you?'

'I have read the translation by Prof. Augustus Schmidt on "The Gifts of the Magi" along with the other letters and documents in the collection. I believe that given sufficient resources, there is a realistic prospect of the swaddling being unearthed. My question, therefore, is are the Vatican Relic Hunters considering a search, and if they are, would you be amenable to allowing me to fund such a venture?'

The Cardinal was nodding lightly whilst weighing his words. 'The Relic Hunters, or to give them their official title, the "Pontifical Academy of Archaeology", are the prerogative of the Holy See and do not make their activities public. I doubt if the Pontiff himself would know of any ongoing investigation. But why are you interested in funding such a thing?' The Cardinal paused, and then, smiled. 'Providing, of course, such an expedition was to take place?'

'Your Eminence, there is someone who means a great deal to me and needs considerable supernatural healing. The natural world of medical science has reached its limit and I am prepared to fund entirely a quest to discover the swaddling.'

'Nikolai Levanevsky?'

'No.' He paused, wanting to frame the words with kindness. 'Nikolai is treading another path and using agents of his own. Naturally, if his outcome is successful, it would please me enormously. But my endeavours are not directly on his behalf.'

'Different paths or different methods?'

'Both, Your Eminence. But if the opportunity presented itself, I would gladly use it on his behalf.'

'And what if we did not discover it?'

'I recognise of course it may not exist, and it is merely a myth or even if you were to discover it, it may not have the power to heal they rumour it to have. Regardless, I am prepared to pay whatever is necessary and risk all to find it on behalf of someone who is without hope. Afterwards, I would return the swaddling to the Vatican for safekeeping.'

Anatoly opened his briefcase and took out a colourful marketing brochure, which the Cardinal instantly recognised. 'In addition, and regardless of whether the project takes place, it would honour me to support the Charity you founded – Agua Ajuda – helping to provide running water and sanitation to the poorest people in Bolivia–'

'Excuse me for asking Mr Artamonovsky, but why would you do that? I don't mean to sound churlish, but you have no history of charitable donations and are not renowned for your philanthropic behaviour. Indeed, many in your own country actually regard your wealth as ill-got.' The Cardinal picked up the briefing paper they had given him. 'A poet and fellow countryman of yours recently said, and I quote, "Fifteen years ago, everything in Russia was owned by the people. Today a quarter of Russia's economy is owned by thirty-six men."'

Anatoly sighed. 'To my eternal shame much of what you say is true. I can only explain it as a moment of inspiration and realisation that has rebalanced my life, a watershed that reminded me although life is precious, it is ever so fragile, and it brought my own into focus. Not a "Road to Damascus" experience, but a significant juncture.'

'That pleases me enormously.'

'I understand people will be naturally sceptical.' Anatoly put the papers back in his case before continuing. 'Tomorrow my office will transfer one-million euros into Agua Ajuda, with no obligation or expectations of reciprocity. If you can help me with my quest, then I shall be grateful, if not, well at least some good will have come from our meeting and if I can be of help in the future, please contact me. Now, Your Eminence, I feel I have taken up enough of your time and wish to thank you for your audience.'

With that, he knelt, took the Cardinal's hand, and whilst he lightly kissed the gold ring of his office, the Cardinal placed a hand on Anatoly's head, leaned forward and whispered in his ear, 'Father Elmer Janssen.'

Anatoly bowed and left.

Chapter Fifteen

~~~

The next day, Anatoly had a meeting scheduled with Erwin Friedrich Escher, head of the Vatican Bank. The official title was the Institute for Works of Religion and had the plumiest address in the world, 'The Apostolic Palace'.

They had provided him with a personal guided tour, a privilege reserved for top-end clients. The guide walked him around, pointing out various art treasures.

'Popes Benedict and John Paul II both had their bedrooms two floors above the bank. In 1982, a scandal engulfed the bank when Roberto Calvi, known as "God's Banker" and head of Banco Ambrosiano...'

Anatoly's ears pricked up. *I wondered if they might skip the dark period in the bank's history.*

'... hung himself under London's Blackfriars Bridge, following its demise. It was the most high-profile bank collapse in Italy's history; prosecutors in Rome concluded the Sicilian Mafia killed Calvi, but they convicted no one. The Vatican Bank was Ambrosiano's main shareholder and lost two hundred and twenty-four million US Dollars.'

The guide ended the tour as Monsignor Marcello De Sica approached; he was the bank's third highest-ranking official and dressed accordingly. An immaculate black silk suit, crisp white shirt, a black tie with a discrete Vatican coat of arms embroidered on it and a pair of black patent leather shoes completed his attire. He was tall, in his early fifties, and had a neat centre parting in his jet-black hair.

The greeting was a gentle handshake. 'Mr Escher is ready to see you now, Mr Artamonovsky,' he said. 'Follow me, please.'

The office of Erwin Friedrich Escher was like entering a time warp into the Italian Renaissance. Frescoes painted by Raphael and his workshop adorned every wall and the entire ceiling. The Bank's governor looked every bit a Swiss banker, right down to his rimless spectacles. He rose and walked around his desk to greet Anatoly; he was ever so slightly overweight, but his grey double-breasted suit concealed it well. His handshake was firm as he welcomed him.

'Are you enjoying your visit, Mr Artamonovsky? I understand Cardinal Poggi has been your host so far?'

Clever, letting me know immediately he is aware of my mission. But why is there a Russian doll looking decidedly out of place on his desk? I won't mention it.

'It has been a great joy for me. His Eminence the Cardinal is a gentle and godly man, far better suited to his pastoral role than perhaps the rough and tumble of banking, wouldn't you say?'

The banker smiled. 'Indeed, he is, and in fact, many in the Vatican would regard banking as a necessary evil. From our point of view, we are merely "giving to Caesar that which is Caesar's" and as you will have discovered during your meteoric rise in business, we sometimes tread a fine line between opportunism and manipulation.'

'And your job?'

'I like to think my role is to ensure we remain on the right side. After all, wasn't it President John F Kennedy who said, "if a free society cannot help the many who are poor, it cannot save the few who are rich"? We are basically a non-for-profit organisation.'

'Maybe, but your accounts show you made a profit of over eighty-six million euro last year.'

'Indeed, but the lion's share of the proceeds – just under fifty-four million – went to the Pope to carry out the Church's mission around the world. Many of our investors willingly give up any profit they would normally gain or leave a generous legacy.'

'Perhaps I can help you reach the many who are poor. I would like to open an investment account with your bank, the profit from which I would donate to the Holy See each year for use at his discretion.'

'I see,' he said. Leaning back in his swivel chair and relaxing, his folded hands lightly tapped the desk. 'That is exceedingly generous of you. How much are you considering depositing?'

A smile played across Anatoly's face. 'US$224m.'

The head of the Vatican Bank raised an eyebrow.

Chapter Sixteen

~~~

Melody's bright red headscarf stuck out among the coal-black hijabs worn by most of the women at Sari International Airport. As one of the primary hubs in and from Iran, arrivals was busy.

'Your passport and documents please.' The immigration officer's request brought her back to reality.

'I'm sorry, I was miles away,' she said, fumbling to present her passport, visa and papers.

'What is the purpose of your visit?' the immigration officer asked.

'Pleasure. A few weeks of sightseeing and visiting a friend. I'd love to visit the Zoroastrian Towers of Silence at Yazd.' Melody said in Farsi.

He beckoned a second officer over. Melody watched them discussing the paperwork, her throat dry and nausea rising.

'I see your father was a senior officer in the British Army,' he said in perfect English.

'He retired a long time ago. He's now a partner in an investment bank. What's this got to do–'

'He has also been an adviser to the British Government, has he not?'

'Yes, but only on fiscal matters. He's an investment banker, he has no connection with the Ministry of Defence. What has this got to do with my visit?'

'Follow me please, Miss.' The second officer said as he invited her through a waist-high gate to an interview room guarded by an armed sentry. Melody scanned the sparse room; a simple table held a white telephone and was accompanied by two chairs. A connecting door led to an even smaller room. She immediately noted the CCTV cameras positioned at the corners of the ceiling.

'Take a seat,' the first officer said.

What has gone wrong? Have they arrested Farrokh?

'Is there a problem?' she asked as she slipped into one of the seats.

'I ask the questions,' he said, looking up as a female officer entered without speaking.

Melody felt anxious. *Is she here to carry out a strip search?*

The officer ignored Melody but grabbed her hand luggage, taking it into the adjoining room to search through it.

'Where will you be staying here in Mazandaran?'

'My hotel reservations are with my visa; you have them there,' Melody said in English. The questions were faster than her ability to translate whilst trying to see what the female operative was doing and also keeping eye contact with her interviewer. She wiped beads of sweat from her forehead whilst feigning nonchalance.

He picked up the telephone and punched in numbers whilst staring at her. Melody could hear the conversation, but he was speaking so quickly in Farsi that she missed parts of it. It was a brief call and as he put the phone down, the other operative returned with her bags.

'You can go now,' he said. Then nodded to the officer who escorted her out and through security. During the whole encounter, neither of them had smiled.

As soon as Melody walked into the arrival hall, she flopped down onto the first vacant chair, her hands and legs still trembling. *What a strange encounter. They acted as though they were expecting me. But if they knew so much and were suspicious, why did they let me go so easily? On the upside, I'm actually in Iran and free to go.*

Eventually, she spotted her friend Farrokh Mokri within a crowd of expectant friends and relatives, standing alongside the more subdued

70

limo drivers holding name placards. Farrokh appeared to be anxiously looking up at the balcony. Melody followed his stare. There was only one man and judging by his chiselled features and pale complexion, he was probably European. Then he turned and disappeared. Afterwards, Farrokh caught her attention and waved.

She made her way over, forcing a smile. 'Who was the man on the balcony?'

'Nice to see you too,' Farrokh said.

'I'm sorry, it's just the face seemed vaguely familiar. Maybe it'll come to me later. Do you know him?'

'No, and maybe you're becoming paranoid. Come, I have a car waiting, a nice Land Rover Discovery with air con. We have a long drive ahead of us to base camp.'

'I'll probably sleep most of the way. I didn't on the plane.'

'Any problems at customs?'

'Two immigration officers interviewed me, wanted to know about my father and mentioned the Army. I felt nervous. They're so officious.'

'Don't worry. They interviewed our cleaner once because she told someone she'd watched Fox News.'

'You're growing a beard,' Melody said, frowning.

'Yes. It's different here, hair is important. For example, Iran's Football Federation has ordered football clubs to stop players with long messy hair, ponytails, hair bands and certain kinds of trendy, shaven beards or they will fine or ban them from playing. Welcome to Iran!'

'It's a bit bushy. Is it compulsory?'

'Pretty much. Beards have a significant cultural and religious association in Iran. Faith has historically been intertwined with rigid notions of masculinity, and the beard was considered part of the natural order for men. Many in the government regard shaving close to the skin as self-harm.'

'Welcome to Iran indeed! Well, I must say I'm not a fan of beards.'

'Nor am I.'

They loaded the car and wound their way through the busy shopping area. 'Would you mind stopping somewhere with toilets?' Melody said. 'I should have gone when I was at the airport, but I was desperate to get out of there.'

'There's a posh shop nearby; they will have nice toilets,' Farrokh said. Minutes later he was pulling up outside Rosha's department store. 'I'll wait here for you.'

As soon as Melody entered, she made her way to the electronics department and purchased three mobile phones, paying for them in cash. She was certain the female security guard at the airport had added a tracking device to her phone and had probably tried to download her contacts. Once in the toilets, she wiped clean the compromised phone, placed it in the waste bin and left it switched on before hurrying back to the car.

They headed north for Chalus before turning east at the Southern tip of the Caspian Sea. Melody could see glimpses of it as the car raced past fishing harbours. She would have liked to spend some time here, but time was a commodity in short supply. *I'm only going to get one shot at finding the swaddling. I can't get caught.*

'Is the distant mountain Mount Damāvand?' Melody marvelled at the stark mountain range against the sunset.

'Yes, but we won't be going so far south. Technically, it's a potentially active volcano.'

'In Zoroastrian texts and mythology, they chained the three-headed dragon Aži Dahāka within Mount Damāvand,' Melody said, and then, in a spooky voice, 'There to remain until the end of the world.'

'Let's hope it's not too soon,' he said, handing her the map. 'From the information you gave us, we head east for about two hundred kilometres and then turn south at Gohar Tepe, just before Behshahr.'

'What are the roads like there?' She unfolded the map on the back seat.

'Single track forest roads, mainly. The Alborz Mountains Range is an uninhabited area, but the base camp we've set up is OK and reasonably well equipped.'

By the time they reached the forested valley, it was dark and progress was slow; the canopy of trees was hiding the moonlight apart from eerie gaps where it cast down a ghostly glow.

'The track narrows further from here to the camp, but it's not far now,' Farrokh said as the car bounced over the track.

Not long after they passed through the remains of two wooden gate posts and entered a clearing. Melody took in the temporary but organised tents and marquees.

'Wow!' she said. 'I wasn't expecting to find a shack here and who lives in the tepee?'

'I kept the shack a secret. It's for you. It must have been a hunting lodge a long time ago, but the guys have patched it up pretty well. We thought you'd be safer and more comfortable there. The tepee belongs to the head chef, Zubeen.' He was still talking as the Land Rover came to a halt outside.

'I love it, thank you Farrokh.'

'Have a look around. Don't get too excited though, it's extremely basic. I'll fetch your things.'

Melody stepped into the shack and explored the interior; they had placed a simple bunch of wildflowers in a makeshift vase in the centre of a scrubbed wooden table where two folding camp chairs were tucked in neatly, looking decidedly out of place. At the end of the room was a rustic wood-burning stove, filling the room with warmth and the scent of wood smoke. A washing bowl, jug and three shelves lived next to it.

'What do you think?' Farrokh walked in behind her. 'The team spent ages making it habitable. There's even a rudimentary toilet through there,' he said, pointing to a door next to the bed.

'I love it, and it's massive, a step up from a tent. Would you thank them for me?'

'You can do it in person tomorrow when I introduce you to them, though some scouts are still out, making a narrow passage through the thickets of sweetbriar and acacias.'

'Where do they camp overnight?'

'There's a second and even more basic camp further up the valley, in a small clearing they use.' He shrugged. 'Do you need anything else?'

'No. They've even put a pot of coffee on the stove.' She turned, smiling. 'I shall enjoy it here, but I would like to visit the other camp tomorrow.'

'Good, I'll see you in the morning. I'll be leaving around 10 a.m. Breakfast is at seven in the big marquee. Goodnight, Melody.'

'Sleep tight,' Melody said, searching for a mug.

Not long after she was sitting comfortably in one of the camp chairs sipping the dark, strong coffee whilst taking in her accommodation when, with a mixture of relief and anxiety, she could feel an episode beginning. *Ah, now it begins…*

A sense of utter despair gripped her. It was overwhelming. It clawed at her, pulling her down. Everything around her spun faster and faster. Her eyes were clouding over. Her breathing became more difficult. She was struggling for breath, gasping. The surrounding space was pure white, with no walls or horizon, like a blank canvas. So quiet, so alone, so vulnerable. Then a total loss of sight, leaving her in pitch black. Gradually the light appeared as a new dawn and colour returned. *Ah! The colour.* An overwhelming sense of peace descended on her…

She was in a wooded valley, standing in a small clearing. She could hear the faint sound of rushing water, perhaps a waterfall, and could smell apple blossom. Several men nearby were hacking away at the undergrowth, bent double and sweating profusely. She was staring up at the valley side. It was high up and faint, but there was no mistaking it.

There it was – the sunlight illuminating the mouth of a cave.

Chapter Seventeen

~~

The London Embassy commander spoke on a secure line with Tehran, where his colleague Commander Zaynab Gilani from Iran's Revolutionary Guard was stationed.

'How did the interview of the British woman proceed, Zaynab?'

'We let her know we were aware of her background and not convinced of her intentions. She had medication in her bag, an anti-depressant. She doesn't seem the type to suffer from anxiety to me. We also put a tracker in her phone but we found it later that day in a waste bin in a ladies' washroom and she hasn't booked into her hotel.'

'I was right to be suspicious. She's resourceful. What's your next move?'

'We've sent a bulletin to ferry terminals, airports, car rentals, hospitals, etc. To report any English woman and use whatever means to hold her until we arrive.'

'What about her friend Farrokh Mokri?'

'We have spoken to her sponsor Mokri and we're briefing the Ministry of Intelligence Service. There is a possibility they already have an interest in him. We would not want to interfere with a MOIS operation. Just keep a watching brief on him at the moment. I believe that given sufficient rope, he or she will hang themselves. The team is monitoring his mobile for chatter and we should be able to find her location through it. Any further intel on what she's here for?'

'I will email my updated report later today. Strange as it sounds, apparently, she has an obsession with a Christian relic concerning the mystical Magi, but it could be a cover. It may be worth getting Mokri in. Let him see his family being interviewed.'

'No, we don't want to spook him too early, and there's the MOIS thing. We need to keep our eyes on the prize, holding an "Oxford University Don on spying charge". With her father, an ex-army chief and a government advisor, she'll make a great bargaining chip. After all, jailing Zaghari-Ratcliffe, the British woman, was how we got the £400m back from the tank deal, and I hope a part of any deal will include the release of my brother.'

'But he's in an Israeli jail. How would that work?'

'The UK Government provides intel for them. I'm sure they could do a quid pro quo. If I can land her, the Revolutionary Council will be more likely to consider it.'

'It seems ages since it happened. Is he OK?'

'We've not had direct contact with him for three years. The Israelis will not even admit they have him. However, after the last prisoner exchange for the Israeli soldier Gilad Shalit, one detainee said he'd been in a cell next to him and so we know he's alive.'

'My prayers are with you.'

'Thank you. Any Intel about the father regarding the embassy siege?'

'It is all in my report. You will have it today. Then we can talk some more.'

Chapter Eighteen

~~

The nurse knocked on the door, and entered. 'Nikolai, your brothers-in-law are waiting to see you. Can you manage that?'

'Yes. Sasha, it's important. Show them in.'

'Only half an hour, though. You know what the doctor said.' She reminded him, frowning.

Two burly minders were standing on either side of his bed when they entered. Their presence surprised Ivan and Grigory, but not as much as Nikolai's condition; it had only been a week since they last met but he looked considerably thinner, greyer and frailer.

'How are you Nikolai? Are they looking after you? Do you need anything?' Ivan asked.

'Three questions and only the last one is important. There is nothing medical science can do for me.' Nikolai paused, needing to conserve energy. 'Do you not understand? My only hope is –' He coughed, then took several breaths. 'I need the swaddling cloth, a miracle cure. Let me remind you, you are rich men because of me.'

Grigory spoke. 'Be reasonable, Nikolai–'

'You're not even sure if this Melody Thornton woman has found it,' he said. 'I'm not interested in how you get it, only results.'

'Nikolai, we are thinking of nothing else. We have strong links through the Vatican and Vasily–'

'Ah! Yes, Vasily Valkov, they call him The Wolf for good reason and just because you're married to my sisters, you don't get a free ticket.' He said, coughing. 'I have instructed Vasily to take charge of this project.

Securing the swaddling is all that matters,' he paused again and took several deep breaths. 'You will report directly to him. I am sending these two gentlemen to assist you; the clock is ticking.' He looked at the men either side of him but he was tiring.

'Do not disappoint me,' Nikolai said, waving them away.

Shortly after they left, the nurse returned. 'I'm glad you had a short meeting. I wanted to hear you finish your story of "Rags to Riches". You were about to leave university,' Sasha said whilst taking his pulse. 'If you're up to it?'

'Seems so long ago now. I graduated with an oil and gas engineering degree in 1972.'

'What made you choose oil and gas for a degree?'

'Sasha, Russia exports only four products worldwide: military hardware, vodka, caviar and energy in the form of oil and gas,' he said, struggling to laugh. 'And because of my connections in the local party machinery,' he caught his breath, but tiredness was pulling at him. 'They assigned me to the State Committee for the Oil Industry.'

'Did you like it?'

'It was an opportunity to be the boss of "Yuganskneftegaz," the giant Petrogas company. Make them efficient, they said... got to travel to America.'

'Going to America. It sounds so romantic. Oh, how I'd love to go to there. Why didn't you stay there?'

'I would have defected, but the KGB were everywhere... watching, listening. I fooled them once. Arranged some visas... took my sisters to visit America. You should have seen their faces, squealing like young girls. I promised...' He was holding back his tears now. 'I promised, one day, they would live there.'

He was drifting away, a smile playing across his face. He loved this feeling, sleep swallowing him, no pain...

Snapshot memories flashed in his mind of the secret meetings with bankers at Lehman Brothers Inc, the decadent nightlife and closer to home, the invites to the Kremlin. Meeting Mikhail Gorbachev, who talked enthusiastically about his perestroika reforms. But the breakthrough with First Secretary Boris Nikolayevich Yeltsin was the game-changer.

'Your reforms have not gone unnoticed, Nikolai. We must move toward a free-market economy and end this senseless quota system for manufacturing.'

Yeltsin pulled him out of the earshot of everyone. 'Nikolai, I'd like to put your name forward to become a deputy of the State Duma. You have a growing reputation for getting things done. We speak the same language and we must drag the Soviet Union out of the dark ages. We are being left behind by the Americans and even Europe is pulling ahead.'

'It would be an honour to have your support, comrade. I must also congratulate you on your appointment to the Politburo and election as mayor of Moscow. Change is coming.'

With that, Yeltsin had simply nodded, moving away to "press the flesh" with other rising stars. His face flushed from too much vodka. Nikolai had noticed this weakness in Yeltsin, his drinking was in danger of getting out of control, along with his other vulnerability – a propensity for glamorous young women.

Nikolai sensed the accelerating pace of change. He had already amassed a small fortune by Soviet standards from the bribes he had taken for infrastructure and capital projects in the oil fields. They stowed away some in cash deposit boxes in Switzerland and invested the rest through Lehman Brothers. Now, he needed to get close to President Mikhail Gorbachev, who talked incessantly about his perestroika reforms. The breakthrough, though, had been with First Secretary Boris Nikolayevich Yeltsin.

His next move held the greatest danger…

Chapter Nineteen

~~

Melody woke as dawn was breaking, lying on her bed in a sleeping bag, but unable to remember how she got there. The milky light was sneaking through the roughly made hessian curtains as she lay listening to the sounds of the forest, wondering if they would eventually become background noise like the clamour of traffic in the city.

She got up and took the journal from her rucksack, making copious notes of the previous night's vision before filling the washbowl; the water was cool on her face, reminding her of the waterfall in the vision. As she dried it, she noticed there wasn't a mirror in the room.

Why don't men understand the simple needs of women?

She used her compact mirror whilst combing her strawberry blonde hair back and tied it in two bunches. Then she took two pills from a container inconspicuously marked 'lozenges' and swallowed them without a drink, noting they were running low. *I should have topped them up in the UK.* She then made her way over to one of the large marquees. The smell of bread baking drifted from it, inviting her in.

'How did you sleep?' Farrokh asked.

'I slept well, which is fortunate. If I don't get enough sleep, I'm like a tall three-year-old. What's for breakfast?'

'Mainly tea, omelette, and sangak bread, but the chef will make you something else,' he said whilst turning to the man serving the food. 'Isn't that so?'

'My pleasure, miss.'

'What you have here is fine. Thank you, chef.' Melody smiled.

'You know a few of them, but I'll introduce you to those you don't.' Farrokh spoke whilst walking over to the buffet table. 'Melody, this is Amooz, who you already know, and is leading the team.'

'Hello, it's nice to see you in the flesh, Skyping isn't the same.'

Melody thought he looked tired and somewhat dishevelled.

'Do you have everything you need?' she asked.

'What I need now is a little luck,' he said, tucking his shirt in.

A young man standing next to him offered his hand enthusiastically. 'I'm Jadu, but everyone calls me Jad, a specialist in drone photography.'

'I'll look forward to reviewing what you've got so far,' Melody said, shaking his hand.

He was about to reply, but Farrokh put his hand on her shoulder. 'But first, you must eat. I'll introduce the rest at the daily briefing. Come, the chef's bread is to die for.'

She chose a selection of food and then headed over to sit with Amooz. 'Tell me about the team you've put together?'

'My first appointment was Dilshod, ex-army and a renowned tracker. He appears soft, but rules with an iron fist and demands complete loyalty. I gave him the task of appointing most of them. He hand-picked them based on their experience. They're mostly ex-servicemen. Zubeen, the chef, has worked with me before as have Jad and Nouri, the technicians. Farzad, the chief archaeologist, was of course your appointment.'

Farrokh joined them, but then his mobile rang. 'Excuse me, I must take this,' he said, moving out of hearing distance.

Melody caught glimpses of him pacing back and forth across the entrance. The conversation seemed animated, and he looked stressed.

'He'll have a heart attack one day if he carries on like this.' The man who spoke had spotted Melody's concern and was now seating himself opposite her at the table.

'I'm the chief guide, Dilshod,' he said. His thick accent showed he was not Iranian. 'I've told him many times, but he will not listen. In my country, they would call him Muammoli ruh – "a troubled soul."'

'Which country is that?' asked Melody.

'I was born in Uzbekistan. Life is simpler there; it is the same in Azerbaijan. Here in Iran…' He shook his head. 'Religion, politics and choosing sides. You cannot even trust the State.'

'Did you live in Azerbaijan?'

'I worked there for a long time.'

'How well do you know this area?'

'I don't, nobody does. Bears and mountain lions are kings here. My primary task is looking for clues of previous inhabitants, but it's been such a long time, the forest has reclaimed it and wants to keep it a secret, but if it's there, I will find it.'

'I'd like a meeting with you later if that's OK. I may have more clues for–'

'Sorry, Melody,' Farrokh said, as he rushed in and gathered his belongings. 'I have to leave earlier than expected. Family issues. I'll call you later.'

'Can I help you in any way?'

'No, no, I'll be fine. I will call you later. It's nothing.'

'Muammoli ruh, Muammoli ruh,' said Dilshod to himself as Farrokh left and Melody followed him. Although Dilshod couldn't hear them, it looked like an anxious conversation.

They cancelled the briefing, which allowed Melody to arrange a smaller meeting. She used the other marquee that also functioned as the communications centre, first aid centre and drone maintenance workshop. Jad had arranged his most recent aerial photos around the walls.

Melody addressed her audience.

'Firstly, thank you all for the monumental effort you've put in to get us this far and, in particular, for my shack, which is delightful and unexpected and has a toilet.' The men laughed, relaxing the atmosphere. 'So, a quick recap, how are we doing and finally what's next? Amooz, could you recap what we know?'

'We started with Melchior's prophesy as discovered by Prof. Schmidt,' Amooz sat up straight. 'Melchior had requested a meeting with fellow Magi, Caspar and Balthazar at the Valley of Ascendency at Behshahr, south of the Caspian Sea. Schmidt also described the area. He said the mountain summits were crowned with cedars and cypresses, referring to it as Belad-al-Irem – Land of the Terrestrial Paradise. They were to meet in the Sanctuary of the Gathering Place, which we believe from other manuscripts to be a cave.'

Melody smiled, pleased her vision was confirmed.

Amooz picked up some notes. 'There are also references to thickets of honeysuckle, sweetbriar, acacias, lindens and chestnut trees, all of which Dilshod has identified after a great deal of searching. They are all found in this valley, but we don't know if this is the actual one referred to in the prophecy, but it is our best guess. Therefore, we're heading toward the cedar-topped range and making reasonable progress.'

'Thanks, Amooz,' Melody looked at Jad. 'Can you bring us up to date with aerial recon?'

'The good news is the military-grade drones we're using are performing well. The bad news is the canopy is a real problem. Flying drones below is extremely difficult and in some places, impossible but, above it, visibility is poor. The chief scout has found clues from contours and different vegetation we've filmed, but it feels like we've plateaued out.'

'Have you got infra-red heat-detecting cameras for the drones?'

'Yes, and a couple of Nano drones we're testing for an IT company, but what would I be looking for?' Jad said, holding up his hands.

'Turbulent water, perhaps a waterfall? The water would be colder than the surrounding environment. I can't explain why now, but I believe the cave is on the Eastern flank of the valley, close to the sound of rushing water.'

'I'll go off track and see if I can locate a river or stream,' Dilshod, the chief scout said.

'I'll load the drones up,' said Jad, making ready to leave. 'Dilshod, can we discuss the best area to start in? We're currently trying to cover an area of five hundred square miles.'

He moved over to the photographs and tapped on one. 'A couple of weeks ago, I saw a Slavonian Grebe flying overhead in this area. I paid little attention, but it wouldn't have been far from water. It would make sense. The area enjoys a moderate, subtropical climate, with temperatures of around 25 °C in summer and about 8 °C in winter, ideal for waterfowl. It's as good a place as any to map.'

'Let's hope I'm not sending you on a wild goose chase,' said Melody, smiling. A few of the men laughed and the rest sat in awkward silence. 'It was a pun, you know, Slavonian Grebe, wild goose… Oh, never mind.'

'Yes, it was a joke, no!' said Jad.

Melody shook her head. 'I'll be in the shack if anyone needs me,' she said, leaving them in the marquee.

Dilshod followed her out. 'Is Farrokh OK? He seemed agitated?'

Melody frowned and then patted him on the shoulder. 'He's got family problems, that's all.'

'The men will become nervous if they think there is a weak link.'

'Amooz told me you demand complete loyalty.'

'I do and the money you're paying is equivalent to three years' wages for most of them.'

'Plus a bonus if we find it.' She said, then regretted minimising the danger.

'Still, keep a close eye on him.'

'You'll be the first to know if I sense any threat.'

Dilshod's question, and the incident at the airport, made Melody consider her exposure. She had spoken to Farrokh several times on one of her phones. 'Jad, can I have a word with you?'

'Sure, can you walk and talk? I need to prep the drones?'

'Can one of your drones take this mobile phone as far away as possible and dump it?'

'I have one that can, but why?'

'I think they will use it to locate us. It's just a precautionary measure.'

'Leave it with me. I have one drone with a grab. Anywhere in particular?'

'I'll show you on the map. I'll be leaving it switched on, but I've cleaned it.'

She thought about Farrokh and his odd behaviour before leaving, as well as the man he seemed to know at the airport. She felt sure she had seen him before. Then a sudden flash of inspiration hit her. She scrolled through the pictures on her phone.

She stopped at one.

It's the same person. I took this picture while training – at Glasgow Central Railway Station.

Chapter Twenty

~~

Why would someone follow me in Glasgow and then show up in Iran? Either it connects them to Sospitas, or I have been under surveillance for a considerable length of time. The latter is concerning, the former would be deeply worrying.

Melody was back in the shack considering the ramifications when another of her encounters began. She used the table to support herself as she made her way to a chair, but before reaching it, she collapsed to the floor. Along came the wave of despair, the loss of her sight and breath, and then the beautiful sense of peace.

She was in a desert; the sun was beating down without a breath of wind. She looked up at an imposing complex on top of the hill. It looked to be a combination of a fortress and a palace. Beautiful yet foreboding, its high stone walls impregnable, the gates shut tight and unwelcoming, whilst the gilded domes of the buildings within shone invitingly.

Amongst a large travelling party, three men were in an earnest discussion. She recognised them instantly from other visions, but she'd rarely seen them together. One of them was Melchior, the elder statesman, the Chief Magi.

Such an elegant man, with your long silky white hair, and, as always, the gold cloak draped over your spotless white tunic. Yes, I have researched you excessively. But what would I give to invite you to a dinner party?

'I'm glad to be moving on. What say you, Lord Melchior or are you still troubled by yesterday's events at Herod's Palace?' Lord Balthazar asked.

What a big man you are, Lord Balthazar, big-hearted, a hater of injustice, loud and such good fun. Any meal with you would be a banquet. But also, I would dearly love to meet your wife.

'It's complicated, my friend, but consider this: there is no Jewish blood in Herod; he is of Nabatean and Edomite descent, whose ancestors converted to Judaism. He calls himself King of the Jews, though many regard this as blasphemy. The birth of a real Jewish King will only compound this,' Melchior looked back at Herod's Palace. 'I fear for the child's safety in this corrupt Herodian Kingdom. Mark my words, our business with Herod is not over. I can sense it, especially as we have to consider the implications of returning.'

'What of the disturbing revelations you had?' Lord Caspar asked.

Ah, the clever one. The Angel whisperer, your weathered countenance cutting such a dash with your purple tunic and green cloak. Teach me the language of angels!

'As for the prophetic messages, I believe a clearer picture will emerge once we have completed what Herod refers to as "our quest."'

Melchior stopped his camel for a moment to address them both.

'There is one thing of which I am certain and, I promise you both, only death will prevent me from fulfilling the mission to deliver our gifts. Ironically, I have Herod to thank for that.' As they moved off, the three men were smiling.

Melody wanted to travel with them.

Don't go, I want to come with you, please, please don't leave me here.

She couldn't move. The caravan continued moving on, gradually fading away like a desert mirage. Her feet were stuck in the sand. She was being drawn down. The sand was up to her knees. The more she struggled, the deeper she went. Now waist high, she was frantically clawing at the sand. Despite that, she was sinking. Her shoulders now covered, she threw her head back to take a final breath and screamed for help...

Chapter Twenty-One

~~

Melody woke on the floor, gasping for air. *Breathe slowly but deeply – in through the nose for four, hold the breath for two, and then out for six. These encounters are more like nightmares, they seem to be increasingly dangerous or violent. Perhaps the medication isn't working.*

She was aching from being on a hard floor. It was dark with barely a flicker of light from the stove. She staggered to her bed and flopped down on it, exhausted.

* * *

The following morning, she found her bag and dug out her medication; not many left. She had one capsule with a glass of water before washing and dressing. She had a quick breakfast and then headed over to the parked vehicle's lot, surprising the mechanic.

'Oh! Hi, how are you? I mean, how can I help you?' he asked.

'I'm fine, thank you. The other camp is where I would like to go. Have you got a spare vehicle?' Melody asked.

'Er, yes, take this Jeep. I've finished with it now.'

Dilshod was nearby and watching her with some concern as he walked over. 'Are you planning a trip?'

'I was looking to visit the second camp,' she said. 'To see the progress and meet the other scouts. Just a little curious, that's all.'

'They may all be out working. Let me send a guide with you.'

'Thank you, I was a little concerned, though I don't want to interfere with the work here.'

'In that case, I'll take you. I'd like to check on the progress myself.'

'That sounds like a plan. Can I drive?'

'Er, yes, if you want to.'

As they drove away, Dilshod radioed the scouts working from the second camp.

The Jeep barely fit on the narrow track, which was filled with potholes. Eventually, it turned into a clearing in the forest. The bivouac was small, with a separate area for cooking and washing, Melody assumed. She pulled up and switched off the engine. The camp looked deserted. She expected someone to be there, but Dilshod had warned her they may all be out scouting.

'Stay in the vehicle whilst I find the scouts.' He said, stepping out of the Jeep and fishing behind the seat for the hunting rifle. 'I shouldn't be too long,' he said, slinging the rifle over his shoulder. 'You'll be safe in here.'

As he walked away, she closed her eyes and threw her arms open. The chattering and squawking of the forest seemed to add to a sense of peace, and even in the isolation, she felt closer to her goal.

Opening her eyes, she took in the scenery. They had cleared an area about the size of a football pitch for the temporary camp. A few minutes later, she left the vehicle, walked to the centre of the clearing and began twirling like a schoolgirl. She inhaled deeply. The smell of the forest was like an intoxicant to her, the air crisp and clean. She scanned the valley's sides, at least a half-mile away in either direction. *Where are you? I know you're out there.*

Whilst scouring the tree line, she missed the bear cub, breaking cover from the undergrowth and heading for the food store. When she saw its mother lumber into the clearing, she stopped. Then looked at the Jeep a hundred metres away, trying to make a mental calculation: the distance to the Jeep, how quickly she could run and how close the bear was.

I won't make it in time and my heart feels like it is going to explode, and my legs feel like jelly. What was the advice if you encountered a bear? Do not run? Or was it to roll up in a tight ball? No, avoid direct eye contact. Do not scream or yell. Speak in a soft monotone voice and wave your arms to let the animal know you are human. The bear was sniffing the air; she can smell me. If she goes to the food store, I'll back away slowly, and melt into the forest.

The bear was again sniffing the air and flicked its protective eyes between the cub and her.

Keep still, they are excellent at detecting movement.

It raised itself to its full height, smelling the air. It looked towards the cub which was still exploring the tents before looking at Melody and dropping onto all four legs.

Stay calm. It's simply trying to better identify what's caught its attention. It is much easier to see, hear and detect the scent of things when standing. Do not make any sudden movements.

The bear raised itself again. This time it let out an enormous roar, then crashed down on all fours, thumping the ground and growling.

Avoid making eye contact, wave my arms, try to speak – why can't I speak? – no sound is coming out, just a squeak and my heart is pounding so fast.

In a moment of blind panic, she ran as fast as she could towards the Jeep. Her legs felt like lead weights and the ground like a sponge. She could hear the bear running, its snorting sound getting louder. *Fifty metres, dear God, help me. Breathe deeply and keep going. Twenty metres, fifteen metres, nearly there.*

She was only ten metres from safety when the bear struck, one claw ripping through her khaki shirt. As she was falling to the ground, another heavy paw swiped the side of her head and just before she lost consciousness, she heard a single crack of a rifle and men's voices. *What a senseless way to die.* Then everything went black.

Chapter Twenty-Two

~~

Dilshod drove the Jeep at a crawl back to the main camp, easing around the potholes.

'We can't just turn up at any hospital. For all we know they could have a watch on them. What about contacting Farrokh? He'll know where to go,' the scout said.

'Farrokh is not reliable now. Under no circumstances does anyone contact him. Is that understood?' Nobody spoke. 'What we mustn't do is choose the nearest hospital. If things go pear-shaped, we'll be easy to find. We'll need time to evacuate the camp safely,' Dilshod said.

'She's unconscious. We need to act quickly.'

'Yes, but she's stable and still breathing. Galugah Hospital is the nearest, but Omidi Hospital is not much further and it's smaller. If her condition deteriorates on the way, we can go to the closest one. How is she now?'

'No change. My primary concern is the concussion. There may be damage we can't see. She may need a CT scan. Luckily, the claw wounds are slight, more of a scratch, but they can carry a risk of infection and even the possibility of sepsis. I've cleaned them with a sterile solution, but I'm only a first responder. I'm not a doctor,' the scout said as they pulled into the main camp.

'The wounds don't seem severe, but I think it's best if I take Miss Thornton. The rest of you stay here. Some of you have a family in Iran. They'd be at risk if they caught you,' Dilshod said. As soon as the occupants left the Jeep, Dilshod set off, leaving them to explain the events to the rest of the team who had gathered for their arrival.

* * *

Dilshod burst through the doors at Dr Omidi Hospital.

'Quick!' he shouted. 'I need help. She's the victim of a bear attack. I'm not sure she's breathing.'

The receptionist was so startled she dropped the phone, then recovered and shouted down the corridor. 'I need a doctor and nurses immediately. It's an emergency.'

Dilshod ran outside.

In less than a minute, two porters, a nurse and a doctor were outside with him.

'I have a pulse.' The nurse said as the porters were placing Melody on a trolley.

'What happened?' the doctor asked Dilshod.

'Bear attack, we think. It knocked her out and there are some claw marks on her back.'

'How long ago?' They headed inside.

'Not sure, at least an hour ago.'

As the group entered the hospital, more doctors and nurses were arriving. They followed the trolley to a triage bay.

The receptionist pulled Dilshod away. 'We don't deal with accidents and emergencies here,' she told him. 'Normally, this hospital is for outpatients only.'

'I panicked and saw the hospital sign,' he said, noting her name on the badge: Soraya.

'She's in excellent hands now,' she said, smiling, 'but we may have to transfer her to Galugah Hospital if there are complications.'

'Would that be necessary? This seems an excellent hospital.'

'We'll see. Can you give me some details about the patient? She doesn't look Iranian. What nationality is she?'

Dilshod was explaining that he didn't know her when a new email pinged on the receptionist's screen.

It had the familiar IRGC logo.

The Revolutionary Guard is actively searching for a foreign woman who promotes Zionist Christianity and poses a threat to national security. We urge anyone with information to come forward.

It included a picture of her passport and a blown-up photograph; Soraya recognised her as the new patient. She read it twice, then smiled to herself; she sent it to her printer and with a satisfied feeling, forwarded the email to junk.

'... I think she got separated from her group. I was out hunting with friends when we stumbled across her – just in time, it seems,' Dilshod said.

'Did she have any form of identification with her? The authorities may find it strange she didn't even have a mobile phone with her?'

'Apparently not. Looks like the bear took her bag. It probably had food in it. We'll go back and do a thorough search once I know she's stable.' Dilshod was relieved the crew had done a thorough job of cleaning all forms of identity from her.

'Take a seat. Would you like a drink?'

'Coffee would be great, thanks.'

After an hour of reading old magazines and propaganda, Dilshod was pleased when a nurse came.

'She has come round but has not spoken yet. We will need to do a few more tests, but we will send her to Galugah for a CT scan tomorrow to be on the safe side. The wounds on her back are slight flesh wounds. We have dressed them and given her antibiotics, but they didn't require stitches. They should heal in a day or two. We'll keep her in overnight whilst we arrange for the scan.'

'I'd like to see her if that's OK. I feel a sense of responsibility.'

'Normally only a relative would be allowed–'

'Just for a minute, please.'

She frowned, but then gestured for him to follow her.

It was a short walk, and once they got there, the nurse left him. It was a sparse room with an iron-framed bed, but was spotlessly clean. Dilshod closed the door.

'Melody,' he said in a low voice. 'Can you hear me? We're on our own.'

She opened her eyes. 'Thank God you're here. I thought I was on my own. What happened exactly? The last thing I remember was a bear and running?'

'We pulled into the clearing just as the bear started chasing you. Dawar, one of my best scouts from the second camp was the first to react. He jumped out of the vehicle and was firing whilst the rest were shouting to distract it.'

'Did he kill it?'

'No. But he wounded it enough for it to take off with its cub. How are you feeling? We were worried about you.'

'I feel groggy and my back stings, but I'm fine… I apologise for not heeding your advice. I feel foolish.'

'You're not the first, but thanks, and please take no more unnecessary risks. There are enough already,' he said, still whispering. 'Look, this is a small hospital. They normally only handle out-patients, but they seem laid-back. They want to keep you overnight, but tomorrow they're transferring you to the major hospital at Galugah for a CT scan. That would require a lot of forms.' He walked over to the window, opened it and looked out. Then turned back to the room, picking up a small white flannel; he dropped it on the floor outside as a marker before snapping the window back shut.

'If you're questioned, this is my story,' Melody said. 'My name is Yalda Khalaji. I am an only child. I was born in Iran with a mixed Iranian and

Swiss heritage. My parents died two years ago in a car accident near where we lived in Bandar Abbas. I was on a camping trip with a friend. Can you remember that?'

'Yes, of course, that makes sense,' he nodded.

'I feel well enough to leave, but I won't discharge myself now. It may seem suspicious.'

'I agree. Stay overnight and discharge yourself tomorrow,' he whispered. 'Here is my phone. Keep it hidden and on silent. All the team's numbers are in there. Call if you need us, otherwise, I will be back in the morning around seven. If you feel at all threatened – call.'

With that, he walked out towards reception.

It was changeover time, and the previous receptionist, Soraya, was talking to her replacement.

'How is she?' Soraya asked Dilshod as she joined him walking towards the exit.

'Not talking, but she seems to have recovered somewhat.'

Once in the car park, she furtively looked around and handed him an envelope before turning and walking away, saying nothing.

He opened it and scanned the contents; he felt sick.

He hurried to the Jeep and headed for camp, constantly checking he was not being followed.

Chapter Twenty-Three

~~~

Melody couldn't sleep. She felt exposed, isolated and out of control in the hospital bed and needed a plan. *Think back to the training. What are the immediate dangers and hotspots and what's my emergency escape plan? What would Stuart's advice be?* While thinking about it, she remembered the dinner they had at Sospitas and his remark about finding her entirely mysterious. It made her smile.

As she was considering this, another of her episodes started. This time, though, there was no sense of peace; she felt afraid, a sense of dread, tormented…

She found herself in a palatial room, marble and gold in abundance. Moving towards an even, more gilded area, the mention of the Magi made her take notice. A man was sitting on a gold throne. He seemed in pain and looked angry.

She was aware of something new, something she hadn't seen before. There were creatures that appeared to be unseen by the humans. Much larger than people and a drab dark grey colour – even the smallest were eight feet tall. She was uneasy and her movement seemed to attract their attention. It was as if they were aware of her presence but unable to see her; their stare was tracking her progress before they lost interest whenever she stopped. One passed close by, brushing against her hand. Immediately, her hand went ice cold.

Melody wanted it to end but several more creatures arrived. They were even larger than the others, almost twelve feet, but boasted the same monochrome grey. They were impervious to the human inhabitants, passing through them as they moved around.

'*Fallen Angels – Evil Spirits,*' the voice in her head repeated.

I want to wake up; I need to get out of here. Then a peace flooded over her and a voice, calm and clear but full of authority spoke in her mind, '*Move closer to the throne.*'

The man on the throne was speaking.

'… should have sent a guard with them; I knew I couldn't trust Lord Melchior and the other Magi – even less so.'

King Herod paused and, unseen by the people gathered near the throne, an Evil Spirit whispered in his ear.

'*Kill all the male children in Bethlehem under the age of two before he escapes.*'

'The Magi said the child would be almost two years old. Therefore, kill all boys under the age of two living in Bethlehem,' Herod said.

'Perhaps, your majesty, it would be wiser to ascertain the identity of this family,' the Chamberlain proposed, feeling nauseous from the order and scanning the room for approval, but finding none. 'The massacre of so many innocent children would diminish your standing as a compassionate king?'

'What do I care about these ungrateful subjects?' Herod said.

'Well, Sire,' he paused. 'There are fresh rumours.'

'More chatter and falsehoods, no doubt.'

'There are rumours the child's mother gave the Magi a piece of his swaddling and it has mystical, or, as some describe it, *supernatural* qualities.'

'What mystical or supernatural qualities?'

'Healing powers, your majesty, some people are calling it "The Healing Cloth". It may work where your physicians have failed,' he said, whilst turning to look at the chief physician, who glared at him. 'Our spies report the Magi are now returning home through Ein Gedi. Would it not be more practicable to relieve them of it?'

'No, don't be foolish. Naturally, we would overcome them, but it would be a bloodbath. Also, our friends in Rome would not approve. These are foreign dignitaries appointed by the Emperor. Besides, they have a disciplined, well-armed and loyal guard. A fight like that would only weaken me. I've made my decision, see to it and bring me this swaddling cloth.'

The King's Chamberlain bowed several times as he backed away.

'Yes, your majesty.'

The King rose and as he sat on a divan nearby; his courtiers scattered and then settled around him as he lay down, their fixed smiles barely hiding their anxiety. He was cursing the stomach pains and dwelling on this so-called healing cloth.

Melody watched as an evil spirit emerged from within King Herod.

Another spirit of a comparable size blocked it. 'Did you plant a seed of doubt in the king about the trustworthiness of the Chamberlain?' it asked.

'Out of my way! I need to speak with a hellion.' Then it moved to one of the larger creatures.

One spirit was heading straight towards Melody. She froze in terror. *Do I move or remain still?* As it passed through, her temperature plunged and she felt physically sick. The spirit stopped and looked around; aware something had changed but could not discover what it was. It eventually moved on...

* * *

Melody woke in her hospital bed, shivering and her teeth chattering. Curled up in a ball, cold and nauseous, she was aware of voices close by.

'Her temperature is only twenty-eight degrees,' a nurse said to the doctor.

'Fetch me a warming blanket and a heart monitor. Hypothermia means a higher risk of wound infection and a greater chance of heart problems. But what I don't understand is why she should end up so cold. If anything, it's a little warm in here.'

'Her temperature's still extremely low.'

'What happened, Mina?' the doctor asked.

'I called in on my routine hourly check. I found her shivering and moaning. When I felt her brow, she was freezing cold. So, I pulled the emergency cord.'

The second nurse arrived, wheeling in the equipment trolley. She set up the heart monitor whilst the other prepared the warm air blanket.

'Who is she? She doesn't look like an Iranian national to me,' the second nurse said.

'Aytan, we have a simple policy here,' the doctor said. 'It doesn't matter who they are, we treat them as though they were a relative of ours – regardless of politics or nationality.'

'It's just there was an announcement on the radio last–'

'Please, Aytan, do not tell me. I'd rather do something wrong in ignorance than have to decide. We save people's lives here, let others worry about saving society.'

'Yes, doctor.'

'She's tachycardic, her heart rate is a hundred and fifty,' Mina said.

'I'll give her 30mg/ml of Amiodarone,' he said. 'Then let's monitor her. Probably best to cancel her transfer to Galugah for a CT scan, at least until she normalises. It is strange, and she is a mystery, that's for sure. What's her temperature now?'

'Twenty-nine degrees, so a slight improvement.'

Chapter Twenty-Four

~~

Dilshod arrived back at camp as the light was fading and made his way into the marquee where the rest of the team had gathered. They fell silent as he entered.

Then Amooz spoke. 'How is she? Is she OK?'

'Her health is the least of our problems. She is conscious and they say the skin on her back will heal quickly. However, they want to move her to the major hospital at Galugah for a CT scan. We need to extract her first thing tomorrow,' he said, taking the note from his pocket. 'The receptionist gave me this. It's an email from the Revolutionary Guard,' he handed it to Amooz.

'Can we trust her?' he asked after reading it.

'She had no reason to warn me,' Dilshod said.

'Jad, there's an all-points bulletin out for her. Where did you dump her phone?' Amooz asked.

'It's on a fishing boat, probably in the Caspian Sea by now, assuming it hasn't already docked. Can we contact her?'

'I left her my phone,' Dilshod said. 'Look, it's a single-storey building. It shouldn't be hard to get her out, though I would prefer it if she simply discharged herself. Extracting her will simply raise awareness. I told her I'd be there at seven in the morning.'

'What about the receptionist? Will she be there?'

'I don't know. I am hoping she works a twelve-hour shift, six till six. But who knows, it could be her day off. Listen, we'll meet up at 0500 hours. Jad, I will need a drone available first thing. I want the ability to monitor the car park and the rear of the building, so choose your quietest one. I'll see you all in the morning.'

* * *

The following morning, Dilshod pulled into the hospital car park and, having satisfied himself that nothing unusual was happening, he spoke to Jad on his radio. 'Jad, can you see Melody's room?'

'Yes, I can see the marker you placed outside it. I'm about to zoom in. There seems to be a lot of activity. Just give me a moment… Yes, there are at least three medical staff, wait a minute, no, there are four now. Two men and two women, all wearing hospital scrubs. I thought you said she was recovering?'

'She was. Text me when she's on her own or if there's any suspicious activity, I'm going in.'

The sight of Soraya, the receptionist from the previous day, brought a sense of relief as he entered the building.

'Good morning. How are you today?' he asked.

'Fine, thank you. Have you come to see the lady you rescued yesterday?'

'Yes. How is she?' He realised for the first time how lovely her smile was.

'I'll ask one of the medical staff to update you. Whilst I do, here's a new magazine for you to read,' she said. After pulling it out from under the counter and having made certain no one was looking, she slipped a note inside the cover. She looked directly at him and nodded.

He settled into a chair and carefully opened the note, making sure no one else could see and read it…

Last night, the local radio station repeated the request by the IRGC for information regarding a female foreign national. It is only a matter of time before a member of the staff here reports her to the authorities. It would be better if you had a believable story. You need a story, or you will lose her!

He had finished reading and put the note away when Soraya returned.

'She took a turn for the worse during the night. But she seems to be slowly recovering. The doctor will let you know when she is recovered enough to talk. If you would like a coffee whilst you're waiting, please help yourself. It's over here,' she said, gesturing for him to follow.

'Why are you helping us?' Dilshod whispered when they were alone.

'The Revolutionary Guard arrested my brother for being part of a peaceful demonstration. Two days later, they found him hanging in his cell. They said it was suicide, but Babak would never have done that. He was so full of life. The RG killed him. I know they did. They were laughing when we went to collect his body. They are evil.'

'I'm sorry about your brother.'

'Thank you. Do you now have a story regarding the woman I can record? If so, tell it when someone else is present.'

'Yes, I will. I appreciate your help.'

'The medical team seems to find her a bit of a mystery.'

'She's a mystery to many.'

'Beware, if the RG shows up, leave immediately and destroy the note I gave you. You won't be able to help her, so save yourself. Good luck.'

Then she returned to the reception area.

Dilshod watched her intently as she walked away. He felt that at another time and place, he would love to know her better. He sighed, then concentrated on composing Melody's backstory. Thirty minutes later, he received a text from Jad – 'She's alone.'

Shortly after, Nurse Aytan came in and spoke to the receptionist, then called Dilshod over. He smiled at Soraya behind the desk.

'She had a spectacular plunge in temperature during the night. The doctor prescribed medication and we're now monitoring her. She is making excellent progress, but I have asked Soraya to cancel her transfer to Galugah for a CT scan. Can you tell me any more about her that may help?'

'Yes. I meant to give it to Soraya when I arrived, but forgot, sorry. One of my team met her friend whilst they were looking for her bag. Apparently, they were on a camping trip, a final jolly before her friend left for a new job today. She was about to report her missing when she stumbled on them,' he said, unfolding a piece of paper and reading from it. 'Her name is Yalda Khalaji. She is an only child. She was born in Iran with a mixed Iranian and Swiss heritage. Her parents died two years ago in a car accident near where they all lived in Bandar Abbas.'

'Did she have a mobile number?' Aytan asked.

'Yes, we tried calling it to locate her bag, but the batteries are probably dead, or it's broken because of the bear attack,' he said, giving the number of the one Jad had placed on the fishing vessel.

'No, I meant her friend so we can update her.'

'She gave it to me. I must have left it at home. But she said she would contact you once she had landed. She was flying to the United Arab Emirates this morning to start her new job.'

'I see. Thank you. I would recommend you don't come back for a couple of hours at least, to give her more time to recover.'

'Thank you,' he said, handing over his scribbled note to Soraya. 'I'll see you later.'

Chapter Twenty-Five

~~

He had been fretting over the lack of an update from Tehran when the call came through.

'What's the weather in London like today, my friend?'

'It's raining, but you already knew that. What progress have you made on the woman?'

'She is indeed a resourceful young lady. We traced her phone through the sponsor, Farrokh Mokri. It somehow ended up on a fishing vessel in the Caspian Sea. The coast guards boarded it, but there was no evidence she'd been there. Someone must have planted it.'

'Presumably, she can't be far away then,' he said, his tone irritable.

'Unfortunately, we caught up with them at Bandar-e-Anzali harbour, but he'd been to Chalus before. Don't worry, she won't get far; we have an all-points bulletin out on her.'

'Has there been any activity on her phone since?'

'No, we're monitoring it, in case someone calls her. The only call she made from it was Mokri, which is odd.'

'How did you find my report? Did it make interesting reading?'

'Yes. The link between her Army Colonel father and the SAS is tenuous. However, his connection with the Black Watch regiment training with the SAS only a year before the siege of our embassy should be enough to make capital out of once she's arrested for spying.'

'The UK Government will try to distance her father from it, though people will assume there is no smoke without fire and they have something to hide. We need to find her Zaynab. If she slips through your fingers, the Council will see it as more than a lost opportunity. I think it's time to get Mokri in unless MOIS has a legitimate interest in him.'

'MOIS are aware of our interest. I'm expecting a call from them today but... hang on a minute...'

The IRGC Intel operator was franticly beckoning him to listen to his phone conversation.

'I'll call you back. A fresh development on this case has just arisen.' The commander put the phone down and joined the intel team.

The intel operator was questioning someone who had called Melody's mobile phone they had recovered from the fishing vessel in the Caspian Sea. 'Who is it exactly you are trying to contact? I want to return this phone to its rightful owner,' the intel officer lied.

'At our hospital last night, we admitted a female trauma patient after a bear attack. This is the only contact number we have. I'm afraid I can't give you any further information without her permission,' Nurse Aytan said, now wondering if she had broken hospital protocol.

'Which hospital is that?'

'Look, I think it would be better if I wait until the person is stable–'

The operator broke in. 'Listen carefully, you are speaking to the Revolutionary Guard Headquarters and we are searching for the owner of this phone. You had better– '

'The phone's gone dead, Sir.'

'Did you get a trace?'

'No, but it's registered to Aytan Sharifi. She lives in Behshahr. There can't be many hospitals in the area,' the intel operator said.

'Inform the nearest agency. I want a team over there. Now!'

A second operative called out. 'She works at Omidi Hospital.'

'Send the team there and get the helicopter ready. Try ringing her back.'

'I have. She's switched it off. Should I call the hospital?'

'No. It may alert them; we need men there ASAP. No wonder she went off-grid. Set up a suitable hospital room near here, ready to receive her. She's injured and I want her alive and kicking.'

'Yes, Sir.'

'What kind of hospital is Omidi? I've never heard of it.'

'My mother went there for treatment. It's for out-patients only, small routine surgery work, mainly for the larger Galugah Hospital,' another agent said.

Gilani moved over to the wall map with his deputy Hossein and put a circle around the hospital.

'Why there? Get me a list of everyone who works at Omidi.'

'Normally you would go to the closest hospital, maybe they specialise in something,' Hossein said.

'It won't have an A&E dept. Were they perhaps attempting to throw us off their track?'

'We found the phone here,' he said, pointing at Bandar-e-Anzali harbour. 'But they had been to Chalus before that. Maybe that's where she lost it or had it planted,' Hossein said.

'An attack by a bear must have been in the forested area,' he said before shouting to no one in particular – 'I want a tracker who knows the forests of Mazandaran.'

'It's an extensive area to cover. Over fifty thousand square kilometres,' one researcher said.

'Yes, but they were close enough to make it to a clinic in Behshahr.'

'The Regional Director of MOIS is on the phone for you, Sir,' the researcher said.

'Tell him I'll call him back – say there's been a significant development.'

One minute later, the same researcher spoke.

'He said to make it as soon as possible, as it is of national importance, Sir.'

A junior member of staff approached him.

'The chopper is ready for you, and your car is outside to take you to the helipad.'

Gilani and his deputy left.

Chapter Twenty-Six

~~

Nurse Aytan thought about the phone call and the potential implications, but was unsure what to do next. The doctor interrupted her thoughts.

'What are the latest stats on our emergency admission from yesterday?'

'She's virtually back to normal. She's had a drink and is ready to eat and is also speaking.'

'Good, I'll examine her,' the doctor said.

'Before you do, can I have a word with you?'

'Certainly, what's happened? Are you OK, you look pale?'

'Can we go somewhere more private?'

His shoulders sank. 'Can it wait?'

'No. It's rather urgent.'

'The patient's consultation room is free,' he said, storming ahead.

Aytan told him the story of her suspicions and the phone call.

'I'm so sorry, I have brought shame on–'

'We can discuss your actions later. The IRGC will almost certainly be here soon. She needs to discharge herself. Wasn't someone with her?'

'Yes, he was here earlier and is coming back.'

'You must have nothing else to do with this patient. I'm going to send you to visit a discharged patient at home. Come to my office and ask Soraya to join us,' he said, running to his office.

Aytan and Soraya arrived soon after.

'Have you got contact details for the man who brought the bear attack victim in?' he asked Soraya.

'No, but he's sitting in reception, waiting to see her. Why?'

'Long story, but the IRGC are probably on their way. She needs to discharge herself right away and we need to show we opposed it,' he said, looking through some papers on his desk. 'Ah, here it is, Aytan. Visit this woman we recently discharged for a routine check-up. Go now!'

Once she had left, the doctor turned to Soraya. 'If they find her here, who knows what will happen to her and possibly Aytan? You know only too well what they're like. Is the man who brought her trustworthy?'

'I believe so. Leave it with me. I'll speak to him, then get her to discharge herself against the hospital's recommendation,' she said, leaving his office and heading for the reception. When she got there, the waiting area was empty. She went outside to the car park, but there was no sign of him. She was going to go to Melody's room when a black Range Rover and two military Jeeps pulled up outside. The soldiers disembarked and surrounded the hospital as four men in civies walked in. *Too late now, no point trying to warn them. What a tragic shame. I feel sorry for them.*

'Can I help you?' Soraya enquired.

'Which room is the bear attack victim in?'

'Room seven. Why?' she asked, but nobody answered. Two men pulled revolvers from shoulder holsters and sprinted down the corridor. They stood on each side of the door. One nodded, and they swept in. The window was wide open, and the room was empty. A soldier was looking in from the outside.

'Search the area. She can't be far away,' he ordered.

The local commander was staring at Soraya.

'Start at the beginning and tell me everything that happened, including all the information you have. Leave nothing out, do you understand?' he demanded as his two colleagues arrived back. 'Well?' the local commander asked them.

'She's gone Sir, she must have climbed out of the window. The soldiers are searching for her now.'

'Get a helicopter out and keep searching. Also, send out a Jeep. They may still be local. You're looking for this woman and probably an accomplice,' he said, handing him a photograph of Melody taken at the airport.

'Yes, Sir.'

'Now,' he said, turning to Soraya. 'Where is Aytan Sharifi?'

Before she could answer, the doctor arrived. 'I sent her to check on a patient.'

'She made a call to the wanted woman's mobile. I need to speak to her urgently,' the commander retorted.

'I told her to call the number. It was the only contact number we had. What was wrong with that?' He turned to Soraya. 'Print off all the details we have regarding this woman. We want to help as much as possible with this inquiry.' He looked back at the commander. 'What has she done?'

The commander ignored him and read the admission details. 'Who was this man that brought her in and where was he from?' He was trying hard not to lose his temper.

'He didn't give his name,' Soroya said. 'He found her following a bear attack and said he did not know her. We had no reason not to believe him,' she said, looking around nervously. 'The following day, he told us he'd met her companion whilst looking for her bag in the forest and she furnished him with the details you have there. Her number was the one Aytan tried to contact.'

'And you didn't find it suspicious?'

'Commander,' the doctor said. 'This is a hospital, not a police station. We do not have your finely tuned inquiring mind.'

'Get me the CCTV footage. I want to see this man and show me the room she stayed in.'

'Certainly, Commander, this way, please,' the doctor said.

When he got back to reception, his deputy told him Commander

Gilani from Tehran would arrive soon and showed him a picture of Dilshod from the CCTV. 'There's no sign of the woman, sir.'

'Find out who he is, and preferably before Gilani gets here, he must be on someone's database.'

Chapter Twenty-Seven

~~

Dilshod checked the mirrors again. 'Lie down on the back seat. They'll be looking for two people.' He said to Melody as they turned onto the major highway, leaving the hospital far behind.

Jad's voice crackled over the radio. 'A military Jeep has just left the hospital, probably searching for you. I'll follow it with the drone to see which direction it's headed and then catch you up. How's Melody?'

Dilshod passed the microphone to Melody.

'Hi Jad, I'm feeling much better. Thank you. My back's tender, but other than that I am fine, concussion seemed to be the major problem. I'm lucky to have people like you and Dilshod looking out for me.'

They had driven for about thirty kilometres on mainly rural roads and tracks when Jad radioed again. 'There's a chopper heading your way.'

Dilshod started looking for cover. Eventually, he simply pulled off the track into the undergrowth and hoped it was enough and that he could get out again.

'Difficult to spot you there, sit tight and wait till I give you the all-clear,' Jad said.

They could hear the helicopter getting louder.

'Listen, Mel, if they spot us, we need to make a run for it. We'll go in different directions that way. At least one of us should make it. I'll go first,' Dilshod said over the deep throb of the helicopter engine as the downdraft made the undergrowth sway around them.

'I'm not sure I can run far,' Melody said, almost shouting over the roar of the rotors.

Whilst they waited for Jad to give them the green light, Dilshod asked her why her condition deteriorated so suddenly.

'I woke up freezing cold. It was strange, but somehow related to a disturbing vision I had that night. By the way, thank the team for returning to the second camp to meet me. Heaven knows what would have happened if they hadn't turned up when they did,' she said, changing the subject.

'I just hope it doesn't compromise the operation. They have a much smaller search area now. Will you carry on?'

'I will carry on until I either drop dead, I'm arrested, or I find it.'

'Good. In that case–'

Jad's radio interrupted him. 'Sorry about the delay. I had to return the drone for fresh batteries. You can head back to camp now; the chopper has left the area.'

'Roger that,' Dilshod said whilst starting the car and reversing back onto the track.

'I'm looking forward to being in my shack again. I love it and for all its limitations, it's my safe space,' Melody said, resting on her headrest.

An hour later, they pulled into the campsite. Several people were waiting to welcome her back and by the time she got out of the car, everyone was there. She was a little embarrassed when they started clapping. She waved and blew a kiss, then turned to Dilshod. 'I think I'll go to my shack now; I'm exhausted.'

'I don't blame you. Get an early night and I'll see you at breakfast. Then we can plan what to do next.'

Melody gave a last wave to the men and ambled to her shack. The stove was burning, leaving a warm, comforting smell mixed with the percolating coffee, and there were fresh wildflowers in a jug on the table. She had wondered how the team would react to her wilful act of disregarding protocols. She poured a coffee and slumped down on a chair; her legs felt weak.

The episodes were becoming more common, intense and dangerous. She felt anxious when the sense of despair enveloped her. *It must be spiritual, why else would I have...*

This time the loss of sight was sudden. In the distance, she could hear the muffled sounds of a child crying. Slowly, the darkness melted away, and the light returned...

The village was on a hillside, the distant bleating of lambs and the chatter of locals going about their daily lives blended. The neat, white flat-roofed houses seemed familiar. *I'm in Bethlehem again. This is where the story of the swaddling started, but is it before Mary presented the swaddling to the Magi or after?*

New sounds filled the air. The slight tremor in the ground turned to constant vibrations, then changed to a monotonous thumping.

She looked down the hill. A patrol of what appeared to be Herod's soldiers were making their way to the village. Two abreast, marching in perfect unison, sunlight reflecting off their helmets and breastplates. The lead soldier halted. The scarlet plumes on his helmet distinguished him from the others. He turned, barking out orders. The company responded, scattering in different directions.

Then she remembered a previous episode at King Herod's Palace and Herod's chilling order. *Therefore, kill all boys under the age of two, living in Bethlehem.*

That's when the screaming started, just one or two at first, coming from the bottom of the hill. The soldiers moved methodically from house to house, more often followed by screaming and grief-stricken cries. People were coming out of their houses to see what was happening, and those fearing the worst were fleeing. But there was nowhere to go. The village was overwhelmed. Women were begging the soldiers, but to no avail.

The wailing was getting louder, and the shouting of butcherers, killers, slaughterers, and child murderers was rising like an unholy chorus.

The soldiers had reached the street where Melody stood and one of them, with a slick, blood-stained sword, kicked the door open of the house right beside her; she could hear the screams from inside. He moved to the next house where a young couple lived with their one-year-old son. She followed him inside.

'Where do Mary and Joseph live?'

'They left over a week ago. We haven't seen them since. Please, please, I beg you, do not hurt my son.' The terrified father was on his knees pleading with him, holding onto his tunic. The soldier brought his knee up into the young father's face, sending him sprawling to the hard dirt floor.

He then headed for the back room in search of the child, but the screaming mother lunged at him with a large knife. 'Filthy murderer.'

He staggered backwards. The knife had skidded off his breastplate and was lodged just below his shoulder; the wall prevented him from falling. He recovered sufficiently enough to slash at her neck. She grabbed her throat and dropped to the floor silently as her husband charged at him. But without a weapon, the soldier simply thrust his sword into him and he fell on top of his dead wife.

Melody stood motionless, the tears flowing freely down her pale cheeks.

Another soldier had moved back onto the street, people started throwing stones at him and hurling abuse, but he put his shield up and ignored them, carrying on with his gruesome task.

The sound of wailing was becoming unbearable. Rising and falling like a concerto. Almost all of them were crying. A few were silently trembling in shock or walking around in a trance-like state. Some were talking of 'the massacre of the innocents', others brought their dead babies out onto the streets. They continued to hurl abuse at the soldiers and curse Herod as the troops left...

When Melody woke, it was dark, the flickering yellow glow from the stove providing the only light. Her pillow was damp with tears.

Chapter Twenty-Eight

~~

After an hour without a sighting, the local commander called the search off. Neither the helicopter nor his troops had made any progress, and so they returned to the local IRGC headquarters in Chalus. Commander Gilani was studying a more detailed map of the area when his deputy interrupted him. 'Just a reminder the regional director of MOIS is expecting you to call back, Sir.'

'Yes, of course, in all the excitement I'd forgotten. Thanks, Hossein. Can you call his office?' he said before turning to the local commander. 'How big is the circle you've drawn around the hospital?'

'A hundred kilometres. I can't see them going too far for treatment,' he said, beckoning the tracker over.

'Clearly, she was in the forested area so we're only looking south–'

'MOIS are on the phone, Sir,' Hossein said.

'You can take it in my office. It's a little more private,' the local commander said.

Gilani picked up the phone. 'I'm sorry about the delay, Sir. We were following up on a lead near Chalus, a British woman we want for spying.'

'That's what I want to talk to you about. It is a delicate matter and I am talking to you with the express permission of the Revolutionary Council. We require you to attend my office and cease all activity in the search for the British woman, Melody Thornton.'

'Our Embassy in London–'

'There's no negotiation here, Commander Gilani,' he said. 'I expect you in my office at some point today. Have I made myself clear?'

'Perfectly, Sir.'

'Good. I look forward to seeing you.' Then the phone went dead.

At first, he felt shocked, but then disheartened. He rang their embassy in Britain, who put him through to the London Commander.

'They want me to shut down the Thornton investigation,' Gilani said.

'Who's they?'

'The RC. I've just had a call from MOIS to close the investigation and attend the regional director's office this afternoon.'

'That's intriguing. Let me know why after your meeting.'

'Listen. Just in case they give me the green light, it is important to understand what she's looking for. We have narrowed the search to an area of forest in Mazandaran province, but it's a vast area. Can you send me the information you have on this obsession she has with a Christian relic? I need to know why she's in this area to narrow down the search.'

'I will, but be incredibly careful. If the Revolutionary Council wants a shutdown, there must be a good reason for her to be on their radar. Do not rain on their parade, Zaynab, and keep in touch.'

* * *

Later that day, Gilani arrived at the imposing MOIS offices and made his way to the regional director's office. The receptionist offered him a seat and although the director's door was closed, he could hear a muffled conversation. It surprised him when, fifteen minutes later, the director opened his door and bid farewell to two Ayatollahs. As Gilani stood, one looked at him and smiled. 'May peace be upon you,' Ayatollah Ahmad Amini said.

'May God protect you both,' he replied with his hand placed over his heart.

'Come in Commander, sorry to keep you waiting, take a seat,' the director said. 'I thought it best to talk face to face, as this is a delicate matter.'

'I appreciate you taking the time to explain why you want the investigation into the British woman prematurely shut down.'

'What I am about to tell you is strictly off the record. Discussing this topic would normally take place only at director level, however, I have permission from the Ayatollah concerned to take you into our confidence,' he said, removing a file marked confidential from his desk, and opening Gilani's file. 'What do you believe is the purpose of Miss Thornton's visit?'

'I was unsure at first but having looked further into her background, I believe she is on an archaeological mission, what for exactly I'm less certain about but–'

'Sorry to interrupt you, Commander. Let me tell you the full story. The Ayatollah I mentioned is an enthusiastic archaeologist himself and after leaving university, had a promising career ahead of him in that field. Following the revolution, though, he felt drawn instead to his present calling. He has maintained an interest in the subject and has long been an admirer of Miss Thornton's research and, under different circumstances, may have invited her to his home, –'

'I'm not sure liking her is a reasonable justification to halt the investigation.'

'You must let me finish giving you *all* the information,' he said. 'The report here says you are prone to impetuous behaviour,' he said, tapping the folder. 'The Ayatollah believes what the British woman is searching for is of great national importance to Iran and so preventing her from discovering it would be a mistake. We are to give her the freedom to search. When the Ayatollah realised her intention to visit Iran, we ensured it would go ahead.'

'What if they had refused her visa?'

'Had the Commander in London turned down her visa, the Ambassador would have intervened.'

'Now, if we treat her like any other tourist, she will become suspicious.

Therefore, the work you have done so far will avoid that, but you are now in danger of causing her to flee the country without completing her mission.'

'And when she discovers this artefact?'

'We have plans in place.'

'My investigation could run in parallel?'

'Your investigation puts ours in jeopardy. To your credit, we did not think you would get this close. She is a resourceful woman, well prepared and equipped by a sophisticated anti-surveillance company based in the UK.' He paused. 'We've had an agent tracking her for some considerable time now.'

'We believed–'

'We?' the director asked.

'The commander at our London Embassy and I considered if–'

'If what, Commander? If you kidnapped this woman, you could somehow exchange her for your brother? Was that your plan?' he said, tapping his file again.

'No, Sir. If we arrested her on a spying charge, bearing in mind her father's army background, it would be possible to trade her, as we did for the £400m the UK Government owed us from the decades-old British tank sale and,' he paused for a moment and straightened his posture. 'Of course, I had also hoped to include my brother's release as he wasn't part of the last prisoner swap with Israel.'

'We had no control over that exchange. It was the Israelis and Hamas. The Israelis would never include an Iranian national accidentally swept up in a Hamas strike.'

'The British Government has a long-standing relationship with Israel and could bring pressure to bear. At the time, he was working for the IRGC.'

'Look Commander, I am sympathetic concerning your brother, I am, but you cannot use your position to benefit your family at the expense of the State. Plus, the British Foreign Office had already agreed to pay back the money they owed us. It was their Defence Ministry that dragged its feet, using the fact that there are international sanctions imposed. Following the Zaghari-Ratcliffe issue, the British Government will not negotiate for another hostage, you can be sure of that. I have made my decision,' he said, standing. 'No one is to know about this. You are not to discuss this with anyone, not even London. The Council would regard doing so as treason. Do I make myself clear, Commander?'

'Yes Sir, crystal clear.'

'In that case, it's been a pleasure meeting you. Your file also says you are ambitious. I agree and look forward to following your career. Good day, Commander Gilani,' he said, shaking his hand.

As soon as Gilani left the building, he took out his notepad; he had spotted a name written on the document lying next to his file before the director removed it. He wrote the name down – Farad El Sayed.

Chapter Twenty-Nine

~~~

Gilani returned to the IRGC headquarters in Chalus and called his deputy Hossein into his temporary office. 'Have you identified the British woman's accomplice?'

'Yes, his name is Dilshod Karimova. Forty-five years old, single and was born in Uzbekistan. He spent eight years in the Army, specialising in surveillance. He now works as a freelance tracker.'

'It pretty much matches up with our expectation that she is searching for something.'

'How was your meeting with the director?'

'Fine, though they want me to scale back the operation on the British woman. Is the Mazandaran forest expert still here?' Gilani asked, quickly changing the subject.

'Milad? I think so. Shall I get him?'

'Yes, and see if there is a drone available. I'd like to have one last shot at finding them. It will depend on whether we can roughly identify where they are and with reasonable accuracy.' He walked over to the map where he began tracing the myriad of roads and tracks leading into the forested area, whilst Hossein went to find the forest expert.

Ten minutes later, he returned.

'This is Milad, Sir, he knows the forest area better than most people.'

'Whilst I talk to Milad, will you see what you can find out about this person?' he said, handing him a note.

Hossein opened it. Handwritten was a single name, Farad El Sayed.

'Right away, Commander.' Hossein quickly retired from the room while Milad held Gilani's gaze with his full attention.

'Have they briefed you regarding whom we are looking for?' Gilani asked.

'Yes, Sir. I have studied several of the British archaeologist papers you provided concerning Iran. In particular, the fabled Valley of Ascendency. It sounds obvious, but it must be in a valley and there is mention of Cedars. This narrows it down a little, however, given the proximity of the hospital. My best guess would be, she's in this area,' he said, drawing a red oval over the map. 'I know it's an immense area, but I can't be any more specific than that, sorry,' he said, standing back.

'No. That is extremely helpful indeed, thank you.'

'Will you be mounting an expedition to the area?'

'No, no. Just some recon work, that's all. I will let you know if we decide to go.'

'Thank you, Sir,' he said, leaving.

A short while later, Gilani was still studying the map when Hossein returned.

'I'd just like to get some aerial shots. Can we get a drone to photograph as much of this area as possible?' Gilani said, pointing to the red outline. 'I have been told to scale back the operation on the woman, but he said nothing about Dilshod Karimova. I would like to interview him. But keep a low profile. Let us keep this on a need-to-know basis, eh? I wouldn't want the director thinking I was going against his wishes.'

'Yes, Commander.'

'What did you get on El Sayed?'

'It wouldn't let me in. My security clearance isn't high enough. It's above my pay grade.'

'Interesting. Use my computer,' he said, gesturing to his laptop on the desk.

'Yes, Sir.'

It wasn't long after that Hossein interrupted Gilani's careful study of the map.

'El Sayed is one of ours, though a sketchy character. He has worked mostly as an agent for us in Palestine with Hamas, and we have used him to conduct several attacks on Israeli targets. Mainly, he's an assassin but has also been responsible for organising several bombings. He was a double agent for us while working with the CIA, but that appears to have ended. It seems he has served his purpose with the Americans.'

Gilani moved over to see the monitor. 'That is interesting. I also think it's worth speaking to the hospital nurse, Aytan. She may know more than the doctor admitted. Do you have a list of all the staff?'

'Yes, anyone in particular?'

'No. But, run the names through the database, you never know what might turn up. I think we should interview the nurse here; it will soften up the other hospital staff.'

Ten minutes later, Hossein left the building and made a phone call.

'He's getting a drone to take pictures of the forest and is going to interview hospital staff to find one of her accomplices, Dilshod Karimova,' he said down the line.

'Anything else?' the MOIS Director asked.

'Yes Sir, he knows about Farad Al Sayed.'

'I see. Carry on as normal for the time being and well done Hossein. Keep me updated.'

Chapter Thirty

~~~

Melody still felt unsettled by the previous vision and the sheer brutality of it. 'Massacre of the innocents', the crowd had shouted. She made notes in her journal. One day, she would write about them.

Bethlehem always seemed such a beautiful and peaceful place. I didn't connect the horror with Matthew's Gospel account.

She made her way over for breakfast, in what she now referred to as the NAFFI canteen. Less than halfway across the compound, she could smell bread being baked and the sound of a drone in the distance. It surprised her; it seemed a little early. As it got louder, she stopped to watch. It was flying towards the camp.

She saw Dilshod run out of the marquee with an assault rifle; he stopped and took aim.

'What's happening?' she shouted.

There was no reply as he continued to aim at the drone. The clack, clack, clack of the automatic rifle shocked her, the sound breaking through the background chatter of animals as the firing continued. The trees became a hive of activity, their branches rocking and swaying as hundreds of birds took to the air. All the team members were out now, watching the drone as it veered out of control, dipping and rising, its sound becoming intermittent and spluttering, and then silence. A hundred metres from camp, it dropped like a stone.

Amooz and Jad were the first to react, running in the direction it fell. Nouri was patting Dilshod on the back, congratulating him. Confused, Melody hurried towards them.

'What is going on Dilshod? Why did you shoot down one of our drones?'

'It's not one of ours. We haven't launched today. It may simply be a civilian craft mapping the area. Most likely it belongs to IRGC, the people hunting you. We will need to up our game if it is.'

The three of them walked hurriedly toward the crash site.

'By the way, how are you today?' Dilshod asked.

'Almost back to full strength. Thanks to you.'

When they arrived, Amooz was taking photos using his phone.

'Let me get some pictures before we take it in for examination.'

'What's your initial impression of who sent it?' Melody asked.

Jad knelt beside it. 'I've seen these before at Air Shows. They're not cheap. It's military-grade and beyond. What's your impression, Nouri? Equipment and communications are your fields.'

'IRGC, possibly MOIS, from the first viewing. There are no markings,' Nouri said. 'If it were standard Army or Air Force, it would have their emblems. A civilian one would have their company logo and even a return address emblazoned over it. It also has a payload bay, quite rare. We need to be incredibly careful. It could have a self-destruct mechanism. I think we should examine it outside initially.'

'Set it up on a bench in the middle of the camp and make sure there's a fire extinguisher handy,' Amooz said as he studied the smoking wreckage. 'Let Nouri have a good look at it. The rest of you grab some food and meet in the marquee.'

Melody felt some concern as she helped herself to coffee and a slice of honey bread before joining the others. She felt comfortable letting Amooz start the meeting, but it was clear from the initial observations her mission had now become much more time critical.

'The plans we made yesterday still stand, but we need to step up a notch in terms of effort.' Amooz turned to Jad. 'Are the infra-red drones set up and ready to fly?'

'Yes, we were going to launch after breakfast. We have narrowed down the search area.'

'Good. Call the four scouts back. I'll brief them on what we know.'

Nouri entered the meeting room.

'Ah, Nouri, perfect timing,' Amooz said, smiling. 'Can you update us on the drone?'

'It's almost certainly IRGC. It has several cameras, a wide-angle for ground scanning, and zoom for points of interest. They may have a recording of Dilshod firing at it. Hard to know, as the operator did not change its direction before he fired. The payload is interesting –it contains a small rover with two cameras and lights, particularly useful if a drone cannot continue. For example, at the entrance to a cave that is difficult to fly into. There are two possibilities. One, we can take the view they pre-programmed it to survey a wide area and have nothing to worry about, or two, they're onto us.'

'Thanks, Nouri. I think they are onto us. Melody,' he said, turning to her. 'Do you want to add anything?'

'I agree with your conclusion,' Melody said, 'and therefore, in the light of this morning's events, I think we should pack up this site and move essential equipment to the advance camp. Leave nothing here you may want again, destroy everything else, leave no clues.'

'Agreed. OK, let's move gentlemen. We are in a short time frame now. Oh, and one last thing, no mobile calls to anyone. Are we clear on this?' Amooz scanned the room like a radar dish. A few nodded, but no one spoke.

The meeting ended and Melody headed for the shack to clear out her meagre belongings. She poured the remains of the coffee percolator into her mug and sat on her makeshift bed to consider future options when another encounter began. It started as usual with her eyes clouded over, but before the loss of sight, she saw her grandmother smiling. Then followed a total loss of sight, and an even deeper sense of despair overwhelmed her...

Chapter Thirty-One

Melody was in the desert again, under a cloudless turquoise sky. The sun was beating down with not even a whisper of a breeze. She recognised the man next to her, Lord Melchior, in his spotless white tunic, his gold cloak draped over the flanks of his horse when another rider drew alongside.

'They have spotted the scouts, Sire.'

'Very well, Captain, the men could do with a break, make camp here. I'm eager to hear what they have to report. Bring Zhakfar with you. I want our chief scout to hear it firsthand.' Hormoz saluted and peeled away barking orders.

When the scouts arrived, they made their way to the hastily set up marquee, helping themselves to the food and drink laid out for them.

Melchior and his entourage entered.

'Don't get up men, continue eating as you report,' the captain said. 'Your mounts are being attended to.'

The lead scout spoke. 'The strangers in Bethlehem were Herod's men, eight in total and hand-picked from what he calls his Praetorian Guard. They captured and tortured one of Joseph's relatives and are now heading towards Egypt. They're running parallel to us, north on "The Way of the Sea" and they appear to be in a hurry.'

Zhakfar laid the map out before them. 'Show me where you think they'll be this time tomorrow.'

'Here,' he said, making a circle with his finger near a known oasis.

'What about Joseph and Mary? How far will they have got?'

'Maybe three or four days ahead, but it could be less. They're probably around this area.' He stabbed his finger near the city of Pelusium.

'Excellent work. Rest a little while. We need to discuss tactics. But you may soon have to leave again on fresh horses.' Zhakfar turned to face the group. His expression was one of concern.

'We'll meet in my tent.' Melchior said, 'Let these men get some well-deserved rest. Captain, I want everyone that will be involved.' He turned to Zhakfar, the chief scout. 'Walk with me. I'd like to hear your thoughts.'

As they walked through the camp, Zhakfar spoke. 'My plan, Sire, would be to send the scouts to follow Herod's men, so when we set up an ambush, there is no retreat. We'll aim for a suitable area, probably the oasis.'

'And your concerns are what?'

'As we're travelling on "The Way of Shur" to the south of them, we'll need to travel fast and sometimes in the dark to get there first.'

'Run it past the Captain, see what he thinks.'

'Yes, sire,' he said, scanning the camp to locate him.

The men, watered and fed, settled down for the meeting in the main tent.

'We now know what we're up against, and time is not on our side. What plan do you propose, Captain?' Melchior asked.

'I agree mostly with the ambush plan Zhakfar outlined to you, but I would also like to send someone to intercept Joseph and Mary. We must be realistic. If our plan fails, they will be at the mercy of Herod's men. If only one slips through our grasp, it could be a disaster. I believe we should send Melker to warn them and find them a safe place to hide.'

'Send someone else,' Melker said, thumping the floor and standing up. 'Don't treat me like a child. I can fight as good as any man here.'

'That is exactly why it must be you. Each of these men,' the captain said, gesturing with his arm, 'are specialists in their field. Joubin with archery, Musa and his swordsmanship, Faraj with horses, Zhakfar our best tracker and scout and it works perfectly in a team, but only in a team.'

'I have never let the team down!' Melker said, moving towards the exit.

'No, Sire. But you are an all-rounder, an excellent archer, a wonderful swordsman. Joseph and Mary will listen to you, trust you, and follow your advice and instruction. You have the authority of being an apprentice, Magi. None of the other men could carry out this task. If we cannot stop all of Herod's guard, if only one of his men slips through, you will be the child's last hope of survival. It is a tremendous responsibility. I believe you are best suited for this task.'

Melker turned to look at his father, Lord Melchior. Melker's face was a picture of resignation. Eventually, he returned to his place and sat down next to his father, who patted his arm.

'If all goes well, we'll meet you at the entrance to the market in a week at Pelusium, though the locals call it "Tahpanhes." Roshan has prepared our fastest horse. Leave now,' the Captain said.

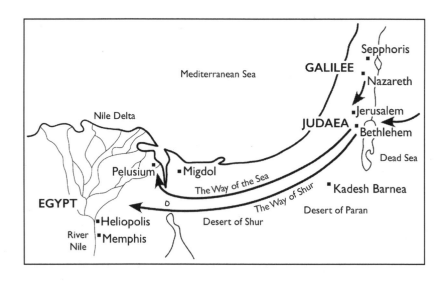

Chapter Thirty-Two

~~

Hossein knocked and entered the commander's office. 'We have the nurse from the hospital in a cell, Commander.'

'Good, let's see what she has to say.'

They were making their way to the cellblock when Hossein's mobile rang. 'I need to take this, Commander. It's urgent. I'll catch you up.'

'OK,' he said, stepping into the lift and pressing the basement button. 'Don't be too long, though.'

As he stepped out, two guards accompanied him down the corridor. 'This interview room, sir,' one said, opening the door.

The commander stepped in to find the Director of MOIS waiting behind the desk. 'Take a seat, Commander.'

He looked around; the two guards were on each side of the closed door. 'I don't understand,' he said. 'What's going on?'

'I thought I'd made myself clear, Commander,' the director said. 'And yet you persist.'

'I have shut the investigation for the British woman down,' he paused, trying to consider how much the director knew, 'as you instructed?'

'How then would you explain the shooting down of a drone?'

'I was searching only for Dilshod Karimova.'

'What then, is your interest in Fared El Sayed?' the director asked.

He made to reply, but said nothing. The commander knew he was in serious trouble.

'Such a waste of a promising career, Commander.' He paused for effect. 'You will relinquish your post here until our investigation is complete.

Do not go back to your office, you can collect your belongings at the reception. Think yourself lucky, commander, several people thought I should fire you.' As he spoke, he nodded to the guards, who opened the door.

Gilani made to leave. He stopped at the door and turned around to say something, then changed his mind and left.

Chapter Thirty-Three

On their deck at the edge of the Black Sea, Nikolai's brothers-in-law, Ivan and Grigoriy sipped from their vodka cocktails while four young women laughed playfully in the heated pool. Grigoriy spoke. 'I didn't like the way Nikolai spoke to us, so ungrateful.'

'I think it's all a waste of time,' Ivan said. 'First, there's no proof this swaddling thing exists. Second, even if it does, it may not work and third, this archaeologist woman may not find it. It's sad, but I don't think he has long to go now.'

'Probably a waste of money. How much is in the fund?'

'About US$20m, after paying Vasily and his two henchmen, but he's burning through it,' he said, looking around. 'Talking of which, where are his minders? They're normally hanging around like a foul smell.'

'I don't trust them.' Grigoriy shouted for the girls in the pool to fetch more drinks.

Vasily, The Wolf, suddenly appeared in the doorway of the french windows. He was the man Nikolai had recently put in charge of the operation. They were both shocked.

'Vasily, what are you doing here? I thought you were meeting the guy who headed up the old USSR Air Force?' Ivan said, panicking.

'I have a message to deliver from Nikolai,' he said, taking out a Glock 17 pistol.

Both men jumped up and ran in different directions. The Wolf aimed and fired. Grigoriy took the first bullet in his thigh and crumpled to the floor, moaning.

Ivan almost made it to the end of the building near the swimming pool when the bullet entered his back. As he arched backwards, the second shattered the back of his skull and he fell face forward onto one of the screaming girls in the pool, all of whom were trying frantically to escape as his blood flowed into the water.

Grigoriy was trying to stop the bleeding in his thigh. 'Listen, I can pay – more than Nikolai. How much do you want?'

The Wolf walked over, grabbed him by the left arm and pulled him inside the villa. 'Open the safe or I'll cut your finger off and do it myself,' he said, holding up a pair of secateurs. 'You choose.'

Grigoriy dragged himself an arm's length to the antique cabinet containing the safe, leaving a trail of his blood across the floor.

'There's no need for this. Nikolai is dying, you know that. I have more money than he will pay you. Let me go and you'll be a rich man.'

'Just open the safe.'

He struggled to move the last few feet before opening the biometric safe. The Wolf then shot him in the forehead as he was about to make a last plea. The assassin emptied the contents of the safe into a holdall he had placed there earlier before casually walking out.

As The Wolf was leaving, four police officers who had been waiting outside entered. He gave them a thick brown envelope and left. The police began taking statements from the women – 'they saw nothing.'

Vasily glanced through the bank statements and then made a phone call to Nikolai. 'I have the bank statements. You were right. They've been skimming off the top. There was also a lot of cash in the safe.'

'Keep half the cash for expenses. Bring the rest here along with the documents.'

Chapter Thirty-Four

~~

Nikolai put the phone down on his bedside table and smiled to himself.

'You know what the doctor said about taking phone calls,' Sasha said, taking his temperature. 'Especially from Vasily. It always makes your blood pressure rise. But I won't tell. Besides, I want to hear the rest of your life story. What were the highlights, those memories burnt into your mind?'

'Why are women so nosey? That's what I want to know?'

Despite being tired, one memory was clear to him.

'There was one event, Sasha, which changed my life forever. I remember it like yesterday.' He stopped talking to catch his breath. 'The only reason I am telling you this is so you don't miss your event when it comes.' He fought desperately against the wave of tiredness. 'It was the morning of the 12th of June 1991 at six-thirty... usual breakfast... rye bread, sliced sausage... the newspaper headline read "Yeltsin wins landslide election". I had told Yeltsin we will only get one shot at this...'

His eyes felt heavy. He was slipping away; sleep was beckoning him. 'Must dampen refinery production... make it look like an accident... downplay the production figures. There was a fire, I remember... refinery in Oblast...'

He was slipping back into the void between reality and flashbacks...

'Is the money in place?' Ivan asked.

'I need to liquidate some of my investments and confirm the loan arrangements I made are still in place.' Nikolai said, pointing to a pile of financial documents.

'Lehman Brothers?'

'Mainly, but in addition, BP, Exxon and Shell have all shown an interest in bankrolling us for privatisation. I already have sufficient cash to pay off whoever is selling the assets. Men that Yeltsin would know and have influence over will sell the shares on behalf of the government.'

'What's your best estimate of the value?'

'Two American banks, including Lehman, have estimated the business value at US$4.4billion, though there's more chance of the snow melting in Siberia than me paying that amount for it.'

'And the proposed voucher scheme?'

'The vouchers must be free. At least, that's what I told Yeltsin's top advisor. They should distribute them equally among the workers and their families. We need them to be exchangeable for shares in the enterprises they work in. Then we can start buying them.'

Yeltsin eventually agreed and even presented it to the Russian Soviet Federative as his idea. They approved the privatisation of the oil sector. Decree №1403 on November 17, 1992.

Nikolai woke. It was dark. Just the strange glow from the various medical monitors illuminated the room. It was also quiet, except for the infernal ticking of the clock, like a countdown of his life. Tick, tick, tick, tick.

Chapter Thirty-Five

~~

It had taken the entire day to pack up and move the camp. They designated two scouts to remain and remove all evidence of their presence.

Now at the second camp, Melody walked to the spot where the bear attack had happened. Although the camp was bigger, she could make out where she first spotted the bear.

'Are you having flashbacks?' Dilshod asked, startling her.

'It seems like an age since it happened.'

Dilshod did not reply. He simply nodded and smiled.

'Well. I think I'll grab a coffee and sort out my new accommodation,' Melody said. 'Though it won't be a patch on the last one.'

She had finished drinking her coffee when she realised how tired she was and probably, for the first time, considered the risk-reward ratio of the venture.

Was it worth all the time and trouble? Not least of all, putting other people's lives in danger. What if someone gets seriously injured or killed? How will I feel if we don't find it? Perhaps my grandmother was prophetic when she told me, 'I pray each day God will use you richly'. Surely this can't be what she meant?

As she lay down on her camp bed, yet another of the encounters began. *If this is using me richly, maybe I should succumb, and welcome the visions as God-given, rather than dread them.* Then the darkness descended.

It started similar to the last one; she was in a wooded valley, a small clearing, the faint sound of rushing water, even the smell of apple blossom. But then the scene changed. This time, she didn't want it to end.

She was inside the cave…

She hadn't been asleep long when the sound of vehicles woke her. Then a familiar voice called out. It was Jad.

'Melody, we're about to launch the drones.'

'I'll be with you in a moment, just unpacking some things.' She left the tent and made her way to the equipment marquee, where a larger group than normal had gathered.

Amooz moved over to greet her. 'Melody, let me show you where we're starting the search,' he said, taking her to the wall maps. 'We think these are the three most likely places to find a water source. If that happens, then we follow it.'

Melody studied the maps. 'We have nothing to lose. Let's send them off. Afterwards, can I speak privately with you?'

'Sure, let's watch the launch first.'

By the time they stepped outside, the entire camp was in a circle around the three drones. Jad began his customary countdown: 'Ten, nine…' When he got to seven, they all joined in. 'Two, one, lift-off.' Melody watched as the drones left at ten-second intervals. A cheer went up, followed by clapping.

'Well done, Jad,' Melody said. 'I have complete confidence in you.'

'Thank you. I'm not sure we'll get another chance after this morning's episode. Anyway, I must go. I need to monitor their progress with the rest of the team.'

'Aren't they pre-programmed?'

'Only to their start coordinates, then we take over manually. We'll let you know the moment we have anything.'

Amooz moved towards her as Jad left. 'You wanted to discuss something; shall we use the canteen?'

'Yes, we can talk over a coffee,' she said as they walked. 'How do you feel the project is progressing? Is everyone still on board?'

Amooz sensed her mood. 'Listen Melody, they all signed up for what we knew would be a bumpy ride. Nothing has changed. We will understand if you want to call it off. But we all feel we are on the final straight and want to stay until the end. Remember, these guys are getting well-paid. If we asked for a vote, one hundred percent would want to continue. They've invested as much as you have.'

'Thank you, Amooz. You're right, sometimes I feel the weight of responsibility,' she said as he settled into a chair in the canteen.

'Is this about Farrokh?'

'No, what makes you think that?'

'There's been a lot of chatter about his state of mind lately. Some don't trust him and think he's sold you out.'

'Dilshod?'

'Amongst others, yes. But Dilshod is an excellent judge of character and a first-class chief guide.'

'I wonder what he makes of me then,' she said, handing him his coffee.

'He thinks the sun and moon rise for you; he's a real admirer,' he said, making Melody laugh.

'I owe him a great deal. After the bear attack, he put himself at enormous risk.' She paused. 'No, I want to talk about a different matter. I trust you, but keep what I'm about to tell you to yourself,' she said, whilst pouring herself a coffee and sitting down opposite him.

'For many years, I have had strange encounters, leading to visions regarding my quest. The closer I get, the more frequent they have become.'

'I have to admit I'm sceptical of anything spiritual, it's outside of any experience I've ever had. How reliable are these encounters or visions?'

She smiled and nodded. 'The previous one was the reason we were looking for a waterfall. It's close to the cave entrance on the Eastern flank of the valley. I had two close together. The second one was inside the cave.'

'You actually saw inside?'

'Yes. They had carved everything out of the rock. There were no added fixtures and only a few fittings. Strangely, the rock looked like marble. The altar table, dozens of statues, benches and even small recesses for candles and torch holders are all hand carved. The ceiling was even more magnificent – dozens of intricate figures, with angelic beings surrounding a central star and a shaft of light emanating from the centre, illuminating a stone bench. It was like being in a cathedral.'

'I don't pretend to know or understand these encounters, but they seem to have got us this far, therefore, we must carry on. To give up now would be a travesty.'

'I know. We are almost there; I can feel it. In the vision, I could even smell apple blossom. Then these words were being spoken over and over: "It shall rest in the Valley of Ascendency in the foothills of Shir and there, in the Sanctuary of the Gathering Place, beneath the Seat of Prayer, it shall remain". We are so close Amooz, I was standing in the Sanctuary of the Gathering Place.'

Chapter Thirty-Six

~~~

Melody felt much more upbeat following the conversation with Amooz and spoke to as many of the team as possible on a one-to-one basis, praising them for their endeavours.

She was thanking Zubeen for the way he had provided such delicious food, on time and sometimes under difficult circumstances.

'Thank you,' he paused. 'I've been meaning to ask. They say you're an expert on the Magi, though we called them "The Three Kings" when I was a boy. Were they Kings?'

'Not really, more governors of a region, though many in what is now Kuwait regarded Balthazar as the King of Arabia. Others, though, would have regarded them as priests in the Persian religion of Zoroastrianism. Today we would call them astrologers, and this was probably the reason the Bible referred them to as The Three Wise Men. Legend has it that each of the Magi had a supernatural power or gift as they called it. Balthazar's was healing.'

'What about the others?'

'The Bible doesn't say. It's mostly myth and legend. Melchior appears to be the senior Magi. His gifting was prophesying, but his son Melker could see into the past a bit like a time traveller and Caspar's gift was his ability to see and talk to angels.'

'So they were like superheroes?'

'I suppose they were,' she said, smiling.

'Which power would you choose?'

'That's a difficult one. I'd love Caspar's. Imagine seeing and talking to angels. I'd have so many questions. But the gift of healing people would be a special blessing, what–'

Just then, a scout rushed over. 'We've found a river. Come quickly!'

They all rushed back to the communication marquee. Most of the team surrounded Jad's screen, the infra-red showing a watercourse.

'Are you sure it's water, Jad?' Melody asked.

'Yes, but we're about to switch cameras from infra-red and go beneath the canopy. Water appears as shades of blue, varying from nearly black for clean water to pale blue if it has increasing amounts of sediment. A shallow stream with a sandy bottom will appear white because of the high level of sand reflection.'

'How far have you followed it?'

'About a kilometre, mostly showing blue, sometimes black.' As he spoke, the image changed to live pictures of the treetops and the drone slowed whilst they looked for a break in the canopy.

'There, nine o'clock,' Nouri said. The drone stopped as Jad changed its course to descend into the forest. 'Also, divert the other two drones into the area in case we have a mishap.'

Jad manoeuvred it through the thick vegetation, then halted as a river came into view. There was loud cheering, hugging, and several team members patting Jad on the back.

'The only decision we need to make now is, do we go upstream or down?' Jad said, clenching both fists in celebration.

'Upstream,' Melody said.

'I agree,' said Nouri, 'but just in case, we'll send one downstream and the third one can follow upstream.'

'Good thinking, Nouri, and well done everyone,' Melody said, clapping. Turning, she could see Amooz beside the maps. He was in a conversation with Dilshod. She joined them.

'We were working out likely routes, depending of course on where it leads us,' Amooz said. 'It's already looking like we can take advantage of the track we made previously from the second camp. We seem to run parallel, therefore–'

Another loud cheer made them return to the monitor. Jad had the drone hovering above a waterfall.

'Mark the coordinates on the map,' Amooz said. 'Jad, can you get back above the tree line? I want to see if we're close to the valley sides. It's the Eastern flank we're interested in, I–'

'Before you do,' Melody interrupted, 'Can you switch on the microphone, and can we all be quiet, please?' The sound of rushing water came through the speakers. 'Yes, that is the sound I heard,' she said, punching the air as a cheer went up.

Jad continued weaving his way up through the small gaps in the trees. Once he was above the canopy, he moved to the Eastern flank and began a methodical search.

'Stay within the sound of the waterfall, Jad. It should be high up, closer to the summit than the valley floor.' He angled the drone, scanning upward and then slowly the camera zoomed in.

There it was, just like it was in the vision – the sunlight illuminating the mouth of a cave.

Chapter Thirty-Seven

~~

It took them a day to reach the area the drone had identified and as Melody stood taking in her surroundings, she could hear the faint sound of the waterfall and even the smell of apple blossom and several men nearby were hacking away at the undergrowth. She stared up the valley side, her excitement growing. It was high up, but again, there was no mistaking it. Even in the fading sunlight, there was the cave entrance. *This is the place.*

Amooz spoke to her. 'I can tell by your face we've found it and, I have to say, not a moment too soon. The two scouts we left behind to clear the camp have reported seeing two police cars outside the hospital we took you to. They passed it on their way to Chalus. Dilshod seemed upset when I told him. He's concerned about the receptionist at the hospital that helped you.'

'I hope she's OK. It was brave of her to put herself at risk. I think Dilshod has a soft spot for her. He's tried to contact her, but keep that to yourself.'

'My lips are sealed. I don't think they have any solid proof.'

'Let's hope so. The government here has huge control over the lives of its people. I'd hate to live here, but we have no control over that so what's the plan going forward?'

'The scouts can carry on clearing a path to the foot of the mountain. It'll only be light for a little longer. We'll bivouac here and start the ascent in the morning.'

'It occurred to me, if this were a regular meeting place, it's unlikely there would be the remains of a track. But they wouldn't hack their way to it each time, so how do we find it?'

'There could be a secret passage. We don't know which direction they would have been coming from. We'll send the drones on a re-con at first light, see if we can spot anything.'

'Good idea, I'll talk to Dilshod, and see if he can find any clues. He knows the area better than anyone.'

Melody wondered if she would sleep that night. Torn in equal measure between being excited but also concerned by the sighting of two further drones, police at the hospital and the consequences if this was not the Sanctuary of the Gathering Place.

Her tent was small but adequate and she settled down to watch footage taken by the drones on her tablet. The cave entrance was exactly as she had seen in her vision, but there were no clues on how best to reach it. She was considering the possibility of the Magi arriving from the other side of the mountain and made a mental note to ask Jad to cover that area in the morning. *How will I feel if we discover it? For so long I have felt compelled, driven almost. Now, though, I feel drawn, destined. More and more, it feels like this is a calling. I used to think of visions as a supernatural tool. But now my grandmother's words "Young lady, visions aren't just for young men" have extra resonance.* She was turning this over in her mind as she fell asleep.

* * *

Melody woke to the early morning calls of the forest and the muffled chatter of the team as they made ready for the day ahead. She peeked outside her tent. The light was just breaking through the grey canopy, shafts of sunlight dotted around like spotlights in a theatre. As she inhaled, she could smell coffee coming from the kitchen tent.

The wash area was a simple table with three bowls. Jad was shaving as she made her way over. 'Morning Jad, can I discuss something with you at breakfast?'

'Certainly,' he said, cupping his hands and drenching his face. 'I'll see you over there.'

Breakfast was a slimmed-down version of the previous camp food, but adequate, and the atmosphere relaxed. The men were chatting and laughing as Melody watched them. It made her smile. She made her way over and sat alongside Jad; he was sipping his tea as though it would be his last drink.

'You do like your tea, Jad.'

'My favourite drink. I cannot do anything until I have at least one, possibly two. What did you want to talk about?'

'There's a cleft in the mountain ridge I'd like to see in more detail and, if possible, a view of the other side of this range, in case that's the way in.'

'Actually, there are two clefts; one is indistinct, but I spotted it when we enlarged the images last night.' He took some pictures from his battered leather shoulder bag and handed them over. 'There, you can just make it out,' he said, stabbing with his finger. 'What makes you think there's a route there?'

'A vision I once had, and although it sounds strange, I saw an angel pointing the way towards a narrow cleft at the bottom of the rock face. It looked narrow, only about a metre wide.'

'Tell me about the angel vision. I'm intrigued by them. My mother used to talk about my guardian angel when I was a boy. She said it was in the Bible.'

'She was right. It's in Matthew's Gospel. Once when Jesus was teaching, he told his disciples not to shoo the children away. He said, "Beware that you don't look down on any of these little ones. For I tell you that in heaven their angels are always in the presence of my heavenly Father".'

'Do only children have a guardian angel?'

'A wonderful question, but you know, I believe that we're all children of God.'

'What did your angel look like?'

'It was a fleeting glimpse in a vision. I was being chased by a drone through a valley when a wild swan flew past. It slowed so I could follow it. Eventually, it took me away from the river, off the beaten track, and as I made my way into a clearing, the swan transformed into a beautiful angel, about twelve feet tall. It was pointing towards a cleft in the rock face where I would be safe. Soon after, I woke up. That's what we're looking for now.'

'I would love to see an angel. I wish I had visions.'

'They're not all dreamlike, some feel more like nightmares. Between you and me, I think they'll end when this is over. I'm convinced more than ever I am meant to find it.'

'Thanks for sharing that. It makes it feel real,' he said, draining the remains of his tea. 'I'll set the drones up. As for the cleft, talk it over with Dilshod and the two lead scouts, though.'

'Remind me of their names?'

'Kurus is the tall one. Dawar is the one with a bandana.'

Melody spotted them immediately. Dawar was meticulously and almost lovingly sharpening his two machetes, the sun glinting occasionally off the blades, whilst Kurus was talking to Dilshod. She strolled over. 'I hope I'm not interrupting you?'

'No, not at all. We were considering our next move,' Dilshod said. Melody showed them the photo and explained what Jad was planning to do.

'We'll start making our way towards the area. It's as good a plan as any,' He said, nodding to Kurus, who left to join his partner.

As two of the drones set off, Melody watched until they eventually disappeared, the faint humming swallowed up by the sounds of the forest.

Chapter Thirty-Eight

～

They had been trekking all day. Melody was sweating and tired. She stopped and looked around. Then began squatting to stretch the life back into tired muscles. 'Dilshod,' she shouted.

He stopped and turned to her.

'How do the scouts know we are still on track?' Melody asked. 'I can't see more than a few yards ahead in this fading light.'

'They do have an amazing sense of direction, but what impresses me most is the speed they slash their way through this undergrowth. It's virtually at walking speed.'

They heard a call from ahead, 'Log warning.'

Melody looked down but became aware they were bunching up and eventually discovered the team in a small clearing.

'The scouts think this is an old intersection and a faint track leads off in that direction,' Dilshod said, pointing.

'I can't see any sign of a track,' Melody said, looking puzzled.

'I know – "sign of a faint track" can sometimes mean slightly different vegetation after the forest has reclaimed a well-worn track. That's what makes them good scouts, and these two are the best I have worked with. We're losing the light now, so I think it's time to make camp.'

'I was hoping you'd say that' Melody said, swatting gnats on her neck. She sat down on the fallen tree trunk to drink from her canteen, fascinated by how quickly the team made camp.

Zubeen provided a light supper, and whilst they ate, the mood was incredibly positive. There was a sense of well-being like they were on the brink of discovery.

Melody excused herself and retired to her tent. She was almost expecting an encounter. So it was no surprise when it happened, except she realised she was looking forward to it, welcoming it. At first, it followed the usual pattern. But when the darkness ended, the light arrived in a flash…

* * *

The sun was at its zenith and there was little sign of life at the oasis. Some houses looked empty and in slow decay. Perhaps this had once been a thriving community, but not anymore.

As the band of men entered the settlement, she recognised most of them as part of Melchior's Guard. *This must be the ambush the Magi had planned.*

Joubin was studying one house in particular. 'A great vantage point from the roof, and located opposite the stables, it's perfect for an archer. I will look to take out those on horses as my priority,' Joubin said.

Hormoz spoke. 'See if anyone lives there. Take Zhakfar with you. I'll look over the smallholding.' As he spoke, he was beckoning Musa and Roshan to follow him. The dilapidated stable had sufficient hiding places. 'They'll probably head for the stables when they arrive, conceal yourselves in here. Zhakfar and I will attack them from behind whilst Joubin picks them off from the rooftop.'

When Hormoz arrived at the house, Joubin was still knocking on the door. An old man appeared in the doorway. He looked them over suspiciously. 'What do you want? I don't have any money.'

'We mean you no harm. In fact, we want to give you some money to borrow your house for the day.' He was holding a small bag of shekels aloft. The old man made to grasp, but Joubin pulled away. 'Deal?'

He nodded, and Joubin handed it over.

'In a short while, some of Herod's men will arrive.' The old man spat on the ground but continued counting the money as Joubin continued. 'It would be safer for you to leave for a while.'

'What, and miss all the fun? I am not fleeing, not at my age. Besides, any enemy of Herod is a friend of mine. Come,' the old man said, beckoning them in and stashing the money bag in his tattered apron pocket.

* * *

An hour later, Hormoz watched from a crack in the door as Herod's eight men arrived at a trot. No longer in civilian clothes, they wore the traditional white tunics of the Praetorian Guard. Three were sporting purple cloaks draped over the horse's haunches, in deference to their status as Imperial Bodyguards. Each of them took in the surroundings.

'They look nervous,' Hormoz whispered to Zhakfar.

Four dismounted but were still looking around as they headed for the stable. Two had hands on their swords. The horses sensed the nervous atmosphere, snorting and stamping their hooves. One of them reared, turning to face Joubin's position on the roof. Its rider glimpsed him as he fired the arrow. It entered below the forehead, throwing him backwards off his mount.

'Ambush!' shouted a guard as the second arrow hit its target, the arrow pinning the cloak to his back.

'Take cover,' the lead guard shouted as another horse reared, causing the third arrow to graze its rider near his stomach. The next arrow hit the cheek-guard of the helmet he was wearing. 'Leave,' he shouted to the two horsemen. They sped off, heading in different directions, leaving their comrades behind.

'Attack!' Hormoz yelled as he and Zhakfar rushed from the house. They were sprinting for the open stable doors when Musa and Roshan appeared. Musa, as usual, was wielding two swords. The guards divided into two groups. Roshan stepped back, waiting for his companions. He defended himself with a makeshift shield and sword, striking one guard's arm as he moved between them.

Zhakfar drew a throwing knife from his bandolier. His throw, whilst running, was perfect; it took one guard heading towards Roshan in the back of his neck, just below his helmet.

The next blow to Roshan's shield caused him to lose balance and he fell on his back. He used his shield once more, but the guard was bearing down on him with a dagger. Zhakfar struck him with a blow to the head as he was about to plunge the dagger in and followed through with his sword. Musa was being pushed back. When one of his attackers peeled off to intercept Hormoz, he realised he now faced three men. He dropped his sword and held his hands aloft. Musa disarmed the remaining Praetorian and forced him onto his knees.

'Bring them both outside,' Hormoz ordered.

As they moved out, Joubin joined them, and Faraj and Bashkir arrived. 'Do we go after the two that fled?' Joubin asked.

'I want to interrogate the two prisoners first,' responded Hormoz. 'Take them to the house we used earlier, tie them up and see if you can patch up the wounded one,' he said to Musa and Roshan.

'I doubt they'll tell us anything. It looks like they had a plan. If cornered, one of them would complete the mission. Did you notice they split up, making it difficult to follow them?' Zhakfar asked.

'Zhakfar and Roshan can follow one set of tracks. Faraj and Bashkir, you two take the other,' Hormoz said. 'You must intercept them before they reach Pelusium where Mary's family are likely to be staying. We don't want to rely on Melker to protect them. He's only meant to be our last line of defence.'

Chapter Thirty-Nine

~~

Nikolai was sitting in his wheelchair with his back to the door as Sasha entered his room. His body slumped forward, not moving. She rushed over and felt for a pulse, breathing a sigh of relief when she found one.

'Ah, Sasha,' he said, rousing, his eyes squinting as he focused. 'I was watching for the assassins, but I must have nodded off... All I do is sleep... the other nurses, they don't care... trying to poison me.'

'No one wants to poison you. It's your medication.' It was then she noticed he was holding a revolver, his right hand clutching it on his lap with one finger on the trigger.

'Nikolai! What are you doing with a gun?' she asked, putting her hand over her mouth.

'Protection!'

'You don't need protection, Nikolai. Nobody is trying to kill you. There are bodyguards all over the hospital grounds. Where did you get the gun from?' she asked, whilst carefully taking it off him.

'Vasily. He understands the risk. But I feel safe when you're here... I have a present for you,' he said, gesturing to the end of the bed. It was a Louis Vuitton bag, a red ribbon tied in a bow on the handles.

'I don't think I'm allowed to accept gifts,' she said, though moving towards it.

'Worry not. I've already cleared it with your bosses,' he said, trying to smile. 'Actually, I don't trust them either.'

'It's worth accepting it just to see you smile. I've not seen that for weeks. It looks awfully expensive,' she said, running her hand over it. As she picked it up, she could feel its weight. There was something inside. She undid the bow and two buckles, then opened it. Again, her hand moved over her mouth. It was full of money, bundles of US dollar bills.

He was fighting hard to stay awake. 'You can visit America... my sisters did... did I tell you? Like young girls, squealing... you can't go yet, though,' he said and managed a faint laugh, causing him to cough.

'But these are high-value bills. How much is in here?' she asked, putting the gun down and flicking through one bundle.

'Not sure ... tired of counting after two hundred thousand... can't concentrate for long... Vasily helped... listen, Sasha, this is your event... life-changing... don't lose it. Now, help me get into bed... so tired.'

'I don't know what to say. I can't thank you enough or think of suitable words. My mind is in a fog.'

She helped get his frail body into the bed, whilst checking his stats and the medication, before looking back at the bag and wondering what to do with the gun.

'I have never seen that much money; it will take an age to count it.'

'I had a machine to count mine... money, money, money... buying vouchers for shares... cash was king... money, money, money... years in pursuit of it, for what?' His head was nodding, his eyes heavy, and he felt the comfort of sleep beckoning him. 'I would give it all for–' The flashbacks started again...

'What is our stake in Yuganskneftegaz now?' Nikolai asked.

'Fifty-one per cent, but we're on course for seventy-five. The Government gets a guaranteed holding of ten per cent,' Anatoly said. 'They valued the business at US$2.1billion.'

'And the forecast if we step up production?'

'Lehman Brothers estimate it at US$6.9billion. Nikolai: you're a billionaire.' He said, hunching his shoulders.

'So are you, but we must be careful. Many will look at us with envy. They will regard what we have done as plundering State Assets. But envy, to quote Yevtushenko, my favourite Russian Poet – "Envy is an insult to oneself".'

'What of your brothers-in-law, buying up vouchers on your behalf? Many say sometimes a little too enthusiastically. Some claim bullying and blackmail.'

'Let them talk. Grigoriy and Ivan worked tirelessly. They forced nobody to sell. Have you set up a way of getting the money into Western Banks? I don't want to have too much money swilling around in Russia.'

'I've devised a transfer scheme, but it will require the services of Grigoriy and Ivan to oil a few wheels. Especially if you're still intent on buying your sister's apartments in Manhattan.'

'I am, and we also need to buy some smaller properties for State Oil Officials in Greece, otherwise, we won't be able to operate there. Finally, we'll require a certain amount of cash to ensure protection against our political enemies and the Moscow Mafia.'

Life was good for them.

Chapter Forty

~~

They came across another clearing, smaller this time. Kurus was already carefully removing a mass of tangled creepers off a high stone pillar.

'What is it?' Dilshod asked, mopping his brow.

'It looks like a statue, but why here in the middle of nowhere?' Dewar said.

'And who of?' Dilshod asked.

They removed more vegetation, revealing first a face, then a male torso.

'Is it carrying something on its back?' Dilshod asked, moving to its side.

Dewar had hacked his way behind, and the rest of the group joined in, unearthing it. They successfully cut the vines at the bottom and then, with one last pull, like carrying out an unveiling ceremony, they revealed the statue.

Melody stepped back; her mouth open. It seemed so out of place and yet, even soiled and covered in moss and lichen, it looked magnificent.

Farzad, the chief archaeologist, was the first to speak. 'It looks like an angel.'

'Yes, it is,' Melody said, 'and it's pointing in the direction we need to go for the cave.' *This is it, all those years of torment, and yet, now I understand why.* As the tears started, she sank to her knees. Most of the group fell silent, and Dilshod knelt beside her.

'Tears of joy or relief?' he asked, patting her shoulder.

'For years, I've been under a cloud of self-doubt. Even when I have had to make a stand against the sceptics, in the back of my mind there was always the nagging thought: what if they're right?' She took her neckerchief off, wiped her eyes and then blew her nose. She smiled and looked up at the team. 'Now I know, I was born to do this. Thank you, all of you.'

One of them clapped, and the others followed, making her smile even more.

Dilshod helped her up. 'Thanks, you've been my rock,' she said, taking a deep breath. She then moved closer to examine the base, scraping away years of dirt and vine suckers to reveal a message.

'It's written in Avestan,' she said.

Farzad passed her a small brush and a canteen of water. 'Can you read it?'

'Something about power, a kingdom and regular, no, the same.' She continued scrubbing, then drenched it with water and stood up. 'The seat of power in a kingdom must be the same seat of prayer.'

The humming of the drones became louder and as they looked up, one was hovering above them as a call came on the walkie-talkie. Dilshod clicked the call button. 'Go ahead, Jad. We think we've found the track.'

'I wanted to let you know there has been more unidentified drone activity. I picked them up on my rudimentary radar. They're not close, just an update.'

'Roger that. What did you find on the other side of the mountain? Is there a way out for us?'

'There's another cave in a similar position. It could be it cuts all the way through, but can't be certain. Over.'

Melody was desperately trying to get the attention of Dilshod.

'Roger that, Jad. We'll keep you informed. Oh, hang on, Melody wants to speak to you.'

'Hi Jad, can you zoom in on us and look at what we discovered?'

After a brief pause, he asked. 'Is that the angel you saw in the vision?'

'Yes. Fantastic confirmation. And the perfect guide to the direction of the cave. Oh, and over and out.'

An hour later, they reached the base of the mountain. Its dark, hard granite face looked impregnable and a lot higher from this vantage point.

'I'll search south. Dawar can go north. I am sure it is close by. We're so close to the mountain now it's hard to see the cleft,' Kurus said.

Dilshod agreed and called for another drink break. They had barely started drinking when they heard Dawar shouting he had found the cleft in the rock face. Melody was the first to react, striding out in his direction. The entrance was over a metre wide and three metres high.

Melody peered into the inky blackness, a stark contrast to the brilliant sunshine outside. Ahead, she could make out the head torch of Dawar and a much larger patch of light further ahead of him, but this was not from the torches. It was different, independent, like sunlight.

Kurus brushed past her as he entered, his large flashlight throwing a beam of light over the walls and ceiling.

Then Amooz appeared alongside her. 'Well,' he said, 'aren't you going in?'

'I imagined the Magi walking in. It feels almost like sacred ground. And yet, it also feels familiar. Like the vision,' Melody said as she walked tentatively into the labyrinth, her eyes focused on the pool of light.

The torch lights ahead had stopped moving. 'It looks like a staircase cut in the rock,' Dawar shouted, his voice echoing.

Where is the light coming from? We are inside the mountain.

The steps were slippery in places and the cobwebs were as thick as net curtains as they spiralled their way upwards. She began counting the steps but stopped at one hundred. They seemed to go on forever, but the light was getting stronger and eventually she reached the top. She stepped forward and gasped.

Chapter Forty-One

~~~

For quite some time, nobody spoke. They simply walked around the Sanctuary of the Gathering Place, taking in the fresco-style carvings.

Melody was the first to speak. 'This is it, people. We've found it. It's exactly as I imagined, and yet I'm still overawed and strangely confounded by it. It's cool but not cold. I expected it to be airless and musty but I keep smelling different things as I walk around, oranges, cut grass, and even a sea breeze. Why? It should be damp, but it isn't and look at the statues. They look like marble, but how can that be in here? And the ceiling is magnificent.'

She sat down on a bench facing the altar table, her eyes straining to take in all the details. Nouri was moving around, painstakingly filming, using a ruler to show perspective for later research. Amooz was clicking away with his digital camera.

Melody gazed upwards. Each of the angels surrounding the central star was different. *Are they depicting distinctive roles? Cherubim, Seraphim, Archangels, Guardian Angels I wonder? I could spend weeks here simply cataloguing them.*

Her eyes followed the light down to the large stone block in the centre. It reminded her of a sarcophagus she once saw in Egypt. Even at a distance, she could make out an inscription. Farzad, the chief archaeologist, was already inspecting it, carefully brushing away dust and cobwebs.

'It looks similar to the inscription on the angel statue,' he said to Melody, as she looked over his shoulder.

'The seat of power in a kingdom must be the same seat of prayer.' She spoke whilst turning to the others. 'Of course. This is the Seat of Prayer. It's beneath the Star and in the centre of the Gathering Place.' The others gathered around, Nouri still filming and Amooz getting close-ups of the inscription.

Melody spoke quietly, almost in a whisper, repeating the phrase. 'It shall rest in the Valley of Ascendency in the foothills of Shir and there, in the Sanctuary of the Gathering Place, beneath the Seat of Prayer, it shall remain.'

'I can see a faint line here,' Farzad said, running his finger around the base of the stone slab. 'Maybe it lifts from here, somehow.'

Melody was inspecting it, but was doubtful.

'It would require more than three or four men. Too heavy for the Magi to do it alone. There must be another way in.'

'Why do you say three or four men?' asked Farzad.

'I'm sure on occasions the three senior Magi would have been here on their own, though we know Melchior's son Melker often accompanied him. Wherever they hid it, they would have needed to do it without force. A slab this size would take a tremendous effort and probably a dozen men, if not more.'

Dilshod moved away from the group and began circling the room, running his hands over the walls, including the recesses for candles and ancient torch holders. 'There's an inscription repeated at the base of each of the three torch holders. It looks Greek to me. Why Greek though, normally it's Avestan?'

Melody gently ran her fingers over the engraving. 'Truly, the triune will be a torchlight in the dark to reveal the sheathe.'

'What does that mean?' Dilshod asked.

Farzad joined them. 'It may be cryptic, truly could be authentic or beyond doubt, triune simply means three. I think the torchlight is torch holders. Reveal is possibly, make known, not sure about dark or sheathe, though.'

'In this context, it could be the enemy, or even Herod. It may even be torchlight in the dark,' Melody said.

'Sheathe means enclosed or wrap,' Dilshod said.

'Or possibly swaddling. Beyond doubt, three torch holders will be light to Herod and make known the swaddling,' Melody said, getting excited.

'I'll go to the torch holder over there,' Amooz said, pointing.

'Dilshod, stay with this one and I'll take the third,' Melody said, taking her place beside it.

She checked to see all were in position. 'On my signal, we all pull the torch holders down simultaneously.' She dropped her free hand and pulled, but none of them moved. She placed both hands on it and tried moving it clockwise. Still, it was solid. When she tried the opposite direction, it moved a little. She stopped and stood back, almost afraid this could be it.

'Did it move anticlockwise?' Dilshod asked.

'Yes. On my mark, try turning it anti-clockwise.' She counted to three, then dropped her free hand and turned the torch holder simultaneously with Dilshod and Amooz. All eyes turned toward the seat. Nobody spoke. Then they looked at one another. Some shrugged their shoulders.

'Nothing,' someone said.

Then it started. At first, there was a slight rumbling sound and a tremor coming from the floor. The light intensified. Melody looked up at the ceiling.

'Look, the angelic beings surrounding the Star are moving.' They were changing their positions, each of them now looking down at the seat. Suddenly, the angels transformed and flew down off the ceiling. They were weaving in between the team, leaving behind a silvery trail. Nouri continued filming it. There were gasps from some as they reached out, trying to touch them. One was laughing uncontrollably whilst another knelt crying, his hands held aloft in a prayer-like pose. Farzad was lying on his back, his eyes closed, silent, but beaming.

Melody stood transfixed, her arms outstretched, her head tilted back. She turned in a tight circle. Several of the angels flew around her, their silver trail falling on her like confetti at a wedding, causing her to laugh. Several of the team also had their arms stretched out above them. Then the singing started. The words were indistinguishable, but the sound was so beautiful, filling the entire cavern. Melody fell to her knees as an angel hovered in front of her, face to face. It held Melody captive; the angel's face transformed into a perfect likeness of her grandmother. *Did Mañana know this would happen?* The angel smiled and a peace she so often experienced in visions overwhelmed her. Melody stretched out an arm, desperate to make contact. The angel moved forward and took her hand. Melody glowed.

It feels as though love is flowing through my veins, or I'm standing in the presence of love. Take me along. I want to be with you. Don't leave me here. The angel's eyes closed and it spoke.

'Chosen, you are now the guardian of the swaddling. Peace be with you.' The words washed over her like liquid song. Then the angel backed away before bursting upwards, leaving Melody holding out her hands, trying to catch the curtain of what she would later call 'angel stardust'.

All the while, the vibrations had increased in intensity as the seat was being pushed up by four posts. A brilliant light emitting from below.

A blanket of fog coming from beneath the seat crept over the floor, and what had started as a slight breeze became a strong wind stirring up the fog, making it difficult to see the angels.

The seat continued to lift. It mesmerised Melody; she felt drawn toward the seat and fell to her knees in front of it. The posts stopped moving; the singing ended and as the mist cleared and the bright light diminished, there on the pedestal base was a beautiful and intricately carved wooden casket.

Farzad, Amooz and Dilshod walked over and knelt beside her.

'Is this it?' Amooz asked.

'I'm afraid to touch it and afraid not to,' Melody said, reaching in under the stone seat and lifting it out. It was heavier than she expected as she placed it on the floor in front of her. 'It's beautiful,' she said, stroking it. As she spoke, the seat sank to its original resting place. She looked up. The angelic beings had gone.

'Yes, this is it,' she said. 'This is it.'

'I see it has two keyholes. Is there a key?' Farzad asked.

'Not that I could see. When I removed the casket, the pedestal base was empty. No sign of any keys.'

The team had gathered around the seat, forming a circle with Melody in the middle. It was quiet, the muffled sound of the forest breaking through again. No one quite knew what to say. Some were still smiling; others were deep in thought. For some, it would have been their first encounter with the supernatural world, but others with a faith would reflect differently. Now though, as they looked at each other, seemingly unable to convey the depth of what they had witnessed, what they had experienced, no words could communicate the wonder of it all. Yet when their eyes connected, each of the parties knew they had been on holy ground and that they would forever share that bond.

Melody wondered if anyone else heard the Angel speak to her or witnessed her glowing, but as no one mentioned it, she decided not to say anything. It felt like a private encounter, a message for her alone.

They spent several hours quietly filming, photographing and taking notes, only occasionally talking about their experiences. They continued to explore the cave but eventually, and with some reluctance, they returned to the temporary base camp. One of the team members who had stayed behind told excitedly of the transformation of the statue.

'It turned into an actual angel and then, in a blinding flash of light, disappeared upwards, leaving behind a silvery trail. Come look,' he said as he took them to the empty pedestal as evidence.

Later, Dilshod pulled Melody to one side. 'What next?'

'I have no idea. I'm still tingling from the experience. Forever is how long I want to stay here. Tonight I want to sleep on the seat of prayer and open the casket, but I know I can't, so let me enjoy the moment. The visions blunted my faith as a young girl. Now I need a little time on my own to process what just happened and then we'll talk.'

Melody turned back towards the cave entrance, holding on tightly to the casket. *Another strange thing, the casket smells strongly of hyacinths. Why?*

* * *

Later, they celebrated long into the night. Amooz brought a case of beer he had hidden to the party and Nouri projected the video film of the cave experience onto a makeshift screen. Demand to see it again was so strong that he put it on a loop. They also wanted a speech from Melody.

The gratitude she expressed was heartfelt and partway through the farewell, she became overwhelmed and cried. The men watched silently as she composed herself and Dilshod handed her some tissue paper.

'It's too dangerous to stay here now,' she said, dabbing her eyes. 'But one day, I promise all of you, we will return and we will carry out a more forensic investigation of the site.'

They cheered loudly, and then she hugged them one by one, desperately trying to hold back the tears, but failing.

Chapter Forty-Two

Melody and Dilshod were studying a map of the region. 'What's your preferred route?' she asked.

'My preferred route would be by road to Turkmenistan and a ferry from the port at Turkmenbashi. They cross the Caspian Sea to Baku in Azerbaijan and from there you can get a flight to Jordan. The hardest part will be to gain entry into Israel.'

'I need an Israeli passport and possibly a Jordanian one.'

'I agree. I know someone in Baku who can help, but he's not entirely reliable or trustworthy. We will need to be incredibly careful dealing with him. But he's the only one I know.'

'Beggars can't be choosers. Contact him as soon as you can. Where would you recommend staying in Turkmenbashi?'

'The Çarlak Hotel. It's close to the ferry terminal and has an international clientele, plus it's big enough for you to blend in. The ferries going from Turkmenbashi to Baku are not passenger ferries, they're freighters which also take passengers. It's potluck. You cannot book in advance and they don't go every day. They leave when they're full.'

'What about the trip to Turkmenbashi? What's the border like and how long will it take?'

'I know several routes through the forest that avoid the Iranian customs border. It takes about eight hours; I will stay with you as far as Azerbaijan. If things go pear-shaped, go to this address. They'll look after you,' he said, handing her a business card.

'How long did you live there?'

'Five years. Don't worry, you can trust these people.'

'We'd better get started then.'

The road trip through the forest was uneventful, though slow-going. Dilshod weaved his way through, using the disused logging tracks. Eventually, he announced they had left Iran and were now in the South of Turkmenistan. 'We are close to the old Silk Road here,' he said, knowing her interest in the journey of the Magi.

'It would have been lovely to visit some sites. How far are we from Ashgabat and the Nissa Fortress ruins?'

'Too far! Are you happy for us to keep going all the way to the Ferry Terminal at Turkmenbashi?' he said, changing the subject.

'Yes, I don't want to stay overnight in a small town. We would be too conspicuous.'

They followed the coast road as far as Okarem, turning inland for Balkanabat where they stopped for refreshments before picking up the freeway.

It was late when they pulled into Turkmenbashi, but it was still lively. The restaurants were open, with many sitting outside and the street vendors still plying their trade. She had the car window open. The smell of spicy street food constantly changed as they drove past their stalls.

They had no problems booking into the Çarlak Hotel and had a light meal in the bar.

'I think I could sit at this bar drinking all night,' Dilshod said, sipping another cold beer.

'I want an early night. I am so looking forward to a long hot soak, I think I may fall asleep in the bath.' Melody said, standing and leaving him behind.

'Goodnight, we need to be up early though to book the ferry.'

Melody simply waved and did not reply. *He's announced to the hotel where we're going. I'll talk to him about it in the morning.*

Having bought some scented candles in the hotel gift shop, along with some overly expensive mineral bath infusions, she had the longest soak she could remember.

Later she snuggled down into the soft bed, revelling in the luxury of it compared to the camp bed and sleeping bags. But another encounter began… She welcomed it, wondering what was in store for her.

She recognised immediately that she was in Egypt. She had spent plenty of time on archaeological digs there, and she felt certain this was Alexandria.

The house had gates leading into a courtyard and two men were standing beside her, one she recognised as Melchior's son Melker. The other was pointing.

'In there,' he said. Melker handed him some coins, and he left them.

Melker opened the gates and walked in. The door to the house was open. As they entered, she noticed it was cool and dark, yet a sense of peace enveloped her.

'Whom do you seek?' a young woman's voice asked. The question drew them in. The same voice, soft and comforting. Melody recognised her. Then, surprisingly, she had the same experience she had once before. Whenever she moved, the young woman noticed it, like she was aware of Melody's presence, but seemingly unable to see her.

'I seek Mary and Joseph from Nazareth. I am Melker, son of Lord Melchior.'

'Welcome Melker, I am Mary. Why do you seek us?'

'Herod is searching for you. Shortly after you left Bethlehem, he ordered the killing of all male children under the age of two. He knows you have escaped.'

'We do not fear Herod,' she said, 'and one day soon, he will have to account for his life, followed by the passing of judgement. Then we shall return to Nazareth.'

She spoke the words lightly but they seemed to hang in the air, as though judgement had already taken place.

'The swaddling cloth you gave to my father has unique healing powers. Herod would seek them for himself, to delay his day of judgement,' Melkar said.

'He cannot delay it. That day is set. As for the swaddling, it was a gift to the Magi. Only they or their ancestors will witness the blessing from it.'

The calm, softly spoken words held them both captive. Melker looked disarmed and completely unable to counter her sense of sovereignty over events. 'But what about your child's life? He is in real danger, if not for yourselves–'

She held up a hand. 'One day my son will give up his life for many, but not yet and not here and not at the hands of this Herodian.'

'Will you at least allow me to take any remaining swaddling back to my father? At least this will ease some of his concerns?'

'You cannot take them. They must be a gift, and this I do willingly. Your father has played his part. For him, the noble quest is over, and he must now return home, knowing that his role was greater than he can ever imagine.'

Mary opened the sacred box Joseph had made for her when they first met. She carefully took out the last of the swaddling and handed it to him. 'Go peacefully and may the blessing of God be on you and all who travel with you,' she said, looking at Melody.

Melody was taken aback, but then bowed in acquiescence. *She can see me, or is at least aware of my presence? How strange.*

Melker realised at that moment that his audience was over. He considered asking if he could stay to protect them, but he now knew that would not happen.

'Before I depart, would you bless me?' he said, kneeling before her.

Mary stretched out her hand and laid it on his head. 'The Lord bless you and keep you. The Lord make His face shine upon you and be gracious to you. The Lord lift up His countenance upon you and give you peace.'

Melody watched, her eyes filling up as Melker wept.

Chapter Forty-Three

~

The sun was shining through the light curtains and after a quick shower, Melody dressed and checked how many pills she had. They were running low; she took one and made a mental note to get more in Baku. She opened the safe and removed the casket. Noticing a strong smell of oranges, she looked it over again whilst sitting on the bed, her hand tracing the fine carving. She was desperate to get it home and have it opened. *I wonder what happened to Mary's Sacred Box. Did she keep it and take it to Ephesus? Is it hidden still at Mary's House on Nightingale Hill?* Her phone rang, breaking into her thoughts.

'Good morning, Dilshod, I'm on my way down,' Melody said before he spoke.

She spotted him in the restaurant and helped herself from the buffet to a simple breakfast before joining him and ordering coffee.

'When we've finished breakfast, I'll go to the terminal and see when the next ferry is leaving. Keep your phone switched on and your bag packed. There could be one ready to leave at short notice. What have you got planned?'

'I'm going to spend some time shopping in the artisan market. I need some fresh clothes, and by the way, you need a haircut. But mostly, I need to wind down after recent events.'

'Be careful, this is not over yet, you still have a long way to go, and as my father used to say, "the Iranian Government's reach is longer than a giraffe's neck".'

As Melody left the hotel, she could see the harbour below. It was not a normal ferry terminal; forklift trucks scuttled around like worker ants. Two leggy angle-poised cranes, silhouetted against the pale blue skyline, were unloading a freighter, as an oil tanker disgorged its cargo into the port's storage tanks. The sheer cliffs around Turkmenbashi Bay formed a stark backdrop.

She walked the short distance into town and had not been there long when she sensed a man was following her. She lost him quickly, using the techniques she had learned and carried on visiting several of the artisan craft shops whilst keeping an eye out for him.

The man who had followed her was now watching Melody from the men's outfitters, the large painted letters across the window hiding him. He noted this was the second time she had visited this vendor.

Eventually, Melody found a speciality coffee bar. She was sitting outside sipping her cortado when the man walked past. *Now I know what you look like.* Just then, a message pinged on her phone.

'*Got tickets. The ferry leaves at 4:30. Meet me at reception.*'

* * *

Later, as they boarded the ferry named Qarabag, the powerful smell of diesel served as a reminder that this was a freight ferry where passengers were secondary. She spotted the man in the queue; he was probably late thirties, with an athletic build and a small scar below his right eye. What caught her attention was that, although dressed casually, he was wearing a rucksack and carrying a briefcase. She decided not to mention him to Dilshod. Whatever it was, she could handle it on her own.

'Our rooms are on the main deck,' Dilshod said. 'I didn't want us trapped below deck. It's five o'clock now, so if we eat later, at say eight, then get an early night, we should dock around breakfast. It's not a restaurant though, more of a canteen.'

'I don't care. I'm simply happy to be on our way. So far, so good,' she said as they arrived at their cabins. 'See you later.'

Once in the dingy cabin, she turned off the lights and positioned herself to watch through a small gap in the curtain. Five minutes later, the man she had identified earlier walked past slowly and even stopped for a moment between the cabins before moving off. Moments later, Melody opened the door, looked down the deck and watched him enter his cabin further along opposite a lifeboat station. *So, you know which cabin I'm in.*

During their meal together, Melody and Dilshod discussed the onward journey. 'At Baku International, you can get a direct flight to Jordan; it has one stop in Azerbaijan at Nakhichevan, near the Jordanian border. Then to Queen Alia airport, Jordan, where you can stay over. I would recommend the Amman Airport Hotel. You're not far then from the West Bank,' Dilshod said. 'I cannot advise you after that.'

'You worry about me too much. I feel confident about getting into Israel, and I will probably hire a private tour from Amman to visit Bethlehem, I feel the need to go there, like a pilgrimage I suppose, and being this close I think I would regret it if I didn't. I have been before as an archaeologist, and it is such a special place. But this time it will feel different, almost a homecoming. I have to go. It's all part of this journey.'

'How far is it?'

'It's about a four-hour drive from Amman. But I need the Israeli passport from your contact to hold up,' she said, getting ready to leave. 'Are you staying for another drink?'

'Yes, I think I'll grab myself a beer. I'll see you in the morning for breakfast.'

'Goodnight then.' As she was leaving, Melody made a quick scan of the canteen. The man following her was not there.

Back at the cabin, she checked the small piece of tape was still in place on the door before entering.

Chapter Forty-Four

~~

Igor was speaking on his mobile. 'She's in her cabin and her minder's in the bar,' he said.

'The casket is what's important. She's disposable, but only after you've recovered the swaddling. Until we have it, she must remain alive. Do you understand, Igor?'

'Yes, Vasily.'

'What about the CCTV on board?'

'I've hacked into the system and disabled it.'

'Good. Call me when you have it.' Then he ended the call.

Igor stood on the deck, looking out to sea. It was rougher now and pitch black. The foaming bow wave was visible only because of the deck lights. He headed to Melody's cabin which was now in darkness. Slowly and carefully, he put the master-key in the lock before glancing up and down the deserted deck. As he opened the door, the deck lights gave him some light. He could make out the shape of her in bed. The man had a piece of tape in one hand and a knife in the other. He closed the door, then stealthily made his way over towards her.

As he pulled the bedclothes back, the lights came on. He realised too late; it was a setup and as he was about to turn, Melody's foot pushed hard against the small of his back, propelling him into the steel bulkhead. His head hit it hard, and he collapsed unconscious on the bed. She put a cable tie around his ankles, then remembered Ryland's advice too late. *The priority is to remove any lethal weapons and then restrict them.* She searched desperately for the knife he had been holding, then spotted it on the far side of the bed. But he was already coming round and turning. He saw her looking at the knife; he also locked onto it and made a desperate lunge to reach it first despite the cable tie restricting his movement.

Melody jumped onto the bed, the bounce causing the knife to fly into the air. She tried to grab it, but it dropped out of sight between the bed and the bulkhead. Melody jumped off the bed as Igor hauled himself up and hopped toward her; she punched him in the throat but instead of folding he staggered forward, grabbing at her throat. Melody brought her knee up into his groin. The leg restrictions caused him to lose balance and as he fell forward, he pushed Melody into the bathroom door; it flew open, and she fell backwards into the bathroom, grazing her head on the washbasin. Dazed and struggling to stand up, she ended up in a kneeling position.

Igor shuffled like a beached walrus toward the bed, then reached under it in a frantic search for the knife. He found it. Now all he had to do was slither his way from under the bed and cut the cable tie. Once free, he stood and rushed to the bathroom, wielding the knife.

Melody was now standing but supporting herself against the washbasin, waiting for him to reach the door threshold.

Not yet, wait, nearly there. Two more steps, wait, now!

Moving forward, she had both hands on the door and forcefully slammed it into him, then stepped back. Picking up a towel, she wrapped it around her left hand and then smashed a glass soap bowl with the other. She stood poised, a glass shard in her right hand waiting for him to lunge at her again. The door slowly swung back open. Igor was standing there, his face frozen in shock, his eyes glazed. The knife blade was in his stomach. He sank to his knees, then fell over onto the floor, blood trickling from his mouth, his body twitching.

She waited for him to stop moving, then checked for a pulse but found none. She went into the bathroom and swilled cold water over her face, before calling Dilshod.

'Can you come to my room as soon as possible and without drawing attention to yourself? I'll explain why when you get here.'

'On my way.'

A few minutes later there was a knock on the door, and she let Dilshod in. He quickly took in the scene.

'Who is he and what happened?' he asked, bending down to check if he was alive.

'I spotted him following me yesterday in the market. His cabin is further down the deck. He broke in tonight. He came at me with a knife and I slammed the door on him. He likely stabbed himself. It was an accident – self-defence – I thought he was going to kill me.' She said, constantly wringing her hands.

'You need to calm down. Are you hurt?'

'Just a bruise on the side of my head where I grazed the washbasin.' She winced as she rubbed it. 'I presume he's dead? I couldn't find a pulse. I have no idea what to do. Shall we put him back in his cabin?'

'No. We need to get rid of his body, leave no evidence, but make sure there is nothing on him for identification,' he said, going through his pockets. He removed a cabin key, wallet and iPhone.

'If you are feeling up to it, check his cabin, but be careful, in case he's not on his own. Let's see if we can identify who he was working for. When you return, we'll dispose of him overboard,' he said, handing over the key and attempting to open his phone.

Dilshod cleaned the blood off the carpet as best he could and was preparing the body when Melody returned. 'Did you discover anything?'

'I have his passport; his name is Igor Chernyshevsky, he's Russian. I also found this brown envelope. There's about ten thousand dollars in it,' she said, handing it over to him. 'You take it for expenses.'

'Are you sure?'

Melody nodded. 'You've earned it.'

'Thank you. He won't be needing it now, anyway. Probably a down payment. I'll keep his phone switched on. Whoever is paying him will want an update eventually, and we may be lucky enough for him to be on the contact list. At least we'll have a name then.' He placed a bathroom towel over his shoulder and then heaved Igor over it. 'Turn the lights off and see if it's all clear.'

Melody cracked open the door and watched a crew member walk past. A minute later she opened it fully, checking in both directions, and signalling the all clear to Dilshod. He covered the three metres of the deck at a jog and hurled the body over; he could barely hear the splash as the body landed in the sea. Dilshod turned toward the bow, feeling the sea spray on his face, and then returned to Melody's cabin.

'The CCTV appears to be switched off. There are no lights on them.'

'We need to finish cleaning up the cabin. There's a small amount of blood on the bathroom door and floor. Then I want to get my head down. I feel absolutely exhausted.'

Twenty minutes later, Dilshod bade her goodnight. 'I'm happy to sleep on the chair tonight if you're worried.'

'That's kind of you, but I'll be fine. See you in the morning.'

'It feels like the sea is getting rougher,' he said, leaving her room before throwing the blood-stained towels overboard and heading for his cabin.

* * *

Leaving the ferry was trouble-free and as soon as they had disembarked, Dilshod disposed of Igor's passport and keys.

Whilst waiting for a taxi, Igor's mobile rang. Dilshod noted the caller ID: 'Vasily'. After a brief silence – Vasily spoke. 'Igor, are you there?'

'Igor is not available at the moment; can I help you?'

'Who are you and where is Igor?' Vasily asked.

'Igor has taken early retirement. Perhaps we could meet and discuss it in more detail.'

175

'Ah! So you are her minder he talked about. Believe me when I say you wouldn't want to meet me.' Then the line went dead.

Dilshod turned to Melody. 'Well, we now know his name is Vasily. He sounded Russian, but he didn't want to meet us. However, I don't think he is likely to give up easily. What I don't understand, though, is why someone would go to such lengths for an artefact, rare as it is. Is there something I don't know but should?'

'Let me buy you a coffee, and I will tell you all I know. On our way, you can contact your friend regarding the passports?'

'He is not a friend, more of an acquaintance, a means to an end, no more. You cannot completely trust him.'

Chapter Forty-Five

~~~

The taxi took them into Baku, where they alighted and then walked through the shopping centre to lose any tags before taking another taxi to the Sapphire Zagulba Hotel.

'How close does your acquaintance live to the hotel?'

'He has a small printing business in a small town called Şağan, a short distance by taxi. We'll meet him as soon as we have checked in. His name is Azim Hüseynov.'

'What's the risk with him?'

'The most common is a hike in price. He offers to do it for one price, but when you go to collect it, he puts the price up, if he believes you can afford it.'

'Is he violent?'

'No, he's a low-level criminal. With him, there is no honour amongst thieves.'

After check-in, they took another taxi to a small industrial estate on the outskirts of Şağan. Melody took in the building as she climbed out of the battered Mercedes. It looked dingy, with rubbish piled up on one side of it. The roof was a patchwork of corrugated sheets, and an advertising sign hung lopsided. It looked dark and empty.

Dilshod knocked on the door and entered. Melody followed. It took several minutes for her eyes to become accustomed to the dim interior. She noticed Azim wore Cuban heels, a grubby suit and a hand-embroidered skullcap tilted backwards.

'Ah! Dilshod, salaam. It has been a long time, my friend. What can I do for you?' Azim said, kissing him on both cheeks.

'We need two passports for my companion here,' he said, gesturing towards Melody, who was messing with her phone. 'An Israeli one and a Jordanian one. How much and how soon?'

He pursed his lips as if to give a silent whistle. 'Expensive, but for this pretty lady, two thousand, and two days,' Azim said.

'Manat?'

'You are joking, my friend. The Manat is almost a worthless currency, US Dollars preferred, though I will settle for the equivalent in Sterling or Euros. Come,' he said to Melody. 'Let me take your picture.'

She looked at Dilshod and he nodded, but it irritated him she was still messing with her phone. Azim led her through to a makeshift studio. There was a blank wall with soiled white paper hanging as a backcloth and an old wooden bar stool in the centre.

'Sit please, for the Jordanian passport you don't need to cover your hair even though it's a Muslim country,' he said, throwing her a red and white scarf, 'but with light hair, you may stick out as a tourist. Also, be sure to wear neck-high tops, showing curves is OK but showing skin is not.'

Melody glanced at Dilshod and rolled her eyes, refraining from saying anything. As a seasoned traveller, she was well aware of the importance of following local customs. She stuck her arm out and dropped his scarf on the floor as if it contained head lice before taking an expensive silk one from her bag and putting it on. He took several shots with and without the headscarf.

'That should be fine,' he said, checking the digital photos. 'They should be ready two days from now. I need to find suitable matches for her age.'

Back at the hotel, Melody was browsing the local tour pamphlets in reception when Dilshod approached her. 'What are your plans for tomorrow?' he asked.

'I rather fancy a tour to the Burning Mountain and Fire Temple. Have you been?'

'Yes, many years ago, isn't it natural gas seeping through the rocks?'

'So they say. Apparently, it has been burning for sixty-five years.'

'Listen, I know you want to be independent. But the next time you think someone is following you, please let me know. It could have turned out differently on the ferry. Remember, I am also at risk.'

'You worry about me too much. But if it makes you feel better, I'll tell you if I suspect someone is tailing me.'

'Good. I have booked a table for dinner tonight at eight. See you then,' he said before heading for the bar.

Melody went to her room and opened the wall safe. The smell of jasmine filled her nostrils. She smiled, took out her laptop, and then closed the safe. She logged in and searched for local taxation and police before taking a pre-dinner shower. It was only when she was about to leave she noticed the empty pill bottle and realised she had not missed them. They were supposed to prevent the visions but she now recognised for the first time that she didn't want the visions to stop, at least not until she had the swaddling in her hands.

Melody spent the following two days doing some local sightseeing, shopping for more appropriate clothing for Jordan and enjoying the tour. She had a last dinner with Dilshod, where he quizzed her more about her trip to Bethlehem and her proposed entry into Israel.

'I am more concerned about getting the passports tomorrow,' Melody said. 'I don't trust him.'

'Neither do I, but we have little or no alternatives. Did you get the US dollars?'

'Yes, plus a couple of thousand extra, just in case. Tomorrow is our last day. I'll miss you. What will you do next?'

'Life will feel dull, that's for sure. Fortunately, the fee for the expedition and the money you recovered from Igor mean I don't have to worry for a long while. I was considering going back to Iran. I'd like to make sure Soraya, the hospital receptionist, is OK.'

'Amooz told me you sounded concerned.'

'The IRG murdered her brother. That was her primary reason for helping. She was nice to us and a great help.'

'What's she like?'

'She's lovely, big smile, large hazel brown eyes.'

'Single?' Melody raised an eyebrow.

'You're very perceptive.'

'It's a female thing.'

'I need to see her again. She put herself at significant risk and yes, I'm attracted to her,' he paused, and Melody thought he looked serious. 'Be careful Melody, this guy Vasily is not likely to give up. I think you should go public about your find, and as soon as possible – you are more at risk in the shadows. Wasn't it Benjamin Franklin who said, "An ounce of prevention is worth a pound of cure"?'

'I promise I will go public as soon as it's practical. But you need to be careful in Iran. They're probably still looking for you after your antics at the hospital. They may use Soraya as bait, and it sounds like you're already hooked on her.'

* * *

The following day, they arrived at the unit of Azim Hüseynov. It surprised them to see an expensive Mercedes outside; it looked oddly out of place against the shabby surroundings. 'Who do you think the car belongs to?' Melody said, gesturing toward the car.

'It could be one of his clients,' Dilshod said, his eyes narrowing to slits as he scanned the surrounding area. Satisfied, he knocked, then opened the door and walked in.

A burly man was standing beside Azim as he spoke. 'What is going on Dilshod? You bring me big trouble. They are saying a man disappeared off the ferry you arrived on. The police may come sniffing around.'

'Lots of people go missing off ferries, probably an illegal migrant or someone wanted for a crime, a drug dealer. Have you got the passports ready?'

'Yes, but when the police get involved, the price goes up to ten thousand dollars.'

Dilshod was about to argue when Melody stepped forward, holding up a brown envelope. 'Here are your options, Azim. In this hand, I have an envelope containing four thousand dollars,' she said, waving it before handing it to Dilshod. 'In this hand, I have a phone with a video of our recent meeting attached to an email. Ready to send to the State Tax Service and the National Police. You have ten seconds before I press the send button. You choose.'

The burly minder was unsure, then moved towards her. Melody stepped backwards, her finger hovering over the phone. Azim put a hand on his minder's shoulder to stop him. 'You cannot bully me; you would be in trouble as well–'

'Seven seconds,' Melody said, staring him down.

'I'll split the difference, seven thousand dollars, and I will accept.'

'Four seconds – Dilshod, call the taxi. We're leaving.'

'Be reasonable, five thousand dollars.'

'Two seconds and we go.'

'OK, OK you drive a hard bargain. I'll settle for four thousand,' Azim said, turning to open a wall safe hidden behind a fading picture of President Ilham Aliyev. 'My mother always warned me about dealing with pretty women.'

Dilshod took the passports off him and checked they were suitable. 'You've done a good job, Azim, as always,' he said, handing over the envelope.

Azim did not reply, and as he was counting the money, Melody and Dilshod left.

'Did you have an email ready to send?'

'Of course, I recorded the first meeting on my phone. Much to your annoyance, if I remember correctly. But he wasn't sure or prepared to call my bluff. Make them feel they have more to lose than you. It's a negotiating technique I learned at Sospitas. Also, have a firm deadline. It keeps you in control,' she said, as they climbed into the taxi.

Chapter Forty-Six

~~

Dilshod finished his lunch and asked, 'What time is your flight?'

'Six fifteen,' Melody paused for a moment. 'Well, this is it, Dilshod. For you, the quest is over, and your mission accomplished,' she said, saluting him and smiling. 'Apart from rescuing Soraya.' Then she looked serious. 'Please keep in touch. I'd like to know how Soraya is. I hope the visit goes well. And it would be great if you could visit me in England.'

'I'll take you up on that and bear me in mind for any future expeditions.'

'You'll be the first on my list.'

'Tell me about your trip to Bethlehem. How will your tour guide get over the border into Israel?'

'They won't. They'll take me to the River Jordan border crossing, then a colleague living in Israel will meet us there and take over.'

'What's Bethlehem like? I've never been.'

'There is something quite mystical about it. For many, it's a spiritual experience. They built the Church of the Nativity in the sixth-century over the site where Jesus was born. The address, incidentally, is Manger Square. In the crypt, they have marked the birthplace with an inlaid silver star. Somehow, though, this time will be different. Previously, it's been about archaeology.' Her eyes met his. 'This time it's different, but I can't explain why. And I have to take the casket with me. It feels more like a spiritual homecoming. It's where it started and I may get a better understanding of what I am to do next.'

'I hope you find what you're looking for. I once worked with a Palestinian, and when I asked him where he was from, he told me he was born in Bethlehem. Imagine having that on your birth certificate,' he said, smiling. 'And after that?'

'I'll stay in Israel and get a flight out. I'm going to Switzerland first to meet a friend who's an expert in this field, then it's home to England.'

The concierge arrived. 'Your taxi is waiting, Miss, the porter has taken your luggage out.'

'Thank you, I'll be out presently,' Melody said, standing. 'So, this is farewell for now,' she said, extending her arms.

They hugged and as they separated, Dilshod spoke. 'Thank you for the journey. I've enjoyed every moment, even the scary bits.'

'This is not goodbye. I promise you we will meet again. Good luck with Soraya and please be careful in Iran.'

Chapter Forty-Seven

It had taken two days to arrange the tour from Amman in Jordan to Bethlehem. The yellow taxi was making excellent progress. Looking out of the rear passenger side window, Melody could see the King Abdullah Canal as they ran parallel with it, heading north on route sixty-five.

'We're close to the Border Control, Miss.' The taxi driver announced.

'Thank you,' she said as the taxi took a sharp left turn onto the bridge crossing the River Jordan. The fake passport lay beside her on the seat, along with the casket in its protective carrying case.

Ahead, the white-painted checkpoint appeared, a stark sentinel sitting directly over the centre of the river. The high fencing on both sides of the road funnelled visitors to a stop at the black border gates. A large gold-painted crown sitting plaintively on top of the building looked oddly out of place.

Am I leaving a kingdom or entering one? Melody mused as she looked at the mountains in the distance, grey and uninhabited.

The taxi driver explained to the border guard that this was the end of his journey. They directed him to an area separated from through traffic. An armed Israeli Guard approached, beckoning Melody to show her papers.

'What was the purpose of your visit to Jordan?'

'Visiting family.'

He was scrutinising her passport, constantly comparing the photograph with her, then spoke into his radio, mentioning her false name several times before spelling it out. A second guard approached.

They were talking quickly, and the car engine noise made it difficult to understand what they were saying.

Have they spotted it's a fake passport?

When both men returned to the immigration station, she could feel the panic rising.

If they question me at length, will my Hebrew hold up well enough? Ah well, here goes.

The soldier returned. 'Sorry for the delay, miss. Your name is similar to someone we need to speak to,' he said, handing her passport back. 'Have a pleasant visit.'

'Shalom,' she said as they moved to a holding area.

The taxi driver pointed to her next host driver. 'He'll take you to Bethlehem. I can go no further.' Melody tipped him and made her way over. The feeling of relief was palpable.

The second part of the journey was in marked contrast to the first. Mainly wilderness had given way to more populated urban areas. They skirted around Jerusalem and headed south, eventually arriving at the Israeli military checkpoint at the West Bank – Rachel's Crossing and the entrance to Bethlehem. The distinct Bell Tower of the Basilica of the Nativity rose defiantly in the distance. The border guards recognised the tour operator, so waved him through.

Melody left the taxi close to Manger Square.

Why is it so quiet today? Has there been a terrorist attack? She scanned the area. *This place is normally a hive of tourists, and why do I feel nervous?*

She paused at the church entrance, the fabled 'door of humility'. During her first visit, the tour guide explained, 'They made it low to prevent looters from taking a cart inside.' She preferred the supposition that regardless of whether you are a king or a pauper, you must bow to enter.

There was a sense of anticipation she had not experienced on previous visits as she descended into the crypt. The click of her shoes on the stone staircase resonated as she spiralled down.

It's so quiet, and although I could see people leaving, nobody appears to be following me in. How strange. Are they closing early?

At the bottom of the stairs, she paused at an altar dedicated to the Magi. *What would they think of my quest? If they were back here today, what would they have me do and how would they feel? What happened after they returned home? Did Melker marry and have children? I feel such a connection with Melchior. I'll miss him if the visions stop.* Melody realised it was the first time she'd felt this way.

Wandering through the crypt also felt different from previous fact-finding visits, more spiritual, like a pilgrimage. Perhaps even the homecoming she had talked to Dilshod about. Then, quite without realising it, the Tombs of the Holy Innocents confronted her. She had barely paid any attention the last time she came. But now it was special, having witnessed Herod's soldiers slaughtering the children. It felt real; it felt personal.

This is where they buried the poor souls.

She was alone, no other tourists there to disturb her. She removed a small posy of flowers from her bag and laid them out. Flashbacks from the massacre raced through her mind. The cries of anguish from the vision disturbed her again. Her eyes filled up and a single tear flowed down her cheek and landed on a tomb. The stone absorbed her offering.

She strolled through the tunnels, lost in her own thoughts, soaking in the atmosphere. *It is so quiet. It's so bizarre.*

Ahead, the dimly lit altar of the Nativity was visible. Two candles in their gold holders flickered, and the oil lamps glowed, making the shadows dance on the cross above it, adding to the sense of being in a hallowed place. Below it, inset into the floor, was the fourteen-pointed silver star, marking the spot where Jesus was born. It drew her forward. She knelt, her hands stretched out, gently feeling the star worn smooth by countless pilgrims. Leaning forward, she gently kissed it and as she stood, words appeared in her mind, dancing like autumn leaves in a breeze. She took out her notepad and scribbled as the words settled.

No one hurries from this place, this space, this place of grace.
Where no love is misplaced.
Instead, hate is displaced at this parallel interface.
The burnished earthstar kissed and worn smooth by love.
Unforgotten by a mourning dove.
The children, carried by soft angels to a loftier place.
Yes, no one hurries from this place, this space, this place of grace.

Melody stood, stepped back a pace and paused, re-reading her words several times before moving on to her eventual destination – the Manger.

She stepped inside the small cave and again knelt.

Was this the place where it all started? Have I done the right thing?

Her trembling hands took the casket out of its case and placed it on the floor, filling the air with the fragrance of frankincense and myrrh. She sensed the start of an episode. But this time there was no utter despair gripping her, or drawing her down, no shortness of breath, no anxiety, just a beautiful sense of peace and joy overwhelming her before total darkness.

Nor was there a vision, simply a voice, one she recognised instantly. 'Bimcom bracha, ani magishah lecha et hamatanah hazo.'

'Instead of a blessing, I present you with this gift,' Melody whispered.

It was the same voice, soft, comforting and confirming. Melody wept.

* * *

Eventually, she left and ended up back in Manger Square calling the same taxi to take her from Bethlehem. She wanted to treat herself to a little luxury and had booked in at the Waldorf-Astoria Hotel in Jerusalem.

She was flying out the following morning but planned to see the Light Show that night at the Tower of David before leaving. The reviews said it was spectacular, and she felt in need of relaxing and being entertained.

Shortly after check-in, she received a text from Dilshod. 'Hi Melody, hope the journey from Jordan to Israel went smoothly. I've had an email from an old friend of mine. He's now living in Jerusalem. If you need help, call him, he owes me a few favours, I'll forward his contact details. He's trustworthy. Dilshod.'

That's sweet of him.

She replied. 'I'm fine, thank you, going to the Light Show tonight to relax. Thanks all the same. By the way, where are you? xx.'

'Iran, take care x.'

Dilshod then sent his friend a text…

The brochure proudly announced, 'The Jerusalem Light Show at the Tower of David Museum brings alive the walls, walkways and turrets of Jerusalem's Tower of David with a vibrant music and light show portraying Jerusalem's often bloody history.'

Sounds great, she thought after reading it. She had dinner early and used the hotel's taxi service for the brief journey to what had formerly been Herod's Palace at Jaffa Gate. It was the perfect antidote to all that had happened as she allowed the show to wash over her.

The show was every bit as good as she expected and when the evening ended, she made her way to meet the hotel taxi. She sensed she was being followed by two people and took evasive action.

One of them was Maria Licciardi, who was following at a discrete distance. A car driven by her accomplice was keeping pace at walking speed.

'Excuse me,' A stranger said, catching up with Maria. 'Could you tell me the way to Greek Patriarchate Street?'

'I'm sorry no, I'm a tourist.'

He was now standing in front of her. 'I forgot my glasses. Would you mind pointing it out on the map, please?' he asked, unfolding it and blocking her way.

'Look, I'm in a hurry,' she said as the crowd swept past her.

'It'll only take a moment.' He held the map in front of her face. 'I'm lost.'

'Move out of my way. You're making me late.' She tried to walk around him, but he shifted his position, blocking her. 'Perhaps I can give you a lift, then. I have just come from the Light Show too.'

She ignored him and stepped onto the road. But by then, there were too many people between her and Melody. She had lost sight of her. The car pulled up alongside and she got in, glaring at the man who had interfered.

He smiled and winked at her as the car raced off. But Melody was already in a taxi, heading for the hotel. Then the stranger sent a text to Dilshod.

'She's safe.'

Chapter Forty-Eight

~~

As the EL AL Flight from Ben Gurion Airport, Tel-Aviv took off, Melody was still considering herself lucky she had passed through security at the airport. She had felt sure they would confiscate the casket. Israel had a rich archaeological history and was extremely vigilant not to let antiquities leave the country. Fortunately for her, customs had viewed her luggage with scant interest by Israeli standards.

She tried to relax by reading an article from the recent issue of *Current Archaeologists Magazine*, but her mind wasn't fully engaged. Leaning forward, she placed the magazine inside the bag and brushed back her strawberry blonde hair, pinning it behind her right ear.

I have made it this far. Soon I will be in Switzerland and after a short stopover, back in England.

'Hi, my name's Suzy,' the woman sitting next to her said, offering her hand.

'Melody,' she replied, whilst taking her hand lightly. 'Pleased to meet you. I see you're a reporter.'

Suzy looked down at the press badge hanging off her rainbow-coloured lanyard and smiled. 'I always wear it when flying. I find I get better service, especially with security. They are worried I may print something bad about them. What about you? What do you do?'

Melody warmed to her, 'Boring, I'm afraid – an archaeologist, for my sins.'

Suzy turned her head, her long ponytail flicking as she leaned into her. 'No, it sounds exciting. Are you going on a dig?'

Melody laughed. 'No, archaeology is ninety-five percent research, four per cent dealing with officials and only one per cent digging. I am going to meet my boyfriend; I have not seen him for a couple of months. It's more of a holiday,' she lied.

Suzy leaned back in her seat. 'My mother is always telling me I should have a boyfriend. "You're married to your job, Suzy. Newspapers won't give you children. A little make-up wouldn't go amiss either. And what about me and your father? We will be dead before we see grandchildren,"' she said, mimicking and exaggerating her mother's voice.

Melody laughed. 'What sort of things do you report on?'

'Listen, Mel,' she said, already shortening her name as if they were old friends. 'Israelis care about two things in politics: religion and security. Despite being a traditional Jew, my family in Hebron are ultra-nationalists. Because of this, I am in charge of security matters, which makes my father happy. How does your mother feel about your boyfriend? Is she hoping you'll get married?'

'I never knew my mother; she died in a riding accident when I was very young. My grandmother, though, was an enormous influence.'

'That's so sad. Did it put you off riding?'

'No. I had desperately wanted a pony when I was eleven. Daddy, though, steadfastly refused, "They're too dangerous; I'm not losing you and your mother."'

'I can understand that.'

'Is it a popular newspaper?'

'*The Jewish Chronicle* is the world's oldest and I like to think the most influential Jewish newspaper. The trouble is, I cannot stop myself from talking to people.' She looked around the cabin, scanning the passengers on board. 'My previous editor, Moshe, repeated the same mantra to me over and over: "Stories always involve people. Watch the people Suzy and you'll be watching the story." To be honest, I've taken this a little too much to heart and become a compulsive people watcher.'

'Does that obsession mean you've always been single?'

'There was a man, called Omar, and we had worked closely together until he took up the post as a reporter for the *Haaretz* newspaper. Sadly, the Palestinians shot him while filming an uprising. The irony of it was Omar was such a staunch supporter of the Palestinian cause.'

'Are you on an assignment now?'

'No, but right now I'm playing a game of "Spot the Sky Marshalls". You see, the guy in the aisle seat – powerful build, neat hair – well, although he's smartly dressed, the pale blue suit looks like he bought it from a department store which seems out of context for a man in business class.'

'If he were a Sky Marshall, wouldn't he carry a gun, and if so, how do they get their guns on board? After all, isn't El Al known to have the airline industry's most impenetrable flight security? Wouldn't it show up at check-in?'

'That's a good question. Perhaps they store them on board, in a safe, and collect them as they board. Talking of which, did you know EL Al has become the first commercial airline to install an anti-missile system on its aircraft?'

'No, I didn't, but I'll remember that in case it comes up on a pub quiz,' Melody said, laughing.

'I'm going to the ladies. It's also an excuse to examine more of the passengers and possibly spot the other Air Marshall.' Suzy left her seat and ambled towards the rear, scanning the passengers as she made her way to the toilets. Her eyes settled on a burly Afro-Caribbean man wearing a polo shirt, chinos, a light cotton blazer, and brown loafers. She decided he fitted the brief perfectly. He was in an aisle seat. He looked muscular, and the blazer could conceal a shoulder holster. Her gaze lingered a little too long and, without smiling, he looked up at her. She quickly averted her eyes. His grimace unsettled her, and she made a note to herself – *'Do not stare.'*

The moment Suzy left her seat, a man sitting behind Melody moved quickly into it.

'I don't want to alarm you Melody, but the man sitting two rows in front, wearing a blue suit, followed you from your hotel.' He continued without looking at her. 'He won't let you leave with the swaddling. You are in real danger. Trust me. You must do exactly as I say.'

Melody felt sick to her stomach, but also trapped and isolated. 'How do you know my name and how can you possibly know he was following me?'

He took a business card out of his top pocket and handed it to her whilst looking behind and leaving his seat. 'I was following him.' With that, he moved back to his seat.

Just then, the man in the pale blue suit made his way back from the forward toilets. En route, his path crossed with the flight attendant, and they had to shuffle past each other. She apologised.

'There is never enough room,' he said. His voice chilled Melody; the accent sounded Eastern European, probably Russian. *Is he Vasily?*

She tried desperately to recall the man who had given her the business card but she'd been too shocked to take in much facial detail. He seemed to be English, with a Northern accent, and in his late thirties. He was wearing a linen suit, a white open-necked shirt and a Panama hat with a brown ribbon.

How did he know my name, and why was he concerned for my welfare? Is he a treasure hunter, simply feigning concern? I can't believe I missed the two of them following me. I usually spot the tags. Damn, probably too concerned with getting through customs.

She looked down at the business card.

Oswald Cox
Close Protection – Personal Security Escort

At the bottom of the card was a PO Box address and a mobile number she momentarily considered calling, then thought better of it.

Suzy arrived back, startling her and causing her to hide the card hurriedly in her purse. *What if she is an accomplice?* She was becoming paranoid. She also realised she needed to visit the bathroom and so would use the opportunity to have a close look at Oswald Cox.

'Excuse me, Suzy.' Melody touched her arm. With a slight tilt of her head and a quizzical look in her eyes, she said, 'I need the little girls' room.' Her well-manicured hand was still gently resting on Suzy's arm.

'I'm sorry,' she replied. 'I was miles away. People watching again, an occupational hazard, I'm afraid.' Suzy rose and straightened herself, smoothing out the creases of her cotton print skirt as she moved back into the aisle. But she suddenly froze.

There were gasps from the passengers, and one soul-piercing scream. Melody followed Suzy's gaze out of the starboard window. Within half a mile, an Air Force Fighter had drawn alongside the Boeing 737.

She looked round to discover an identical fighter on the port side. Several passengers were using their phones or cameras to film the Military Aircraft as the two planes maintained their positions alongside. The flight attendants were scurrying around, trying to calm things down, despite its obvious threat.

Unknown to the passengers, the pilot had pressed the red panic button, sending an automated SOS as soon as the MiG fighters appeared on his radar. An operative in the Israeli Mossad office in Rome picked it up. The co-pilot began transmitting a message to the oncoming MiGs, stating their civilian status, and requesting they identify themselves and change their flight course. There was no response.

The Director of the Israeli National Intelligence Agency in Italy made two telephone calls. An emergency meeting of the cabinet was called after the first notification. The second was to his counterpart General Vito Marcelo in the Italian SISMI (the Military Secret Service, run by the Defence Ministry). General Marcello called his colleague at the Italian

Aeronautica Militare where they deployed two Typhoon Eurofighters to intercept the MiGs, along with a Sikorsky S-61R Combat Search and Rescue helicopter.

Melody looked at the flight information screen above her. EL AL Flight ELY28 was cruising at 34,000 feet over the Adriatic Sea. To the east was the coast of Croatia and to the west lay Italy.

'They're Russian-built MiG 21 Fighter Aircraft,' Suzy said in a low voice. 'I've seen them at air shows and, judging by the chequered red and white markings, I'd say they're Croatian.' She opened her small shoulder bag and pulled out a notepad with her mobile phone.

She filmed; first the jets and then inside the passenger cabin, pausing slightly at a woman to the rear of the plane who was almost hysterical. Melody watched Suzy sit down again and make some brief notes before looking back out of the window.

'Oh no, they're armed,' Suzy said, making Melody's heart lurch. 'What's going–'

Suzy stopped talking as the pilot made an announcement…

Chapter Forty-Nine

~~

Fania Landver, Israeli Deputy Minister of Defence, urgently tried to contact the Croatian Ministry of Foreign Affairs. Meanwhile, her assistant called for the head of the Croatian Consulate to come to her office. They had sent a police escort to his residence to collect him.

The Israeli Intelligence Serious Incident Room was situated half a mile beneath its headquarters. Dozens of experts, operatives and high-ranking defence chiefs Fania referred to as 'Brass' sat inside. The facility was the size of a small cinema and full of high-tech surveillance, satellite communication equipment, computers and television monitors. It was completely self-sufficient and able to withstand a direct nuclear attack.

Fania covered the mouthpiece and shouted to no one in particular, 'I want eyes on people. How are we doing?'

The satellite operator piped up in an equally loud voice, 'Nearly there, Minister, just aligning the satellite. Two minutes to visual.'

Fania slammed the phone down and turned to General Kadish Shamir, of the Israeli Air Force.

'Flush the F-16s,' she said and then followed with a question. 'How long will it take them to get there?'

She was now looking at his aide, Colonel Rafi Ginzburg, expecting him to respond, but he fixed his gaze on the general; he didn't take orders from politicians, they had to be wearing a uniform and be, at least, a general.

General Shamir answered her. 'Probably not in time, but the Italian Eurofighters have already taken off; they're our most trusted allies in the region, but we should send a couple of F-16s, anyway.' He nodded to his aide; the Colonel moved to a phone to carry out his instructions, knowing they already had assets over the Adriatic Sea.

'However, we need a calm voice, ma'am,' the General continued. 'Two MiGs, two Eurofighters and a couple of F-16s buzzing around a commercial aircraft carrying over hundred and fifty civilians,' he paused. 'We don't want anyone becoming trigger happy. Our navy has nothing in the area, but the US are moving a Nimitz-class aircraft carrier further north up the Adriatic to provide help if it's required.'

An operative touched Fania on the arm.

'Yes?' said Fania, with a withering look at this personal intrusion.

'This is the passenger log for the flight. At first glance, there's nobody of any political or military significance on board.' She handed it over, and Fania scanned the names, but none stood out.

'I want a profile on all these people – where they've been, what they've been doing – hell – I want to know what they had for breakfast. Prioritise them by age, children and pensioners last. Start with non-Israeli males aged between twenty-five and forty. In my hand – five minutes.'

Another operator called out, 'We have the Croatian President, Mr Josipović, on a secure line, Minister.'

Fania looked round. Her eyes narrowed as she strode across the room. 'This had better be good,' she said in a growl, snatching the handset from a serious-looking staff member. 'Mr President, what the hell is going on? I'm having trouble stopping the Brass from flushing the bombers,' she lied.

'All I can tell you, Minister, is we have accounted for all our military aircraft. None are presently over the Adriatic. Whoever this is, they are not Croat and if they enter our airspace, we will shoot them down with our anti-aircraft missiles. Other than that, I cannot help you unless you want us to send our fighters up.'

'That will not be necessary. Thank you, Mr President. There's already too much hardware deployed; we'll keep you informed.' She put the phone down and turned to a large bald-headed man reading a report and flicking through some photos. 'What else do we know, Avi?'

She was addressing Avraham Feinstein, the legendary Station Commander, who had a fearsome reputation; even the cabinet was wary of crossing him. Avi had ordered hits on at least a dozen Hamas leaders and had a bodyguard of four Mossad agents wherever he went.

'We have the photos of the MiGs taken by the reporter on board – Suzy Marash; she sent them to her editor. The call signs and markings are false, and our weapons analysts believe the armaments are blanks, used for training only. They flew out of an ex-military airfield in Albania at 1400 hours. The Albanian Government sold the airstrip years ago for re-development to a Russian and Italian business consortium, but nothing happened. So far, we have had no vocal contact with the pilots, who are ignoring requests to identify themselves or standoff; it ties in with what Mr Josipović said.'

'Am I missing something, Avi? This doesn't smell like Hezbollah, Hamas or Islamic State. No demands, no threats; what are our agents on the inside saying?'

'The Iranians wouldn't sign off on this, Fan. It's an escalation Iran would have no control over, and without their funding, it couldn't go ahead. Our guys have gone deep, so I think you can rule them out. As for Hezbollah, if they got hold of MiGs, we'd be bombing airfields in Lebanon by now.'

'Who can tell me what the pilot's telling the passengers?' Fania asked in an irritated voice.

A junior operator monitoring cabin activity answered, 'He's told them it's part of a NATO anti-terrorist exercise.'

The satellite operator interrupted Fania. 'We have visual.'

Six people moved towards a large screen showing a satellite view of the Adriatic. They zoomed in on the Boeing, seeing the MiGs on either side and the Eurofighters in a single formation behind.

General Shamir spoke quietly to Fania, 'It's on NBC, Al Jazeera and Sky News that an El Al Jet is being hijacked by the Croatians. The source was a passenger on board, working for the Jewish Chronicle; the Italians are asking what we'd like them to do.'

'Only surveillance, for now, General. I'm not sure how good their aim is. If the MiGs lock on, tell the Italians they have our permission to deploy.'

Fania moved over to watch the breaking news on the TV monitors. She turned to address everyone. 'Is someone getting all this down for me? I'm giving a briefing to the Cabinet in ten minutes and I don't want to be standing there with my knickers down.' This brought about quite a few smiles and tittering, but no one laughed out loud.

The junior operator monitoring cabin activity spoke up. 'They're about to enter Italian air space, Minister. The Eurofighter pilots are getting twitchy; they're carrying Paveway II air-to-air missiles and have switched on their infra-red search and track system.'

'What the hell does that mean?' A code breaker asked.

'It means they've locked onto their targets, but the MiGs are unaware of it.'

'Clever, very clever,' he said, nodding and pursing his lips.

Fania was about to instruct the EL AL pilot to stay out of Italian airspace when an operator interrupted.

'The MiGs are moving away and separating.'

'Track them and keep the Italians on station with the Boeing,' Fania responded, relieved.

Avi pulled her to one side. 'We need to get that plane on the ground, Fan. The nearest airport is Bologna, but I suggest Treviso, north of Venice, as they probably won't let us land at Marco Polo Airport. They have a civilian airport and the Istrana Military Airbase within ten miles of each other; it'll give us time to arrange our assets.'

'I agree. How long to wheels down?'

'Thirty minutes, max,' he said confidently. 'I can let the pilot know and get permission from the Italians.'

'Let's make it happen, Avi. Oh, and warm up the Lear Jet. I want you and a team over there to debrief the passengers and crew. Try to keep the Italians away from the Boeing. I want our forensic team to be the first boots to go in. Also, leave the air marshals on board.'

The satellite operator became animated again. 'Our F-16s and the US aircraft carrier are now in range of the MiGs and are seeking operational guidance, Minister.'

General Shamir moved to his side. 'Tell the Americans to stand down. We will take over now. Ask our boys to monitor, unless threatened.' He spoke as he was moving towards Fania. 'We have limited options, Minister. If they land in Albania, we will never see them again; it is virtually a third-world country and their military airbase is defunct. We cannot escort them back here. The thought of two MiGs entering Israeli air space is unacceptable, and the Italians will not take them. My preference would be to ask the Maltese to let them land there. We have assets on the ground in Malta and they have an airfield the Brits used to run, plus, they only have a few fixed-wing aircraft for coastal patrolling, so they won't see them as a threat, and I know the Air Force Commander.'

'Make the call, General,' she said before turning to Avraham Feinstein. 'Who have we got in Malta, Avi?'

'Small office in Valletta: two civvies and two agents, one of whom I know and trust; I'll shake and bake them.'

She moved back to the satellite operator. 'What's happening now?'

'We have requested the MiG pilots to acknowledge our demand to land in Malta but they are maintaining radio silence and are about five minutes from entering Albanian air space, headed for what was Gjadër Airbase.'

'Tell the F-16s they can lock on.' She looked at Avi and General Shamir.

They both nodded. 'Oh, and give them one more chance to alter course.'

'The pilots report "no response", ma'am.' The operator said in a flat tone. Everyone was looking at Fania when the room fell silent.

'Avi?'

'We have to send a simple message to all our enemies, Fan – shoot them down.'

'General?'

'I agree, Minister, if we don't deploy now, we'll lose them and, politically, it could look as though they escaped on your watch.'

Fania held up both arms to address everyone. 'Listen up team, has anyone got anything to say?' She paused for a moment, looking at each person in the room individually. 'Now is the time to speak, before we pull the trigger.' No one moved or spoke.

She turned to face the General and nodded.

Everyone in the room moved to look at the screen as General Shamir gave the order to engage and to put the pilots on the speakers.

The pilots' voices crackled over the intercom.

'Echo Five, maintain vector.'

'Copy that, Lima Seven.'

'Echo Five, keep the target locked and missile primed, over.'

'Roger that, Lima Seven.'

'Deploy on my count, Echo Five, ceiling at thirty-five, over.'

'Bogies now twenty-five miles and closing Lima Seven.'

'Five, four, three, two, one – deploy ATAs and nose up.'

'Lima Seven, air-to-air deployed and on target, banking starboard one eighty degrees over.'

'Roger that, Echo Five, missiles on target, rendezvous at thirty-five triple zero, bearing two seventy, maintain radio silence, over.'

The team watched in silence as the two missiles closed on their targets. There was a slight flash of light, a puff of smoke, and then an empty area where the two MiGs had been, only one mile from Albanian air space.

Fania was about to ask for the passenger profiles when she realised the young woman she had spoken to earlier was standing in front of her. 'Your briefing papers, Minister, and our preliminary report on the passengers. Believe it or not, there are two private detectives on board.'

Fania raised her eyebrows. 'One could be a coincidence, but two, we need to talk to them. You hearing this, Avi?'

'Who else we got, Shayna?' was his retort. 'A British woman who spent time in Iran but came into Israel via Iraq and Jordan. She's an archaeologist–'

'How old is she?' Avi asked.

'Thirty.'

'Not a gap-year backpacker, then.'

'Unlikely. She's a Doctor of Philosophy, a wealthy family, educated at Oxford; her father's a retired Army Colonel.'

'An establishment academic visiting Iran – interesting – flag her up. Who else?'

'A Russian on a business trip and an African American who's not had a conviction in the US but the FBI considers menacing and malignant. You already know about the reporter. We're still running checks on a few others.'

'Any unusual groupings on board?' Fania queried.

'There's a Catholic Priest with two nuns.'

'Now I know I'm in a disaster movie,' quipped Avi.

Fania ignored his comments, moved over to the giant whiteboard on the wall and started writing as she spoke. 'Listen up again, people. Let's join the dots. We have a Russian connection with the MiGs; I want to know who sold them and who bought them. We know they flew from Albania; find out how the Government missed them. Is the Russian passenger linked to them and what is the Italian connection? I want airport footage of the passengers at the terminal. Who did they meet or talk to? And background info on the two detectives, and inform the sky marshals to keep a watching brief on them.'

She pulled Avi to one side. 'When you talk to the suspects, no bruises, I want us to walk away clean on this one. We have precious few friends in Europe. I don't want to upset the Italians. I also want to know more about the reporter and this woman who has been to Iran and where she went afterwards. They have ordered me to brief the cabinet in a few minutes.'

Fania turned to address everyone present. 'Well done, team. Good work today. Now let's see if we can solve this riddle. If anyone plays hardball with you, use my name. Don't let the grey suits hold you up. I will be back in an hour and expect progress and a press release. Because of this shooting down, the doves will be all over us like a cheap suit.'

Then, turning to Avi, she whispered. 'Who will you leave in charge while you're in Italy?'

'Shayna,' he said flatly.

'Are you sure, Avi?'

'Yes, she reminds me of you when you were her age.'

'God help us,' she said, before turning and sweeping out of the room.

Chapter Fifty

～～

Avi had to pull in a few favours to get the Italians to agree to the aircraft landing at Treviso Airport rather than Istrana Military Airbase. The Eurofighters escorted the Boeing 737 until its wheels touched down, before peeling off and heading for Istrana.

The airport was temporarily closed. Fire trucks and ambulances lined the single runway. They instructed the pilot to taxi in a holding bay away from the main airport building, inviting a plethora of emergency vehicles.

Melody looked at the airport signage as the aircraft taxied past the modern glass-fronted main terminal.

Aeroporto di Treviso A Canova

She had been here two years earlier on a trip to Venice after feeling in need of a distraction from her research into the Magi. She'd flown in from Germany, where she had visited Cologne Cathedral and the reliquary said to contain the bones of the Biblical Magi. *Will this obsession with them ever end?*

The pilot's announcement from the speakers interrupted her introspections. His voice was calm, almost soothing.

'They have required us to proceed to a holding bay and await further instructions. I'm sorry for the diversion and hope to complete the journey as soon as possible. This will depend on the Italian authorities permitting us. I will keep you informed. This was a NATO training exercise we accidentally became involved in.'

The cabin was buzzing with chatter and conspiracy theories. Passengers were chatting with each other and removing their seat belts, even though the plane was still taxiing.

Meanwhile, the control tower was instructing the pilot to secure the aircraft and prepare for a boarding party of the Italian Police.

'Negative,' was the pilot's taught reply. 'This aircraft is the property of the State of Israel. We are awaiting boarding authority by my government.' He then spoke to his co-pilot, 'We need to delay them until our Mossad team arrives.'

The control tower was hailing them again. 'This is Commissario Renzo Ponti of the Polizia di Stato. A boarding party is approaching you. If you do not open the front passenger door voluntarily, we will open it by force.' He paused, allowing the silence to add weight to his words. 'You are now on Italian territory, and the Central Directorate for the Anti-Terrorism Police has ordered me to secure the aircraft prior to a thorough search. Do you understand, Captain?'

The co-pilot pointed towards an oncoming truck with its blue lights flashing, followed by a mobile boarding ramp, or what the crew referred to as 'air-stairs.' The pilot responded to the oncoming convoy. 'Let's have a word with Rivka. As the senior cabin crew member, she will need to know what's happening and can brief the air marshals. And, whilst you are explaining the situation, I will talk to the Commissario and try to contact our agents again. We can't allow them to blow the door off. It'll terrify the passengers and we'll be here for weeks for repairs,' he said, before switching the microphone back onto the control tower. 'Commissario Ponti, thank you for your frankness. There will not be any need to force an entry into the aircraft. I have asked my superiors for permission and expect full compliance with your wishes shortly. Can I also request your officers are not deploying guns when they enter the cabin?' The pilot was trying to sound calm but authoritative to avoid alienating his hosts.

'Thank you, Captain. I appreciate your co-operation. I will pass on your concerns to my deputy, who is leading the boarding party.' Following a brief delay and terse requests from the Commissario, they opened the passenger door. The mobile boarding ramp was driven into position.

A female flight attendant stood with her back to the flight cabin, facing the passengers as two Italian police officers entered the cabin carrying pistols. They made their way towards the rear of the aircraft, followed by the flight attendant.

The punch to the stomach of the leading officer took him completely by surprise. He crumpled to his knees. The air marshal who delivered it moved swiftly, twisting the officer's arm and taking the gun from him. The second officer was too slow to react and the flight attendant behind him delivered a blow to his throat, followed by a rabbit punch to the back of his neck. As he fell, she wrenched his arm behind his back and disarmed him as well.

Suzy Marash wished she had filmed it; they completed the entire episode in less than ten seconds and revealed Suzy had been hopelessly wrong in identifying who the air marshals were. She watched closely as the one disguised as a flight attendant now turned towards the front of the cabin where an immaculately dressed police officer stood smiling; he slowly clapped his black leather gloved hands.

'Buona Ben fatto!' he said. 'I warned them you would challenge them. They do not listen to me – my wife and children are the same! However, having assisted you in your time of need, I would have expected a warmer reception.' His two colleagues were now trying to stand as they recovered from their injuries.

'And you are?' The disguised air marshal didn't smile.

'Forgive me,' he replied, whilst clipping his heels and bowing. 'I am Sostituto Commissario Marco Casale, at your service.'

'The captain was quite clear he would not allow the brandishing of weapons, Commissioner.'

'Deputy Commissioner,' he said, correcting her. 'Like you, I take orders from my superiors and suggest we put this unfortunate incident down to one of over-enthusiasm on both our parts. Now, if I could speak to your captain, we require you to evacuate the passengers to enable us to carry out a thorough search.'

The air marshal stepped forward and picked up the internal phone, punching in the flight cockpit number. 'Captain, the aircraft is secure and the police deputy commissioner would like a word with you.'

The captain opened the cockpit door and invited the deputy commissioner in. 'Thank you, Sir, for assisting us with your air force regarding the two MiGs following us. It's still not clear what their intentions were and my apologies for the overzealous behaviour of our air marshals.'

The deputy commissioner had been scanning the cockpit but seemed satisfied nothing was untoward. 'Thank you, Captain. As you know, the airport was closed at great inconvenience to accommodate your landing and, therefore, I would appreciate the immediate evacuation of the passengers to allow for an inspection of the aircraft. I'd like to turn this around as quickly as possible to allow you to continue your journey.'

'Certainly. However, I am also expecting a team from our consulate to arrive and my government would appreciate it if you would allow us to interview the passengers.'

Melody had watched the events unfold with increasing anxiety. Her head reasoned it was a coincidence, but her intuition insisted it was not. Unfortunately, she couldn't make a connection.

The captain spoke again on the intercom. 'Would all passengers please make their way to the terminal building, and ensure you take all of your hand luggage with you. I am hoping this will not take long and we can continue our journey. In the meantime, please enjoy the Italian hospitality.'

Suzy Marash spoke quietly to Melody. 'This makes little sense. Why are they searching the aircraft if this was a NATO exercise? There must be another explanation.' She broke off to listen to some other passengers who were making similar deductions and quite a few stating they did not want to continue their journey on the aircraft, regardless of any search.

Keep calm. I need to think of how I can keep the casket safe or prevent them from searching my belongings.

The co-pilot made an announcement. 'Because of the uncertain duration of the search and the late hour, we have arranged accommodation and transportation with hotels in the city for all passengers. Once you have disembarked, they will direct you to your transport and, if allowed, your other luggage may follow as soon as they complete the search. Once again, I'm sorry for this further disruption to your journey.'

Melody sighed with relief; the announcement had given her more time to plan what to do next. As she moved into the aisle, she noticed the man sitting behind her, who had introduced himself as Oswald Cox. He was smiling and allowed her space to leave before him.

Should I trust him? He seemed genuine enough, and if he were intending to hurt her, why would he reveal himself? I need more information about his involvement.

She felt alone and wished Dilshod was with her, he would know exactly what to do in this situation; she also regretted insisting that Stuart must not get involved.

If only he were here now. However, I've got this far without Sospitas, but I need to get some distance between myself and the other passengers.

Chapter Fifty-One

~~

The Israeli Lear Jet landed at Istrana Military Base. Avi, the head of Israeli Intelligence, was being briefed by Ezra, the local agent, as they walked across the tarmac with armed bodyguards and Mossad agents. They headed towards a small convoy of vehicles, including two bullet-proof Range Rovers, an Italian Police escort car and two motorcycle outriders.

As soon as Avi seated himself between his most trusted agents, the motorcade sped out of the airport and headed east on the Via Castellano. Six kilometres later, they turned south onto the Via Noalese, heading towards Treviso Airport.

Avi was now speaking. 'Let me get this straight. The Italians have taken the passengers off our plane and are planning to send them to three different hotels without interviewing or searching them. Somebody tell me I'm wrong.'

Ezra was sitting uncomfortably in the front passenger seat and twisted round to reply but Avi was not listening. He was going to replace him when this was over. He clearly had little or no influence. Now he was considering how to salvage the operation. He spoke again, cutting into the agents' explanation. 'Have we got the list of which passengers are in which hotels?'

Ezra felt relieved as he handed over three separate lists headed by the hotel name. 'We've highlighted those of interest, and we have a safe house near all three hotels and have hacked into their communications network.'

Avi took them without acknowledging him and began scrutinising the names. He handed the first page to the agent on his left.

'You've got one detective and the Russian. Start with the detective.' He handed a second sheet to the other agent. 'The African American the FBI considers menacing and malignant looks interesting. After him, shake down the other detective and the Brit, Melody Thornton.' He paused before addressing Ezra. 'No doubt you've got some Vatican contacts?' Ezra was nodding enthusiastically. 'Then look at this Catholic Priest. Let's see if there's a connection. Drop me off at the Hotel Continental.'

'Yes, Sir. What I still do not understand is what they expected would happen, when all they have achieved is diverting a civilian plane to Italy.'

Avi did not reply immediately. He was considering this simple observation. *Maybe that was the intention all along. What if the sole intention was to divert the plane along with its passengers, crew and cargo? Who had the resources to send the fighters and what is unique to Italy and who or what are they after and, just as important, who are they?*

'Take me to the safe house instead. I need to speak to Shayna at the Serious Incident Room. I'm expecting that she will have gathered more intel since we left.'

* * *

Meanwhile, another private jet landed at the Istrana Military Airbase, where six men disembarked and made their way to a blacked-out minivan waiting on the apron. Their identities were neither sought nor given. It left the base and headed toward Treviso at high speed.

Chapter Fifty-Two

By the time Avi and his team arrived, the temporary communication room was ready and manned by two technicians. Banks of CCTV monitoring screens were showing various scenes at the three hotels.

'Get me Shayna on a secure line.' Avi said to no one in particular.

'They're all secured, Sir.' As Ezra spoke, he was punching the numbers in and passed over the handset.

Avi pressed the speakerphone and replaced the handset. 'What you got, Shayna?'

'The airport footage confirms that at least three passengers were interested in the British woman, Melody Thornton, who has mixed heritage. Her mother was born in Iran. Her family fled to Egypt following the Iranian revolution in 1979. Later, her mother married a British banker and an ex-army colonel in England. The Russian is Vasily Valkov, also known as The Wolf. He's an assassin and wanted in several countries. We're following up on a lead. He recently met up with a retired chief from the now-defunct USSR Air Force.'

'Is it where the MiG fighters came from?'

'No hard proof yet, but it's our best bet.'

'I want him interviewed,' he said, nodding to an agent. 'What about the priest? Is he clean?'

'He's not your normal parish priest. He works for Cardinal Poggi, who heads up the "Pontifical Academy of Archaeology" or "relic hunters" as it is more commonly known. Plenty of run-ins with several authorities around the world in his quest for artefacts. The nuns are simply his secretary and researcher.'

'Find out what he's currently searching for. I think there may be a Vatican connection with the British woman. Let's see if they are after the same thing. Who else have you got?'

'You will not like this. One claiming to be a detective is Farad El Sayed, born in Iran, another one with a sketchy background in the despised Ministry of Intelligence and Security, now works privately but has many connections with the authorities in Iran.'

'How the–' Avi closed his eyes and took a deep breath to contain himself. 'How did an Iranian ex-MOIS agent get on one of our aircrafts?'

'He's travelling under false papers, claiming he's American.'

'I really want to talk to this guy. What about the other detective?'

'Felix Breunig, an Austrian American, retired early from the NYPD as a captain in homicide. He now works independently to recover stolen or lost property for insurance companies and wealthy clients.'

'And the African American?'

'Still working on him. We think he's ex-CIA and called Landon Bailey, but not much else. I'll let you know as soon as we get something more concrete.'

'Shayna, find out who owns the ex-military airfield in Albania.' Then Avi pressed the disconnect button and turned to his staff. 'Which hotel is Farad El Sayed staying in?'

'Hotel Focalare. Do you want us to interview him?' Ezra asked.

'Hell no,' barked Avi. 'I want him brought here. We will take him home with us, back to Israel. Put a team together. I want this one alive. Where is he now?'

The operator monitoring the CCTV at the hotel responded quickly. 'Drinking in the hotel bar. He's on his own.'

Three men stepped forward to carry out his instructions. Avi raised an arm. 'I want this done quietly.'

'He's moving, Sir. Looks like he's headed for the phone booths.'

'Get moving. I don't want this guy giving us the slip; he'll be expecting us to look him over after the plane diversion.'

The three men left.

'Where is he now?'

Both technicians were frantically trying to locate him. 'He's not appearing on any of the monitors.'

Avi was scouring the screens. 'Where's the goods entrance camera?'

They made more movements on the keyboard, and a loading bay came into view as a laundry van pulled away.

'Get the registration number.' Avi banged his fist on the desk and then turned slowly to Ezra. 'Use your police contacts. Find the van now. And can someone explain why we were only watching the front door?'

Chapter Fifty-Three

~~~

The blacked out minivan with its six English occupants headed across Treviso to a farmhouse in Del Daino on the eastern edge of the city. Dino, the Italian driver, took advantage of the blue flashing lights concealed in the grill. The front seat passenger had worked constantly on his satellite laptop since leaving the airport.

'You'll want to listen to this, boss,' he said. He took off his headphones and handed them over to the man sitting behind him.

Ryland listened intently before handing back the headset and turning to his associates. 'The Israelis are going to snatch an Iranian who's trailing the Christmas Fairy.' The team smiled at this attempt at humour. 'I'd like us to get him first; he may be useful as a bargaining chip. His name is Farad El Sayed, and he's staying at the Hotel Focalare. Sage, show them a picture of him.' Three of the men looked at the photo and nodded.

Stuart Toulson wasn't listening; he was speaking on his phone in Italian to his friend Sostituto Commissario Marco Casale.

The driver made a sudden diversion whilst the three other men checked their weapons. They left the vehicle two blocks from the hotel and, as they melted into the city, Dino continued his high-speed sprint to their rustic hideaway.

As Dino was hiding the minibus in the barn, the owner of the farmstead greeted the others warmly. 'You will be safe here. No one will bother you. Come, I will show you to your rooms. Any friend of Commissario Marco is a welcome guest.'

The technician unpacked his two laptops and the various monitoring devices he'd brought from the van. Few knew his actual name. They always referred to him as Sage. He headed up covert surveillance at Sospitas. 'How much danger is Miss Thornton in?'

'A great deal,' Ryland replied. 'There were originally four people tracking her movements, but because of the heavy-handed tactics of the Russian, Nikolai Levanevsky, we now have Mossad involved. If the snatch team is successful, we will be down to three and possibly get the Israelis out of our hair. Have we got the list of people who are the greatest threat?'

'Yes. Our Intel team put The Wolf – Vasily Valkov – at the top, followed by Farad El Sayed, who may, by now, already be in our possession. Then, in descending order, the Israeli Mossad team, Felix Breunig, a Private Investigator and Oswald Cox, who we believe is working for the Vatican. On the flip side, the air marshals, Bill McGann, and Hannah Weil could be useful if need be.'

'Anyone on the list staying at the target hotel?'

'No, the two air Marshalls are there. Oh, and the reporter, Suzy Marash. They booked Avraham Feinstein in, but as you know, he went to their safe house instead. They are at the Hotel Continental. Miss Thornton has not left her room since checking in. I made a reservation for one of our guys, Tyke. He spent a lot of time here in a kidnapping negotiation two years ago. He's already in situ and has bugged her room.'

Ryland was opening a case containing a syringe and a glass vial. 'We don't know if the Christmas fairy has found what she was searching for. Remind me of the connection with Farad El Sayed – who's he working for?'

'It's difficult to know at this stage, he could work solely for Miss Thornton's "so-called" friend–' Sage was leafing through a notepad on the desk. 'Ah, here he is, an Iranian, Dr Farrokh Mokri, but Mokri may be a frontman for the Iranian Government.'

'Some friend he–'

'The Wolf has left his hotel,' Sage said urgently. 'He's heading for the Continental. I'll brief Tyke and the rest of the team.'

'I'll head over there. Tell them I'll meet them there,' Ryland spoke whilst checking his handgun and picking up the case. 'This man is extremely dangerous; we need him off the scene.'

Chapter Fifty-Four

~~

Melody was considering her options when the phone rang, startling her. She stared at it, considering who it might be and whether she should answer. It stopped and she cursed herself for her timidity. Now she would wonder for the rest of the day who it was. Her mobile phone showed a new message.

Meet me at reception. Suzy x.

She felt relieved, not least for having a reason to leave the room. It felt like a prison. She picked up her handbag, moved to the mirror to check her hair and was making her way out when there was a knock on the door. Melody froze momentarily, then tiptoed towards the door to peep through the spyhole. The electronic lock clicked, and the handle turned.

'Ciao Servizio in camera,' the middle-aged housekeeper said as she entered. Melody breathed a sigh of relief. She brushed past Melody and placed the flowers and chocolates on the dressing table, smiled knowingly, and left. Melody picked up the Hotel Focalare card and read the message – 'We need to talk. Oswald.'

She placed the card in her bag. On her way to the door, Melody could feel another episode about to overcome her.

She dropped onto the closest chair as a wave of despair overcame her, losing her sight quickly followed and then the lovely sense of peace...

She could see her friend Farrokh arguing with the Russian passenger, it was the same man that Oswald Cox had warned her about on the plane. Then the scene switched to a villa where the body of a man dressed entirely in black who was floating face down in a swimming pool, followed by another scene where Suzy, the reporter, was with her at a wedding; they were laughing and chatting together.

Gradually, she came out of her trancelike state. She needed time to think. Maybe Cox was genuine after all. She sent a message to Suzy, 'Can you come to my room instead, please?'

'Sure, no problem, x.'

Several minutes later, there was a knock at the door. Melody felt relieved; Suzy may help her. But as she opened the door, three burly men dressed in dark suits filled the frame. 'Miss Thornton?'

'Yes, but who are–'

One man pushed her back into the room whilst two of them brushed past her, staring around the room. 'We're investigating the incident leading to your flight being diverted. We work for the Government of Israel.' He looked her up and down before continuing. 'This shouldn't take long. What was the purpose of your visit to Israel?'

'I answered these questions at the airport, and I don't see what relevance they have–'

'Just answer the questions, Miss. Our government does not take kindly to having one of its civilian aircrafts threatened. The security CCTV showed they failed to check your hand luggage properly. Would you mind if we have a look now?' The other two men had already begun searching the room.

'Which government is that and have you got a search warrant?'

The lead man turned on her, his face only inches from hers. 'We're investigating a terrorist act on an Israeli passenger airline and you're in the frame. My advice to you is to co-operate. You got that, Miss Thornton?' He pushed her backwards and she landed in the armchair by the door.

Despite feeling extremely anxious, she tried to sound calm. *Turn the tables and appear in control.* 'If you don't leave, I'll call the police.'

'Where do you think I found out where you're staying? The police are just as concerned as we are.'

'Really? Why aren't they here then?'

The other men had completed their search; they looked at him and shrugged their shoulders, showing they had discovered nothing.

'Listen, Miss, you need to talk. Where had you been prior to Israel? What countries have you visited?' He leaned over her, his hands on each of the chair's arms. His jacket hung open, and she could see he was carrying a gun in a shoulder holster.

'Have you got a gun licence for Italy?'

He raised his voice. 'This is not a game. You're dealing with a government, being English won't–'

A loud knocking on the door interrupted him. The three men looked at one another and the leader nodded to his colleagues, who had already taken out their handguns.

The knocking became louder.

'Are you alright, Mel?' Suzy shouted from the lobby.

'It's my friend Suzy Marash. She's a reporter with–'

'We're fully aware of who Miss Marash is.' The agents holstered their weapons and opened the door.

Suzy took in the situation.

'Friends of yours, Mel? Maybe I could get a picture of all of you?' She switched her phone to the camera.

'They work for the Israeli Government. They're just leaving, aren't you?' Melody stood.

'I thought I could smell Mossad. Can I see your identification please, gentlemen, or do I need to call security?' Suzy said, stepping into the room.

All three ignored her. As they were leaving, the lead agent placed his foot on the door to prevent Suzy from closing it and turned to Melody. 'This matter is not over, Miss Thornton. Whichever way we look at this, you are at the centre.' He turned to Suzy. 'You need to decide which side you're on. People have lost jobs for interfering in a legitimate investigation.'

'Good day, gentlemen,' Suzy said.

Melody breathed a sigh of relief as the door closed.

'What was all that about Mel, what have you got involved in?'

'Can we go down to the bar? I could really use a strong drink. I think oddly enough, I may also need a priest to confess to.' *I'm so glad I left the casket in the safe at reception.*

Chapter Fifty-Five

~~

Melody was being watched as she left with Suzy. When the lift doors closed, Vasily Valkov padded across the landing and entered her suite. The search started in the bedroom.

'He's now in the bedroom, Tyke. I've unlocked the door. It's the first room on the left. He will have his back turned towards you.'

'Roger that,' Tyke replied, adjusting his earpiece. Vasily was unaware of the door opening, and whilst concentrating on the contents of a travel bag, he felt a stinging sensation on the back of his neck. Even before his hand could reach it, he fell into unconsciousness.

* * *

Vasily felt like he was coming out of a drunken stupor. His vision was blurry and he was sleepy. He tried to wipe his eyes, but realised he was being restrained. He blinked continuously, trying to focus on the fuzzy figures surrounding him.

'He's coming round,' Tyke said. 'He'll have full vision in a moment. I'll keep watch on the landing.'

Vasily was trying to get his vision clear and could just make out one man bent over him.

'The thing is, Mr Valkov,' Ryland said, 'we have little time and you only have two options.'

'I need a drink of water,' he said whilst taking in three of his captors. They all wore balaclavas.

'Option one involves me pouring a copious amount of vodka down your throat,' one man said, holding a syringe and a bottle. 'Then injecting you with a drug that will make it appear like you've suffered a heart attack. That's after they eventually fish you out of the River Sile and carry out a post-mortem.'

'I presume option two involves me living?' Vasily was trying to focus his vision.

'Indeed, it does but, and here's the rub, it requires you, The Wolf, to go home to Omsk.' Ryland spoke whilst waving some paperwork in front of his face. 'A private jet will take you to Dubrovnik, where you will start your onward journey.'

'What about my client? He will not be happy you have interfered. He may come after you.'

'Let me worry about Nikolai Levanevsky and let me make it perfectly clear to you. At no point in the future will you try to contact Melody Thornton, her family or anyone connected to her. If you do, we revert to option one. Do you understand?'

Tyke hailed Ryland in his earpiece. 'The women are leaving the bar.'

'I will need to get my belongings,' Vasily said.

'I see you have sensibly taken option two. Your holdall is here with all your possessions, including your false passport minus the Glock 17 and silencer. My men will release you now but accompany you outside to the loading bay where a car is waiting to take you to an airport.'

'Nikolai will not be happy, Mr-?'

'Goodbye, Mr Valkov. Trust me, you will never see me again, because if you do, I would be the last person you would ever see,' he said whilst nodding to his two accomplices. 'Take the stairs. I wouldn't want him to meet Melody in the lift.'

* * *

Melody was feeling more relaxed as she left the bar. 'Thank you for your offer of help and listening. I needed a friend.'

'It's a fascinating story,' Suzy said. 'Are you sure about meeting this priest, Father Johnston?'

'Janssen.'

'Whatever. Can you trust him? After all, he works for the Vatican?'

'I am finding it difficult to trust anyone,' Melody said, turning to leave.

'I'll check up on him,' she called after Melody as she left. Suzy was about to go back to her room when she realised she had left her notepad on the table. As she recovered it, the female air marshal approached her.

'Miss Marash, can I have a word, please? My name is Hannah Weil.'

'Hi, Hannah, I mean yes, sure, and call me Suzy. Congratulations on tackling the Italian Police, so impressive.'

'That's what I'd like to talk to you about. I know you're a reporter and that you witnessed my action on the plane. But keeping my identity as an air marshal secret is especially important, not only for passenger safety but also for mine. Passengers must believe that I am just a member of the cabin crew. I'd prefer it if you keep it to yourself.'

'You don't need to worry, dear. I would never expose you, like never.'

'Thank you, that's a relief.'

'Would you mind giving me your number? I'd love to do an article about female air marshals in the future, anonymously, of course, smashing the glass ceiling, etc.,' she said, handing over her notepad.

'No problem,' Hannah said, taking the pad to write. 'I see the name of the priest, Father Janssen, here. If you intend to interview him, you had better be quick. Between you and me, I understand there are some irregularities,' she said, handing back the notepad. 'They haven't informed passengers yet, but I understand we may fly out tomorrow. Although several passengers are so spooked by events, they're making alternative arrangements.'

'What were the irregularities?' Suzy asked, trying to sound only mildly inquisitive.

'They don't give specific details in the security briefings, but don't worry, they rarely materialise. They're super cautious and, as he's close to the Vatican, he probably wouldn't fly on anyway.'

'OK, great. I'll see you tomorrow, possibly.'

Chapter Fifty-Six

~~~

The phone call was being routed through six countries. 'You don't know me, and trying to trace this call is pointless,' Sage said. 'You'll waste valuable time, and you won't find me. I need to speak to Avraham Feinstein. It's a matter of great urgency.'

Stuart and Ryland were listening in on the conversation.

'If Mr Feinstein were contactable, what is the nature of your business with him?' Ezra asked down the line.

'We know he's at the safe house with you and probably listening to this conversation. We're on the same side as you and we have a package we believe you may wish to take back to Israel.'

A new voice spoke. 'This is Avraham Feinstein. Who are you and what is the package?'

'We are an international company involved in several activities, including, but not exclusively, personal protection, anti-surveillance, and hostage negotiation, we-'

'What's the package?' Avi demanded.

Stuart nodded to Sage. 'Farad El Sayed.'

After almost a minute of silence, Avi spoke, his voice measured and calm. 'Tell Mr Toulson to meet me at the Chiesa di Santa Maria Maggiore at one o'clock.'

'He'll be there. Try to keep your bodyguards discrete. It is, after all, a public place and a church.' The line went dead.

'Well, he quickly discovered who we are,' Sage said.

'Yes, but he doesn't know the why,' Stuart said and walked over to the map as Sage printed off a picture of the church and pinned it on its location. 'Get El Sayed packaged for transport. See if we have an asset nearby and I want men here, here, and here.' Stuart said, tapping the map. 'Then get a man in the clock tower next to it.'

'Our host says there's a tobacconist nearby. That's also a safe house,' Sage said. 'I'll get the details.'

'Ryland, take him there and stay with him. I'll go inside on my own. Feinstein has spent a lifetime dealing with hardened terrorist groups. He'll expect this to be easy and he'll want to hear what the deal is before reacting.'

'Are we leaving after?'

'Not quite. There are some loose ends, which I prefer to think of as operational experience opportunities. I have asked Marco to collect Melody's luggage and transfer it to our plane. She'll be leaving with us, probably tomorrow.' Stuart put on his jacket. 'I like to wear my Sunday best when I go to church.'

* * *

The church was cool as he walked down the aisle. Two elderly ladies prayed silently on the rear pew. The smell of burning candles and incense lingered. Ahead of him was the stocky figure of the Mossad Chief, sitting with his back to the altar. As Stuart neared, Avi gestured for him to sit.

Stuart spoke. 'Behind the altar in the Lady Chapel is a fresco of Madonna Grande, though I prefer the name Lady Mary. She is with her child, the infant Jesus. You have chosen the perfect location. They built the church in 1473, they bombed it during the Second World War, and yet, here it is, as beautiful as it is magnificent.'

'Some say you're the best negotiator in the world, Mr Toulson.'

'And yet, not all are successful.'

'Mexico?'

'One can never plan for every eventuality. I can't imagine you were enthusiastic about the release of over a thousand terrorists for the one Israeli soldier, Gilad Shalit.'

'Perhaps. Though many in my country would claim it was a bargain,' Avi said, unbuttoning his jacket. 'Plus, the message it gave to the world was that one Israeli is worth a thousand Palestinians. Have you brought me a bargain?'

'Which brings me back to the fresco of the Lady Mary—'

'Mr Toulson, I didn't expect you to be religious. Nevertheless, I must congratulate you on your skilful manipulation of the police, most likely with the help of Marco Casale. No doubt a down payment for negotiating his daughter's release from her kidnappers.'

'Your Intelligence is impeccable. However, I don't charge individuals, they're pro bono. Only corporations and insurers pay, and they do, handsomely. On this occasion, I am working on behalf of a friend.'

'Ah yes, the redoubtable and,' Avi smiled, 'strikingly attractive Melody Thornton. We have her at centre stage in this mystery. Is she your bargaining chip?'

'Miss Thornton inhabits a different world to ours. I'd like to keep it that way. She has spent years searching for what she believes to be a piece of swaddling cloth the Mother of Jesus gave to the Magi.' Stuart paused. 'There you are. We are back to the Lady Mary.'

'If it's only a simple artefact, why so much interest, and why were you not protecting her on the plane?'

'Miss Thornton's naivety is rather beautiful. I'd like to preserve it. She doesn't know we're here. She insisted on doing this on her own.'

'And yet. Here you are. Is the artefact valuable?'

'Legend has it that it possesses supernatural powers to heal people. Her research eventually led her to explore an area in Iran close to the Caspian Sea. We are not entirely sure if she found the item causing so much trouble. However, the Russian oligarch Nikolai Levanevsky is dying from liver cancer and is prepared to go to extraordinary lengths and pay any amount of money to possess what he hopes will cure him. He hired Vasily Valkov to recover it.'

'Where is The Wolf now? He seems to have gone to ground.'

'We persuaded him to live in exile in his native country.'

'Where does Landon Bailey fit in?'

'Ah, Mr Bailey is my man on the ground. Call it a watching brief. Only if her life was in imminent danger, then he would intervene.'

Avi was nodding. 'We know Oswald Cox is working on behalf of the Vatican, but who is El Sayed working for?'

'Ah, the bargaining chip,' Stuart said. 'Almost certainly the Government of Iran. Apparently, a senior member of the Guardian Council has a child on life support, but, of course, you already know that.'

'You assume too much, Mr Toulson.'

'It is often said Israel has more spies in Iran than a dog has fleas. A vulgar saying, though true. Although "spies" is such a loaded word, I prefer the term "emissaries." Similar, no doubt, to the ones you used to steal Iran's nuclear files. We think he's using an old university colleague of Miss Thornton as a contact, a man called Farrokh Mokri.'

'Unfortunately for Miss Thornton, Mokri's family is being held by Iran's security force, and once MOIS gets their hands on you, you're rarely seen again. He is merely a pawn of theirs and will do their bidding. You cannot trust Mokri.'

'That's interesting, Avi. We wondered where they were. I hope you don't mind me calling you Avi, surnames are so formal, don't you agree? We should work together more often. What we do in our respective fields can be a lonely existence. El Sayed was also working for the Americans. The CIA thought it was better to have him inside the tent, so to speak. He handled the cemetery bombing, but the Americans gave him an alibi.'

'They're supposed to be our friends. I always felt it was him, so much so, I didn't bother looking for anyone else. Presumably, if we back off, you hand over El Sayed?'

'Ah, the "zone of possible agreement", I was told you are candid,' Stuart said whilst standing up from the oak pew. 'I can assure you there will be no consequence from your politicians back home. When this is over, we will package this to gild your reputation further. Do we have a deal?'

'We do indeed. I also have some information you may not be aware of. I'll call you once we have our man.'

'The Tobacco Shop on Via Carlo Alberto. He's in the storeroom.' Stuart held out his hand. 'If I can be of any help in the future, please contact me.'

Avi gave him a firm handshake. 'You can count on it, oh, and good luck with Miss Thornton,' he smiled again. 'Whatever your intentions towards her are.' He looked around at all the mosaic artwork and the fresco behind the altar. 'Until we meet again, Stuart.'

Chapter Fifty-Seven

~~~

As Stuart left, he was aware of three of Avi's bodyguards in deep conversation as a blacked-out Range Rover pulled up. Two got in the back whilst the third man held open the front passenger door for Avi.

Stuart spoke into his lapel microphone. 'Ryland, they're coming to collect him. Is it safe to leave him? They'll be there in two minutes.'

'Yes The Wolf is still out cold. By the way, Sage told me Miss Thornton had a long meeting with Suzy Marash and was planning to visit the Vatican Priest. Do we need to do anything?'

'I'm more concerned about the other private investigator, Felix Breunig. What's the latest?'

'He's an Austrian American, retired NYPD Detective, works mainly for insurers recovering stolen goods, fairly low-level stuff. But this time, another billionaire Russian hired him. We believe him to be Anatoly Artamonovsky, who for years was Nikolai Levanevsky's right-hand man. They parted company on good terms shortly after the privatisation of the oil and gas industry. They're staying at the Carlton Hotel.'

'Leave now and meet me at the Carlton. I think it's time to ask him what he is searching for or what he believes is missing.'

'Another interesting fact, Anatoly's financial records show he deposited 224 million dollars into the Vatican Bank.'

'Interesting. He who pays the piper, often calls the tune.'

Chapter Fifty-Eight

~~

Suzy was desperately trying to contact Melody about the priest, but she had switched her phone off. Suzy was about to go to the Carlton Hotel when her phone rang.

'Is that Suzy Marash?'

'Yes, who are you?'

'My name is Oswald Cox. I am commissioned by Cardinal Poggi on behalf of the Vatican. The reason I am calling you is I believe Miss Thornton's life is in real danger. She will not answer my calls and I understand you have a friendship with her.'

'I'm not sure I'd call it a friendship, but why should she trust you or your friend, the priest, Father Janssen, who incidentally has questions to answer over some irregularity? She wants to meet him. I advised her against it.'

'There must be some mistake–'

'Typical of the Vatican, covering up for each other.'

'No, you must be mistaken. I left Father Janssen in Israel. He had an important meeting and could not make the flight. As far as I am aware, he is still there. She cannot be meeting him.'

'But he was the priest on the plane with two nuns?'

'Again, you are mistaken. I don't know who the priest on the aircraft was, but it wasn't Father Janssen. I know him well and have worked with him many times. He and Cardinal Poggi left it to me to contact Miss Thornton. Believe me, we only want to help her.' There was a long pause. 'Are you still there, Miss Marash?'

'Yes, I need to get help. She'll already be there, with this man, pretending to be Father Janssen.'

'I know who to call,' Cox said. 'Don't panic, leave it to me. I'll contact you as soon as I hear anything.'

Chapter Fifty-Nine

~~

Melody walked the short distance to the Carlton Hotel. As she was about to enter, she noticed a flurry of activity in the car park. An army Jeep arrived, and two soldiers disembarked.

She was expecting Father Janssen to meet her in the lobby and was looking around, wondering where he was when one of the hotel staff approached. 'Miss Thornton?'

'Yes, I'm meeting Father Janssen. My name is Melody Thornton.'

'He's asked me to show you to his suite,' he beckoned a porter. 'Take Miss Thornton to suite 319.'

'This way, signora,' the porter said, guiding her to the lifts and the third floor. He knocked twice on the door. 'Il tuo visitatore è qui, padre,' he spoke whilst opening the door and then leaving.

'Ah, Miss Thornton, please come through to my temporary office,' The priest said, beckoning her in. 'Please, please take a seat. These are unusual times, are they not?' There was only one nun present from the flight, dressed on this occasion in a grey two-piece suit and although she still wore a veil and coif, it made Melody feel more at ease. 'This is Sister Maria,' he added.

'Thank you for seeing me. I'd like to discuss a delicate matter with you.'

'Certainly. However, can I ask you to turn your phone off first? It's a Vatican protocol.'

'Yes, of course,' Melody said, switching it off and placing it on the coffee table.

'Let me start at the beginning. I am sure you are aware of the reference in the Lost Gospel of Joseph, and the swaddling being presented to the Magi. The subsequent unearthing of some manuscripts called "The Treasures of the Magi" by Prof. Schmidt and–'

'The question I have is, have you found it?' His abrupt interruption and manner unsettled Melody. She was about to protest, but he continued. 'It is number two on the list of artefacts the Holy See has charged me with recovering. We have been aware of your interest for some time.'

'Forgive me, Father, but when you say recover, it implies you somehow own it or have previously owned and lost it.'

'All writings, manuscripts and artefacts relating to the Christian faith belong to the Church of Rome. Surely you see that.'

'No. I disagree entirely. The notion that the Church of Rome has jurisdiction, in this case, would be preposterous.'

'Be as it may, the question remains unanswered, or let me put it another way, where is it now?'

'I cannot answer that,' she said, reaching into her bag, lifting out the intricately carved wooden box and placing it on the coffee table. It mesmerised the priest. He leaned forward, his hand stroking the surface like a mother would a newborn infant. 'As you can see, there are two keyholes. The integrity of the casket is extremely important, and therefore I would like to have it X-rayed to determine the mechanism. At this stage, the casket could be empty.'

'We can take over from here, Miss Thornton. We already have the resources available. Your efforts will not go unnoticed.'

'Father Janssen, I have little doubt the ultimate resting place for the casket and any contents, if we find any, may and I stress, *may* eventually reside in the Vatican, but not now,' she said, raising her voice and moving to take the casket. As she did, his hand landed hard on top of it.

'This is the end of the story for your part in its long history, Miss Thornton!'

As he spoke, the woman masquerading as a nun produced a gun and moved toward her, placing the gun to her temple.

'As you can see, Maria is no more a nun than I am a priest.' He turned to his accomplice. 'Secure her for now. Then we'll need some kind of diversion. We don't want the Army intervening.'

'It won't do you any good, you know.'

'Au contraire, Miss Thornton, it will provide me with US$15m and save the life of an extraordinarily rich man,' he said, standing to take the casket into the bedroom.

Maria was attempting to tie Melody's hands behind her back so laid her gun on the floor. Melody put her feet against the table and hurled herself backwards, unbalancing her assailant. As Melody landed, she grabbed the gun, rolled over and stood. Maria was also rising and as soon as she had, she kicked the gun from her hand and made a lunge toward it. Melody punched her in the throat before bringing her knee up into her face. The woman simply staggered back two paces, blood flowing freely from her nose, before launching another attack. The fake priest was desperately trying to train his gun on Melody, but the two women were interchanging positions so often, it was nearly impossible. Kicking was Maria's favoured method and so Melody had to match her, landing a second punch on her nose. Eventually, she grabbed Maria's foot and twisted her over. Now she threw herself toward the gun, but as she curled her hand around it, she felt the hard metal of the priest's gun on the back of her head.

'I don't want to shoot you in here, but I will if I have to.' As she knelt up. He turned to Maria. 'There's a more suitable case for this in my bedroom. See if it will fit.'

Maria was still wiping blood from her nose and glaring at Melody, who simply smiled back. Maria moved forward, raising her arm.

'Enough,' the fake priest said, 'now go.'

She took the casket and moved reluctantly down the corridor and into a bedroom.

'Unfortunately, Miss Thornton,' he said, gesturing for her to stand and pushing her towards the open veranda windows. 'You will be the distraction we need. Suicide from a balcony should occupy the Army.'

Chapter Sixty

~~

Stuart was making his way to the Continental when his phone rang. 'Stuart Toulson,' he said.

'Avi here, the package you gave me is safely on its way to Israel. Thank you, Stuart. And, as promised, I have some information you may not be aware of. Two days ago, they discovered Father Elmer Janssen's murdered body floating in a hotel swimming pool in Tel Aviv. The two nuns are missing. The priest on the flight is an imposter using his identity.' There was a click as the phone went silent.

Stuart called the ops room. 'Where's Melody now? It's urgent,' he said into his lapel microphone.

'She's at the Carlton Hotel, meeting the Vatican Priest. Are you OK? You sound anxious.'

'The priest is an imposter. Ryland, are you listening to this?' He did not wait for an answer. 'Ryland, meet me at the Carlton. I'm on my way.'

'I'm just passing it. There's a military checkpoint outside, checking the papers of those entering. What's going on?'

'Go in, see if you find this so-called priest, Father Janssen. I'll be there shortly.' Stuart was running and finding it difficult to talk. 'Sage, try contacting Melody.'

'Already tried several times to log onto her. She's offline. Also, there are Army checkpoints at all the major hotels.'

As Ryland approached the hotel, he noticed one soldier waiting in the Jeep, engrossed in his mobile. As he was about to climb the steps, two other soldiers stopped him. He scanned them both; they looked like reservists, one was overweight and smoking, and the other was young and looked nervous. The heavily built one asked for his I.D – 'Le carte per favore.'

'What's going on, guys?' Ryland asked, handing his passport over.

The soldier did not answer. Instead, he looked up from his passport, then directly at his comrade and stepped back, his hand moving towards his holster. 'Il Fermo!'

He was not fast enough to stop Ryland dropping him with a punch in the throat. Pivoting, he spun the other soldier round, taking his pistol and lunging with him towards the Army Jeep. The driver had been texting and by the time he realised what was happening, it was too late. As he was leaving the vehicle, Ryland slammed his human shield into the door, disabling both men. By the time they had recovered, they'd lost sight of him.

He picked a spot on the river where boats were moored; he scaled the low wall, and within two minutes, he was heading towards town in a speedboat.

'It seems they're looking for us,' Ryland said. 'Stay away from the hotel. I've commandeered a boat on the river. Meet me at the bridge on Via Roma.'

Stuart changed direction for the new rendezvous. 'Sage, we need a way into the Carlton, an escape route, and the location of Melody and this priest. Send the rest of the team over for an extraction. Then pack up and prepare the plane for departure. Better warn the medics on the jet to prepare for casualties. One last thing, ask Landon to look in on Suzy Marash. She was speaking to Melody before this meeting. We may need to take her with us.'

'Roger that.'

Stuart tapped a UK number, that he'd not used for some time, into his phone. 'I haven't time to explain, but we're in Treviso and the military are trying to arrest us. No idea why, but somebody wants us out of the way. We need them off our backs for a quick extraction. See what you can do. We're bringing Melody home.'

Just as he hung up, Sage spoke into Stuart's earpiece. 'Front and rear are both guarded, but there's a staff entrance on the west side of the building. I have disabled the door access control system. Punch in any four numbers. Melody is on the third floor. Suite 319, let me know when you are there, and I'll unlock the door. The corridor is empty now. I'm packing up and the boys are on their way. You will need to leave by the same route and the plane is being warmed up. Incidentally, the chatter on the Army airwaves is someone reported overhearing you talk to Ryland about a terrorist attack.'

Stuart had reached the bridge as Ryland was coming up the steps. 'I'll let you know when we're on the third floor. Disable the lift from stopping there. I want one man at the staff entrance, one on the stairway and one in the vehicle. I'll try to arrange a police escort to the airport.'

'Got it,' Sage said.

'And make sure this channel is open for all of us. Are you OK, Ryland?'

'Sure, just a couple of volunteers, rookie grunts, but the incident will flush out some regular soldiers. We will need to move fast.'

Sage spoke. 'There's a way to the staff entrance just off the Largo Porta Altinia. The cinema won't be open now, so it should be quiet.'

Chapter Sixty-One

~~

Felix Breunig was in his room on the second floor of the Carlton Hotel briefing Anatoly. 'Update me, Felix. What do we know so far?' Anatoly asked.

'Remember, you instructed me to tread lightly. Information has been difficult to get under those circumstances. What I can say is several of the interested parties have vanished or are lying incredibly low. Farad El Sayed seemed to disappear the day we arrived, quickly followed by Vasily Valkov.'

'Anyone else?'

'The genuine surprise was the sudden departure of Feinstein and the Mossad team today. I thought they would be in for the long haul. Miss Thornton is presently having a meeting with Father Elmer Janssen. As for Oswald Cox, he works for the Vatican and reports directly to Cardinal Poggi. Not sure what his plans are regarding Miss Thornton without–'

'Ah, speak of the devil,' Anatoly said, holding up his hand whilst answering his mobile. 'Your Eminence, how lovely to hear from you.' Anatoly was nodding, his furrowed brow revealing his concern as the Cardinal spoke. 'That is disturbing news indeed. I'll call you later. Are you sure he is in suite 319?' A slight pause. 'Thank you.'

He turned to Felix. 'The priest is an imposter. I fear she is in real danger. He's on the floor above. We must move quickly.'

'Did you say 319?' Felix asked whilst recovering his gun from the wall safe, screwing on the silencer and moving towards the door. 'Are you armed?'

'No, I've never needed one.'

'Stay here then.'

'No. I insist on coming with you.'

'In that case, take this.' He took a small handgun from an ankle holster. 'Pretend you know how to use it.'

'I do. I'm just not accurate, so I don't carry one.'

They made their way up to the next floor. 'I got this keycard off the housekeeper just in case,' Felix said, removing a plastic card from his wallet. They were now on either side of the door. Anatoly nodded. They both took out their weapons, then Felix inserted the card. A faint click, a green light, and they were in.

It was a short corridor leading into the living area. They could hear muffled voices. Felix picked out snatched words, 'distraction, balcony, suicide.' They spun into the room simultaneously as Janssen was attempting to push Melody through the French windows towards the balcony. Felix strode forward and put the gun to the priest's head.

'Put the gun down and release the girl,' he demanded, his voice calm but authoritative.

It was a voice Melody had not heard before. She turned her head slightly; she could just make out a man holding a gun to the priest's head as another man came into view.

'We seem to have a Mexican standoff,' Janssen's imposter said.

'I don't think so,' said Anatoly, moving closer and pointing his gun at him. 'If you release her, you walk away, alive and free. We don't want the authorities involved any more than you do, but if you don't–'

'What about your friend, Nikolai Levanevsky? Don't you want him to live also?'

'I am not–'

They all heard the door open and quickly close. Anatoly approached the corridor slowly, not sure if someone had entered or left. No one was there. He hurried to the door and stepped onto the landing. A woman in a nun's headdress was heading for the stairwell. He went to the lift, but even though he pressed the call button several times, nothing was happening. He considered going back to the room, but followed her instead.

'If you kill the girl, I'll kill you,' Felix said, pressing the gun harder in the fake priest's scalp. 'Walk away now and you live to fight another day. Anatoly will probably return with the police. This is your last chance.'

The priest quickly pulled Melody towards the door, making sure she was between them. He backed down the corridor, aware Felix had his gun aimed at him. He opened the door, then pushed Melody hard into Felix and fled.

'That was a close call,' he said, helping her to her feet. 'The tip-off came just at the right time.'

'Thank you, but who are you and what's this about a tip-off and what do you want?' Melody asked rubbing her aching arm.

Chapter Sixty-Two

As Suzy Marash came out of the bathroom, Landon grabbed her from behind and covered her mouth to prevent her from screaming. 'I mean you no harm, Miss Marash. In a moment, I'm going to let go of you. Do you promise not to scream?' Suzy nodded, and he let her go.

'If you mean me no harm, why didn't you knock on the door like normal people?' Suzy snapped back, remembering him from the aircraft as the man who unsettled her.

'Would you have answered if I had?'

'Probably not,' she said before mouthing an obscenity.

'My name is Landon Bailey, and I am working for an organisation protecting Melody Thornton. Now, regardless of what you tell me, I will leave at the end of our conversation. What happens after depends on what you tell me. So far, we know she was meeting a priest called Father Elmer Janssen. Unfortunately, the real Father Janssen is dead, murdered in Israel, and this man is impersonating him. If you value keeping Melody and yourself safe, you need to tell me everything you know. We will probably leave today, and they have allowed me to take you with us, providing you want to, and we extricate her from her present difficulties.'

'Oswald Cox told me he's an imposter. I'm not sure I can help you much.' Suzy said, flopping down on an armchair. 'I've tried to contact her–'

'Try to think of it this way. Assume they have taken Miss Thornton hostage and tortured her, and she has told her assailants everything. Would that compromise you? Now tell me what you know.'

Chapter Sixty-Three

~~~

Stuart and Ryland passed by the cinema and turned right down a narrow passage leading to an apartment block. They picked the lock of the communal gate, crossed the gardens, scaled a wall and crouched behind shrubbery near the staff entrance. Two kitchen staff were having a cigarette break. 'Damned nuisance. Unfortunately, I can't speak Italian,' Ryland said.

'Cover me if things turn sour,' Stuart said as he walked out and addressed them. 'Cosa stai facendo, torna in cucina sono un ispettore sanitaria.' The two men panicked, stubbed out their cigarettes and disappeared into the building.

'What did you say to them?' Ryland asked when he caught up.

'I told them I was a health inspector. Take the stairs, I'll find the service elevator.'

As Ryland climbed the stairs, a nun in a grey two-piece suit passed him, smiled and nodded. Ryland noticed her shoes were out of keeping and she was wearing make-up. He smiled, but as he passed, he turned and drew his gun. Unfortunately, a staff member was passing behind her in the corridor below, preventing him from firing. She had turned at the same time and was aiming at him. As she fired, Ryland was already moving. The bullet grazed the side of his head and he lost his balance.

She was about to fire again when Anatoly appeared behind him on the stairs, took aim and fired. The bullet narrowly missed her and the chef's presence was still preventing Ryland from returning fire. She took advantage of his dilemma and grabbed the chef, using him as a shield before knocking him unconscious with her gun and escaping along the corridor towards the staff changing rooms.

'Are you OK?' Anatoly asked Ryland.

'Just a graze. Who are you?' he asked, ignoring Stuart, trying to hail him in his earpiece.

'My name is Anatoly. My associate is with Miss Thornton. She may still be in danger. I must hurry back.'

'Stuart, I've taken a flesh wound. Go immediately to 319. I'm on my way.' He was speaking into his microphone.

The service lift stopped on the third floor. Stuart stepped out, took a quick bearing of the room numbers and ran towards 319. When he arrived at the door, he stopped and took his gun out of its shoulder holster. Ryland and Anatoly appeared at the far end of the landing. He waited for Ryland to take up position on the other side of the door.

Ryland turned to Anatoly. 'Put the gun away, leave this to us,' he whispered.

'We're armed, and we're coming in,' Ryland shouted. Then, in a synchronised move, both he and Stuart spun into the corridor with their guns pointing forward, cautiously making their way forwards. 'Put down your weapon. We're armed,' Stuart said. As he and Ryland turned into the living area, Ryland dropped onto one knee.

'Come in, Mr Toulson. Melody is safe and unharmed.' Came the reply.

'Stuart's here?' Melody asked, bewildered.

As they entered the room fully, Melody was sitting in an armchair, nursing a bruised arm. When she saw Stuart walk in, she got up and walked over to him. 'It's lovely to see you, but how did you know I was here?' She shook her head, then hugged him.

'We were just keeping a watching brief. That was until the fighter jet incident, then we decided you may need a little extra help.'

'It looks like Ryland was correct when he told me the world and his wife knew what I was doing,' she said.

'We eliminated three interested parties, but the couple impersonating the priest and the fake nuns slipped through the net. To be honest, I am amazed you have made it so far. Will you excuse me for a moment? I need to speak to Felix about the priest,' Stuart said.

She could see Ryland checking the perimeter from the balcony and joined him. 'Hi Ryland, pleased to see you again.'

'Good to see you too,' Ryland said. 'What do you know of Felix and Anatoly?'

'They are not a danger to me. Felix has explained their interest. It's a long story. I'll explain it to you later.'

As they stepped back into the room, Stuart walked over to her and put his hands on her shoulders. 'Well, Melody,' he said, kissing her on both cheeks. 'We'd better get you home.'

Chapter Sixty-Four

~~

Ryland touched his earpiece to talk to the team. 'We're bringing the "Christmas Fairy out,"' he smiled and Melody shook her head. 'We'll use the main entrance, bring the cars around. Sage says the checkpoints have gone. Let's make sure the walk to the car is safe.'

By the time they had reached the ground floor and left the lift, Melody had five men with concealed weapons protecting her. She thought this must be what it feels like to be a president or prime minister. Sage was waiting at the top of the hotel steps. Below, the blacked-out minivan was waiting with a police escort.

'I need to call at the Continental to collect my things, and I'm worried about my friend Suzy. Also, my luggage is still on the flight. I can't leave without it,' Melody said.

'Suzy is waiting on the jet. She packed up your hand luggage and we've already transferred your other luggage,' Stuart said.

'Oh. It seems you've thought of everything,' she said, stepping into the van.

Anatoly leaned inside and spoke to Melody. 'We're not coming with you. Felix and I are going to see Cardinal Poggi. It was his tip-off that led to our intervention. I'll contact you once you're safely home.'

'Please do. You and Felix probably saved my life. I have something important to tell you, but not here, not now.'

Anatoly smiled and nodded. 'I look forward to it,' he turned and shook hands with Ryland and Stuart. 'No doubt we'll meet again.'

'No doubt. We're trying to locate the priest and Maria, the imposter nun. I understand she made off with the swaddling casket?' Ryland said.

'Apparently, but as your head wound can testify, she'd gone before we could stop her. She will almost certainly be making her way to Nikolai by now.'

The journey through Treviso was uneventful. The police escort used sirens and blue lights to guide them through the traffic. Security waved them through at the airport and onto the tarmac, pulling up alongside the Gulfstream G550.

Marco Casale was waiting at the steps. Stuart walked over, along with Melody. Marco shook his hand. 'So this is the young lady causing so much distress?' Marco said, smiling at her.

'It is indeed, and I hope you don't get into too much trouble for what you've done for us,' Stuart said.

'Listen, my friend, if I hadn't helped, my wife would have killed me and if she didn't, my daughter would.' They both laughed. 'Anyway, I may retire, we'll see. But before you leave, I need to speak to Ryland. I didn't have time to thank him after the rescue of my daughter.'

Melody blocked his way. 'Stuart told me on the way here that we couldn't have done this without your help, thank you so much,' she said, stepping forward and kissing him on both cheeks.

'Perhaps I should keep her here,' Marco said, smiling.

They said their farewells, and as Melody entered the cabin, Suzy was excited to see her and desperate for the full story. 'Come and sit next to me,' she pleaded, also pointing to Melody's bag she had brought along.

'Later, let me catch my breath,' Melody said, leaning forward and pretending to whisper. 'I think Stuart wants a debrief.'

Thirty minutes later, they were in the air, heading for the UK. Melody was sitting next to Stuart.

'I was happy but also surprised to see you when you appeared at the Carlton,' Melody said. 'I'm glad now you ignored my insistence on allowing me to complete this project on my own.'

'Tell me what actually happened today. You didn't seem overly concerned that they had stolen the item you'd spent years searching for.'

'She stole a fake one. On the journey out of Iran, I had to spend some time in Turkmenistan waiting for a ferry. I had a replica made by a local artisan; it was virtually identical. The original was still in my luggage on the aircraft.'

'How do you imagine they tracked you?'

'An old college friend of mine, Farrokh Mokri, I confronted him, following one of my episodes or visions where I saw Farrokh talking to a Russian who was on the plane. He called him Vasily. He confessed to me MOIS was threatening his family. Vasily was working for the Iranian Government.'

'His nickname is The Wolf,' Stuart said. 'An extremely dangerous individual. He was working for a Russian Oligarch called Nikolai Levanevsky, who is terminally ill.'

'The secret police now have the Mokri family held hostage, did you know?'

'Yes, the Mossad team told me. We do not expect the outcome to be a good one. They also tipped us off about the identity of the priest. But please do not mention any of this to Suzy. She may print it and it may compromise them.

'I had my suspicions at the airport in Iran. There was a connection between him and someone I didn't recognise at first, but later I found his picture on my phone. He had been following me in Glasgow. They must have been using me to lead them to it.' She looked directly at him. He seemed even more handsome than she remembered. 'How long have you been tracking me?'

'Once Ryland brought me his report, we agreed on a watching brief. There were too many variables and the "Mission Risk Assessment" was remarkably negative.' He paused and put his hand on hers. 'Since we dined together at Sospitas, I have thought about you often. I am hoping to see more of you.'

'I'd love that, but I thought you'd regard me as too dippy to consider any involvement.'

'My view of you hasn't changed from when we dined together. I still find you entirely mysterious, though I agree some would say dippy.'

She punched him playfully on the arm. 'I'm looking forward to an uninterrupted dinner with you this time.'

'Me too,' Stuart said.

'How did you meet Marco or Sostituto Commissario as he introduced himself on the aircraft?' She imitated his Italian accent.

'He was head of the Drug Enforcement Agency. A local drug lord, whose business he had interrupted, kidnapped his daughter so he asked us to negotiate.'

'How much did he have to pay?'

'Nothing. In the end, Ryland and his snatch team rescued her. The drug barons are ruthless, but not clever.'

'I don't suppose there were any arrests or charges made.'

'Well, as Ryland would often say, no one got away and there were no prisoners.' After a long pause, he spoke again. 'I have to ask you, is the swaddling in the casket?'

'I don't know. It has an intricate two-lock mechanism, and the casket alone is a valuable antiquity. I want to do more research and have it X-rayed before attempting to open it.'

'Have you spoken to Brodie recently?'

'No, it would only have worried him, and he would report back to my father. Why? Have you been in contact?'

'He was extremely worried about you.'

'My father! Why have you spoken to him?'

'Your father has been deeply concerned about you, and it was your father's contacts through NATO that had the Army checkpoints removed. I had little or no choice.'

'I see,' she said, her tone sharp. 'I need to catch up with Suzy. Will you excuse me?'

'Melody, I'm sorry I–'

'It's OK,' she said. 'It's just I suddenly feel like an actor, being watched by others directing things. Look, I am grateful, I am, but I need a little space right now.' She left her seat, joining Suzy.

'Who's the dishy guy?' Suzy asked. 'You kept him a secret. Rich, handsome and a hero. If he proposes, you must say yes and invite me to the wedding. I'll be your Maid of Honour.'

'It's complicated. Can we talk about something else?'

'Let's talk about me writing the story. Oh, and the film rights from the book.' They both laughed a little, but mostly from a sense of relief.

'Why was the Italian police officer so pleased to see you?' Suzy asked.

'That, my dear, is a story of its own. I swear you couldn't make this up…'

Chapter Sixty-Five

~~

When the jet landed at London City Airport, the helicopter was waiting. The discrete logo of the 'Cherished Anti-Surveillance' on its side brought memories flooding back. Melody wondered if she had overreacted with Stuart. She chided herself for not being able to forgive and forget easily. *Also, I need to speak to Stuart regarding Suzy.*

They had agreed on the flight, though Stuart was reluctant for the helicopter to take Melody and Suzy to Oxford.

'If you insist on going to Oxford, and again, I advise against it, I must insist you have some element of protection. At least two of the close protection guys, discretely keeping watch. It's not over yet,' Stuart said. 'You fooled the impostor priest, but when he discovers it's a fake, he'll come looking for you. We have discovered he is an ex-mafia hitman called Salvatore Lombardi *or* 'the Viper'. Even the nun, Maria Licciardi, Lombardi's long-time lover, is dangerous. Her nickname is the Praying Mantis and there may be more out there.'

'I promise you, Stuart, as soon as my business in Oxford is over, I'll stay at Sospitas, that is as long as you'll agree,' Melody said, her hands pleading.

'I only want what's best for you and, of course, you can stay at the retreat. At least I will know where to find you and it will be the safest place for the casket, don't you agree?'

'Yes, thank you, Stuart, you're wonderful,' she said, moving forward and kissing him on the lips. Stuart looked lost for words as he walked away and Melody turned to Suzy.

'We'd better make a start.'

'Are you sure you want to go straight to Oxford? After all you have been through, how can you possibly leave Stuart behind?'

'I'm feeling terrible. I probably shouldn't have done that,' Melody said, still feeling a tingle on her lips. 'Despite how terribly ungrateful it may seem. I've tried to explain to him, I sometimes feel manipulated in his company.' She suddenly realised she didn't want to talk about Stuart. 'Anyway, I'm desperate to start the research and Brodie will have the most contacts.'

'I must admit, the thought of visiting Oxford is exciting. You never know, I may meet a handsome don.'

'Don't hold your breath on that one, but you will enjoy the city and Stuart's booked us in at the Randolph Hotel. It's my favourite.'

'What's it like, quintessentially English?'

'Yes, but also modern and it's got a spa,' Melody said. 'Are you sure you don't mind sharing a room? I don't want to be on my own tonight.'

'To be honest, Mel, I'd prefer that myself. Hotels can be lonely places. Can I meet Brodie tomorrow?'

'Yes, but behave. No flirting, I'm on business here.'

* * *

Suzy loved the hotel, and the two minders were so discrete, they were almost invisible.

'They call one of them Tyke. He's the one with a haircut like a marine,' Melody confided to Suzy. 'I don't know the one who looks like Brad Pitt, though.'

'Should I ask him?'

'Hell no. You must pretend you don't know them. If you blow their cover, Stuart will have a hissy fit.' They both giggled.

'I thought you didn't care what Stuart thought,' Suzy said, teasing her.

'None of your business. Anyway, who was that on your phone earlier. Boyfriend?'

'I wish. Anyway, I told you, I don't have a boyfriend. Unfortunately, it was my boss on the paper. I have to convince him to play the long game, get a fantastic story eventually, rather than just a good story now.' Suzy then changed the subject. 'Which rooms will they be in?'

'Who?'

'The minders.'

'Close protection personnel, if you don't mind, and if I know Stuart, it'll be next to ours, with an interconnecting door and a key only on their side.' They both giggled again. 'I haven't laughed in ages. It feels good. It feels like I'm on the last lap.'

'You have been through a lot recently.'

'Let's go to the restaurant. I'm hungry and in need of a large glass of wine.'

'Why don't you call him tonight? I can see it's bothering you.'

'I will. He's been so generous and kind. It is such a strange feeling. I miss him already, yet when I am with him, I feel boxed in.'

'Then tell him. Don't let him slip through your fingers. If you do, you'll regret it. Did you see his face when you kissed him at the airport?'

'Barely. I turned away as quick as I could. It was an instinctive gesture. Why? What was his reaction?'

'Well, first I think he blushed slightly, then a cheesy, wide smile. I thought he was going to faint. All the other guys looked down at their feet, embarrassed.'

'You're exaggerating. But I will text him later. Thanks for reminding me.'

'The fainting bit was a white lie, but all the rest was true. Incidentally, is he picking up the tab for the accommodation? My expenses only go to two-star hotels.'

'You don't have to worry about money whilst you're in the UK. You're a guest of ours, plus Stuart will pay for the hotel. It's pocket money for him. The artwork in his office alone is worth more than my house.' That set them both off laughing again.

Before going to bed, Melody and Stuart exchanged a flurry of text messages. The last one from her read: 'Would you investigate Suzy's background for me? She seems nice, but just to be on the safe side, would you check out her story?'

'Certainly, and let me know the moment your business with Brodie is over x.'

The next text was to Dilshod.

'I'm back in the UK. Are you still in Iran?'

'Yes. Soraya the receptionist from the hospital and her family are under low-level surveillance. They turned down her visa to visit Europe. We meet up often but have to be careful. Have you opened the casket yet?'

'I'm meeting a locksmith soon. Stay safe xx.'

Melody went to sleep feeling safe for the first time in quite a while.

Chapter Sixty-Six

~~

The following morning they had an early breakfast and walked to Magdalen College. Melody was pointing out features to Suzy as though she were a professional tour guide. Suzy was soaking it in like a tourist and loving every minute. Melody couldn't see the minders, but she knew they would not be far away.

They were being watched, but not just by the minders.

Brodie was excited to see Melody. 'It's such a relief seeing you back safe and sound and, of course, your friend.' He turned to her. 'Welcome to Oxford, Miss Marash.'

She smiled politely. 'Please, call me Suzy.'

'Did you find a locksmith with knowledge of antiquities?' Melody asked, ignoring the pleasantries.

'Yes, he'll be here at eleven o'clock. I presume you have the casket with you?' he asked, a little too eagerly.

Melody lifted a case from the side of her chair and placed it on the desk. Bodie watched, transfixed, as she opened it and removed the protective foam. Hidden from view only by a soft linen bag, she removed the packaging from the desk and slid the casket out of its bag.

'Wow. It is magnificent,' Brodie whispered as he put a pair of white gloves on. His hands caressed it. 'Even if it's empty, it's such a treasure. The intricate carving, the rich history it holds, and the stories and visions it creates. This will mean so much to so many people. The entire world will talk about it.'

Suzy spoke. 'Put your nose near a keyhole and tell me what you can smell?'

Brodie looked bemused, then lifted it; he was frowning but inhaled like a sniffer dog. 'It smells like wild garlic.' The quizzical look on his face made Melody and Suzy smile.

'It's a distinct smell for everyone and changes daily, sometimes more often. It's a complete mystery,' Melody said, sliding it back into the bag and pulling the drawstring.

Brodie turned to Suzy. 'I was wondering if you'd like a tour of the college, Suzy?'

'Yes, of course, please, I'd like that.'

Brodie buzzed his secretary. 'Would you be kind enough to take Miss Marash, err Suzy, on a tour please?' Shortly after the door opened, the secretary gave a weary smile and Suzy left.

'I wanted to ask you how you are and about the visions,' Brodie said. 'Have they ended now? I didn't want to ask in front of Suzy.'

'I'm feeling much safer, thank you. As for Suzy, she knows the full story and wants to write it up. We'll see.'

'The visions?'

'I haven't had an episode recently and even though they continued right through to Egypt, somehow the story doesn't feel complete. What I can tell you is the sense of dread over them has lessened and there's been a reawakening of my faith.'

'You should write a book about the Nativity story from the Magi's point of view. I think it would fascinate people.'

'Perhaps I will, a behind-the-scenes story. Stuart has invited me to stay at Sospitas once this is over. I'll have plenty of time on my hands then. The title could be "The Treasures of the Magi or The Untold Nativity Story."'

'How is Stuart? I rather thought he would accompany you here,' Brodie said, probing.

'He was in excellent form when I left him in London,' she said. 'Now, tell me about the locksmith.'

'Ah yes, he'll be here soon. He is a forensic locksmith and spends a lot of his time in court working for the Crown Prosecution Service as an expert witness regarding safes, keys, antique locks and the techniques used to crack them. He uses photography, microscopy and tool mark identifications. Some may say he's boring, others that he is a simple stickler for detail.'

'What about antiquities?'

Brodie picked up the notes he was reading and continued. 'He has a doctorate and lectures around the world on the history of locks. Bizarrely, his name is John Bolt, which he always mentions the irony of.'

'Impressive. How much detail did you give him?'

'As little as possible. We need to explain the confidentiality of this to him "face to face" and no mention of the swaddling. Otherwise, we'll have a media storm.' Brodie was questioning her on the possibility of the casket being empty when Suzy returned with his secretary.

'Brodie, I want you to sign me up to do my M.A. here. I have got to come to this college,' Suzy said. 'I'm not leaving your office until you agree.' She was laughing. But there was an element of truth.

'I'm sure we could accommodate you, Suzy. We love foreign students. Could you get someone to sponsor you?'

'That could be difficult. I only know Melody, and she's flaky.'

They were all laughing as his secretary announced: 'Mr Bolt has arrived. Should I show him in?' This started Melody and Brodie laughing again, much to the consternation of the secretary. Brodie nodded and stood to greet him.

'Welcome again, Mr Bolt. This is Melody Thornton and her associate Suzy Marash. Ladies, this is John Bolt, the eminent locksmith I spoke of.' They all shook hands and settled down.

'Melody?' Brodie said, offering her the opportunity to speak.

'What we have here is an antiquity from between AD 1 and 60,' she said, tapping the box. 'Probably Persian. Judging by its intricate design, it's rare and extremely valuable. We would like to open it without causing damage. That Mr Bolt is where you come in. Brodie assures me if anyone can, it is you. Brodie has arranged for us to X-ray it later today, and the results made available to you. What's your first impression?' She took the casket out of the bag, presenting it to him.

'A fascinating object, to be sure,' he said, putting on white linen gloves. 'It certainly looks first century, but the locking mechanism would have been ahead of its time, pretty much state-of-the-art for the period. The Romans had locks, but nothing this advanced. The owner must have been both wealthy and secretive. I have only come across one like this before.'

'Were you successful in opening it?'

'Yes, the two keys are different, naturally, but you must turn them at the same time. If you unlock one on its own, it locks the other, and vice versa. I would need to spend some time making the keys, probably out of carbon and plastic first, so as not to damage the mechanism. How much access to it would I have?'

'I was hoping you would have enough time today to complete your initial investigation, along with the X-ray scans to take with you. We'll be taking the casket to Hertfordshire in the next couple of days. Is that a problem?'

'If it is, I will contact you. Hertfordshire is closer for me, anyway.'

'Just to warn you, Mr Bolt, a member of our security team will accompany us to the radiology department. It's an insurance thing, I hope you'll understand?' Brodie said, standing to show this part of the meeting was over.

'Of course, I perfectly understand.' He picked up his well-worn leather attaché case and followed them out of the room.

X-ray of the casket did not take long, and it was obvious from early observations the casket looked empty, except for what appeared to be a small piece of parchment attached to the underside of the lid. They continued concentrating on the locking mechanism.

'What are your initial impressions, Mr Bolt?' Melody asked as they were leaving the facility.

'I am confident about making the keys and will be in touch soon. I'm rather sorry it looks empty.'

'We'll say goodbye here then if you don't mind, it's closer to the main entrance. I look forward to hearing from you soon.'

They all shook hands, and as soon as the locksmith was out of earshot, Brodie spoke to Melody. 'How are you feeling?'

'A little disappointed, but not surprised,' she said, placing it back in the linen bag. 'It felt empty, though I couldn't be sure. The thing is, last night I unlocked and unpacked my suitcase. When I had finished, I slid it under the bed.'

'I don't understand,' Suzy said.

'I didn't lock it,' Melody said.

'Because it was empty,' Brodie nodded. 'Why would you?'

'Precisely. Why would you lock something if it were empty and where are the fragrances coming from?'

Chapter Sixty-Seven

~~

Vasily Valkov slipped into the UK on board a Russian cargo ship. A car with diplomatic plates whisked him away from the Port of London. It headed for the M40 Motorway and Oxford.

The Ambassador spoke first. 'Remember, your primary aim is to recover the swaddling cloth.'

'I know what I have to do,' Vasily said.

'So, revenge isn't on your agenda, then?'

'I won't pass up the opportunity if it presents itself.'

'These people protecting her are not amateurs, as you discovered once before.'

'I don't need reminding.'

'Yes, you do. Moscow will not be as forgiving a second time. This is not about Nikolai Levanevsky. There is someone higher up the chain of command and for the record, let me emphasise, someone extremely high up is depending on this. Do you understand?'

'Perfectly.'

'Good.' He turned to the driver. 'Drop him off at the railway station.'

Vasily stepped out of the car and walked away. He did not bother looking back as the car sped off.

Later that morning, Vasily watched as Melody and Suzy left the hotel and made their way to Magdalen College. He also spotted the two-man close protection team. Once they were out of sight, he walked into the hotel and checked in with his false passport.

'Thank you, Mr Lebedev. I'll let you know the moment your case arrives. Have a pleasant stay. Will you be dining with us tonight?'

'Unfortunately, no, I have a prior engagement.'

Once upstairs, he found and entered Melody's room, planting a hidden camera and listening device before making a more thorough search. He then moved on to the minder's room next to it and repeated the process.

Back in his room, he set up the laptop, poured himself a large vodka, placed his gun beside him on the bed and waited.

Chapter Sixty-Eight

~~

Stuart Toulson was meeting Enano Domingos, Senior Vice President of Angola's state-owned oil company, Sonangol. 'We produce 1.4 million barrels of oil each day, Mr Toulson, and yet many of our children are starving. How can that be?'

'It used to be 1.8 million.'

'OPEC – we have to do their bidding. They say cut production, we ask by how much, it's a club we have to belong to. We have no choice.'

'It's a vulgar phrase and yet it seems apt to say there are perhaps "too many snouts in the trough" – BP, Chevron, Exxon Mobil, Total and the Chinese all taking a share and is it possible some of your own officials are feeding from it?'

'We have no control over the multinationals, we needed their investment and expertise, it's those within our organisation the president wants to root out.'

'Is that the president of the company or the President of Angola?'

'Inciteful, Mr Toulson! No one from the company knows I'm here today. You could say I'm the president's Envoy.'

'How much is missing?'

'Two billion dollars is our conservative estimate, we–'

Stuart's emergency phone was vibrating. 'Please forgive me, Mr Domingos. This call is an emergency. It won't take long.' He stepped out of the room to take it. The phone was for critical situations only. 'Yes Sage, what is it?'

'The Wolf is back in the UK. Worse still, we captured him planting surveillance equipment in Miss Thornton's and the close protection team's room. We think the Russians brought him in. He has a Russian passport in the name of Yuri Lebedev, and he has booked in at the same hotel.'

'Who have we got in Oxford?'

'Tyke and Boston are the C.P. team. Ryland and two of our extended team, Sharpe and Gilford, are staying at a different hotel close by. I've already given them a heads-up; they're already planning for an extraction.'

'Any news on the whereabouts of Lombardi and his sidekick, the Praying Mantis?'

'Last intel we had was they were in the Black Sea area. Presumedly visiting Nikolai Levanevsky, they've been below the radar since.'

'Tell the C.P. team to keep Miss Thornton and Miss Marash away from the hotel until Ryland gives the green light. Ryland may need Tyke later. They work well as a team. Keep me informed, twenty-four-seven.'

'*Damned Russians.*' Stuart then made a call to Avraham Feinstein.

'It's nice to hear from you again, Stuart and so soon,' Avi said.

'We have a wolf in sheep's clothing. Vasily Valkov has surfaced again in the UK and before we deal with the inconvenience, I wanted to see if it was a package you would be interested in, and also to thank you for the intelligence regarding Father Janssen.'

'What are your options?'

'One, we can eradicate the problem permanently. Two, we hand him back to the Russians, knowing he would not leave the Embassy alive, having embarrassed them again. The third option is we parcel him up for you to collect from our private airstrip.'

'Let me talk to my intel team,' Avi said, and then the line went dead.

Chapter Sixty-Nine

~~

Ryland and Gilford walked into the Randolph Hotel. Gilford made his way to the foot of the staircase; Ryland approached the receptionist.

'How may I help you, Sir?' asked the receptionist. Ryland made a note of the name on his badge: Adam.

Ryland opened a small leather I.D. wallet, showing his photo and an MI5 badge. 'Keep smiling whilst you answer my questions, Adam, do not draw attention to us.'

The receptionist was now grinning widely and nodding. 'What room is Mr Yuri Lebedev in?'

'215, Sir,' he replied, still grinning from ear to ear.

'Shortly, an ambulance will arrive with two paramedics. Mr Lebedev is not well, do not interfere. Is that clear?'

'Yes, Sir.'

'Is he still in his room?'

'Yes, Sir.'

'Give me a passkey.'

'Is he a Russian spy?' he asked, still smiling.

'I'm not at liberty to inform you of his status. Now, the key, please.'

The receptionist handed it over whilst glancing at Gilford, who had one hand inside the breast of his dark suit.

Ryland headed for the stairs, talking to Sage on the way whilst Gilford followed.

'Sage, room 215, have you got control of the lifts and doors?'

'Roger that. Let me know when you're outside his door.'

Ryland had the tranquiliser gun while Gilford had a SIG Sauer Mosquito and silencer for backup. 'We're near his room. Once we are in, send in the ambulance extraction team, on my count, 3,2,1.' The door clicked, Gilford opened it and Ryland swung in, dropped on one knee, and fired at the neck of Vasily in one movement. Vasily instinctively moved for the pistol beside him on the bed, but collapsed before he reached it.

They could hear the sirens of their ambulance arriving. 'It looks like we're back to "option one," Mr Valkov,' Ryland said as he and Gilford made a sweep of the room.

They assembled his meagre belongings next to him for the extraction, apart from his Glock 44 pistol, which Ryland locked and shoved in the rear of his waistband. They left the room with the door slightly ajar and walked calmly down the stairs, passing the two Sospitas paramedics on their way in. Ryland walked to the reception desk and gave Adam the door pass.

'You have served your country well today, Adam. Well done. But speak to no one about this. I need Lebedev's passport and any other belongings he left with you.'

Adam found his passport in the safe and handed it over. 'It's all we have of his, but he said a suitcase would be arriving.'

'The safe in his room was empty. Did he leave anything in a safe deposit box?'

'No Sir, nothing.'

'If a case arrives, ring this number immediately. They'll know what to do,' Ryland said, handing him a business card, falsely branded as MI5.

'Thank you, Agent Carlyle, I will.'

'You can send in your housekeeping staff now. We have removed his belongings. Mr Lebedev will not be returning.'

Adam was still beaming as they left the hotel. He couldn't wait to tell his friends.

Chapter Seventy

~~~

Stuart took the call. It was from Avraham Feinstein.

'Stuart, I would appreciate it if you delivered the package we discussed earlier to the Russian Embassy. It's a quid pro quo with another agency–'

'Before you go, Avi,' Stuart said, 'I wonder if you could do me a favour. I believe the Russians could help on this one. I'll send the details encrypted. It's delicate and I would prefer it if there were no collateral damage on this extraction.' Then the line went dead.

The following day, they tossed the unconscious body of Vasily Valkov out from an unmarked minivan outside the gates of the Russian Embassy. He was wearing a wolf's mask. Two Russian GRU agents, who were waiting for them, opened the gates, recovered the body and carried it inside.

Chapter Seventy-One

~~

Ryland met Melody and Suzy in the deer park of Magdalen College. They strolled along the 'water walk' alongside the River Cherwell, and explained the danger they had narrowly avoided. 'Stuart wants you both to go to Sospitas. It's not safe here, and it's impossible to guarantee your safety. Also, you're now putting the close protection team at unnecessary risk.'

'Yes, of course. I'd hate it if any of you were hurt,' Melody said.

'Grab your things from the hotel. We have men stationed there. After you've packed, they'll take you to Sospitas. It's not a long journey.'

'Is Stuart there?' Melody tried to sound nonchalant. Suzy looked at her and opened her eyes wide whilst leaning her head to one side. Melody ignored her.

'He was an hour ago.'

Suzy linked Melody's arm. 'How exciting is this? Tell me about Sospitas.'

'It's called Sospitas Retreat, and it's a cross between a health spar and Fort Knox.'

'And Stuart will be there.'

'Your wanton matchmaking will not draw me!' Melody said, looking up defiantly.

The welcome back from the hotel concierge surprised Melody. 'If you need any help, please let me know, Miss Thornton. Call me when you're ready and I'll send someone up to collect your cases. Just to let you know,' he said, in almost a whisper, 'there is a man on your landing.

Ignore him, he's security. A guest took ill and had to go to the hospital.'

'What a shame. What happened?'

'A Russian tourist, heart attack, I believe.'

Ten minutes later, they climbed into the blacked-out minivan, along with Ryland, Tyke, Boston and two other men Melody did not recognise. They headed out through the city and were soon making excellent progress on the M40. 'How long will the drive take?' Suzy asked no one in particular.

'An hour and twenty-nine minutes. Our ETA is 2231 hours, ma'am,' the driver said.

The two women stifled a giggle at his military precision.

Chapter Seventy-Two

~~

Salvatore Lombardi and Maria Licciardi were sitting in the back of the Land Rover Discovery. At first glance, it looked like an ordinary Traffic Police Land Rover. Two of the occupants had SCAR 17S Combat Assault Rifles resting on their knees. Milo, a huge Italian ex-Mafia hitman, was sitting in the passenger seat, running his hand over his shiny bald head. The car waited, hidden from view in a newly cropped field. The open gate allowed access to the winding country road.

Once again, the getaway driver glanced at his watch. 'They'll be here at approx. 2200 hours.'

'Is the roadblock ready?' Maria asked, whilst inspecting her neatly manicured hands.

'Yes, as soon as they pass us, I'll signal them to set off smoke bombs. It'll make it look like there has been a serious accident.'

'What about the ramming vehicle?'

'Approximately one mile behind them.'

* * *

Ryland was nervous. Earlier, he had noticed a transit van had followed them for some distance before it eventually fell behind. Even the open gate made him suspicious. Farmers rarely leave an open gate unless they are working in the field.

'Slow down Sharpe and watch out ahead,' Ryland said, drawing his pistol. The others followed suit. 'Gill, keep an eye out behind for a transit van.'

'Who are you expecting?'

'Lombardi and Licciardi.'

'Maria Licciardi held me at gunpoint.' Melody said, looking behind.

'Leave them to us,' Boston said, 'and as a precaution, lie down on the seats and keep your heads down.'

'Why? What's happening?' Suzy asked.

'Just a precaution. It could be nothing and this vehicle is bulletproof.'

'Smoke eight hundred metres ahead, boss,' Sharpe said.

'Transit van coming up fast with a police car following,' Gill shouted.

'Slow down on the next bend Sharpe, Tyke, and I will bail out. I think they're going to ram us.'

The transit driver saw the minivan slowing and sped up, but as he reached the bend, two men were now leaning back into the hedgerow. The passenger in the transit opened his window and fired indiscriminately. Tyke was firing at the tyres, Ryland at the driver who hit the brakes at the same time as the bullet drilled a neat hole in the windscreen and hit his forehead. As the driver slumped forward, the van careered past them, out of control, and ploughed into the hedges on the bend.

'I'll get the passenger,' Ryland shouted, following the van whilst changing the magazine and pulling The Wolf's Glock 44 pistol from his waistband. He resumed firing at the passenger with both guns. Tyke turned his attention to the fake police Land Rover; it had come to a screeching halt and three passengers disembarked with combat rifles. Hopelessly outnumbered, he turned and ran for the cover of the transit. He could also hear gunfire ahead. Ryland had opened the passenger door of the transit and pulled the dead body onto the tarmac before clambering inside as the automatic rifles opened fire. Tyke used the open door for protection and returned fire. He considered the options. Three pistols against three combat rifles were poor odds. They were spraying bullets all over the van and twice Ryland had to lie flat in the back of the van, but as he got up for the third time, he noticed a wooden box behind the double passenger seat, inside were two Armalite AR-10s combat rifles. He shouted to Tyke and slid one of them out of the door onto the tarmac.

Tyke had kept them pinned down by hitting one man in the arm, forcing them to climb back into the Discovery. Now the Discovery headed directly at them. The passenger was again firing a constant volley as they approached, and one of them was firing from the open sunroof.

Ryland kicked open one of the back doors of the van and aimed at the driver of the approaching Land Rover, the reflection from the windscreen making it difficult to pinpoint his exact position. He fired off ten consecutive shots, moving from left to right. The second, third and fourth hit the driver in the head and neck, causing the car to slew round broadside before coming to rest across the road, allowing Tyke to recover the Armalite rifle. Three passengers jumped out and started shooting again.

The minivan Melody was in had stopped before the last bend, two hundred metres from where the smoke was spiralling upwards. Boston got out and climbed onto the roof with his sniper rifle. He could see three armed men. Two of them must have realised there was a problem and sensed their plan was unravelling. They were running in the minivan's direction. Smoke was now hiding the third man. Boston took down the lead runner with a headshot. The second man spotted him and returned fire. Boston did not flinch and fired two shots into his chest. 'Just one target left.' Boston shouted as he jumped down. 'Gill, you take the one round the bend, Sharpe, stay with the targets. I'll go back and assist the others.'

To the surprise of Suzy, Melody sat up and leaned over the back seat, rummaging in a Karki holdall. 'What are you doing, Mel?'

Melody pulled a pistol out of the bag and opened the door. 'I've had enough of this woman. She tried to kill me once before. It ends here.'

She could hear Sharpe calling for her to stop, but she ignored him and followed Boston, who had jumped off the roof and was running towards his stricken colleagues.

Boston joined Tyke behind the transit as Ryland continued to pin them down with rapid firing. Milo moved to the rear of the Land Rover and opened the boot. He emerged carrying a six-shot automatic M32 Grenade Launcher. As he fired off the first, Ryland threw himself over the passenger seat. The first grenade hit the open rear door, pushing the van further into the hedge and knocking Tyke and Boston off balance; the second one whistled past and through the hedgerow exploding when it hit a tree in the field. The two other assailants trapped them, keeping up a barrage of fire and preventing them from leaving the safety of the van.

Melody arrived at the bend and instantly recognised Maria and Salvatore firing at the transit. She dropped onto one knee as her eyes met Maria's. The memory of the hotel meeting flashed in her mind. Maria aimed at her and began firing.

Don't move, concentrate, take aim, pull the trigger slowly, and breathe in and hold. Her first shot hit Maria in the chest, the second her shoulder as it threw her off balance and she twisted, and the third hit her temple, killing her.

Melody felt the downdraft from the helicopter before she heard the rotors, then the distinctive clack, clack, clack from its front-mounted machine guns as the continuous burst of fire from the helicopter exploded the grenade launched at it. The chopper pilot then concentrated on the Land Rover. Within ten seconds, it also disintegrated. Milo, the man with the launcher, lay dead on the road. Salvatore looked at the body of Maria, then an escape route – a gap in the hedgerow – and made a run for it. The chopper flew past him and two men in fatigues abseiled

274

down to block his escape. Ryland, Tyke and Boston were now following, their guns aimed at the fleeing assailant. Sharpe reversed the minivan up behind them, with Gill hanging out of the side door.

Salvatore realised it was all over and dropped his weapon, holding up both hands. Melody walked up to join them.

'Are you OK?' Ryland asked Melody. holding out his hand to take the gun. She was violently shaking, then bent over and vomited. As she straightened, she handed over the pistol.

Ryland turned as the helicopter was landing in a field nearby. 'Melody, I need you to get in the chopper. Can you take Suzy with you?'

She nodded but couldn't speak.

'Sharpe, use the minivan to get them there. We'll stay and clear up here,' he yelled above the noise of the helicopter engines.

Sharpe burst the minivan through the gate, making a beeline for the helicopter. Two minutes later, it took off with Melody and Suzy on board. Melody was convulsing. Suzy reached for her, hugging and stroking her hair until they landed. Stuart was waiting at the helipad and took her directly to her room, where a doctor spoke to her before a nurse administered a sedative.

The team removed any trace of them being at the site before bundling Salvatore into the minivan and setting off across a field to pick up a different road and continue their journey to Sospitas.

* * *

The following day, Stuart Toulson was speaking to the Commander of Hertfordshire Police at their headquarters in Welwyn Garden City.

'We can probably put this down to a county-line drug feud,' the commander said. 'but what about Salvatore Lombardi? How will we explain him away?'

'Ah yes, the Viper. You needn't worry about him. A friend of mine at MI6 will contact you shortly. He is a "person of considerable interest" I understand. They'll pick him up from Sospitas,' Stuart said.

'Why would MI6 have an interest in him?'

'They don't, but the CIA does. Therefore, handing him over would be good P.R.'

Chapter Seventy-Three

~~

Stuart was having breakfast with Melody. 'How did you sleep last night?'

'I can barely remember any of the last few days,' Melody said. 'It must be the sedatives. I still feel a little woozy. The nurse was more than helpful. She gave me her mobile to call anytime.' She paused for a moment. 'I don't know what possessed me to get involved in the shooting. I keep getting flashbacks. What was I thinking?'

'Did you make an appointment to see the psychotherapist? Even hardened soldiers have PTSD. You'll need help.'

'Yes, the doctor was insistent. Look, I'm also sorry I overreacted to your intervention when we were flying home.'

'It's understandable. I know you wanted to do this for yourself. When we reviewed the mission profile, there was potential for conflicts of interest and many of them were a significant threat. We tried to keep as low a profile as possible, but when they diverted the flight to Italy, I considered it appropriate to increase our involvement at the risk of alienating you.'

'I'm glad you did. I became so focused on finding the swaddling, I often lost sight of the dangers.'

'Any regrets?'

'I should have stayed in the car yesterday, stupid of me, and I regret asking Farrokh Mokri to assist me. I put him and his family at risk. His family being held hostage by the Secret Police is down to me. He had no choice but to help them. I believe he gave them the wrong co-ordinates, which allowed us time to evade them. I'm not sure of his or his family's status now.'

'I'm trying to find out what the situation is. I still have some connections in the Middle East. But do not build your hopes up. Iran is a tightly controlled country.'

'Thank you, it would be wonderful if you could.'

'I understand the locksmith is arriving later today along with our dear friend Brodie.'

'Yes, today is the day I finally get to open the casket and discover its contents, if it has any. I felt certain it was in there, but now I'm unsure. Can I ask if it's OK for Suzy to stay here? She's not ready to go home yet and I need her at the moment.'

'Of course, I want you both to feel as comfortable as possible. We did a background check on her and she's clean as a whistle. What next, though, is it over now?'

'No, whatever happens when we open the casket, I still need to see Anatoly and possibly Cardinal Poggi. It's the least I can do.'

'We presumed Anatoly was working on behalf of Nikolai. They were close business partners for a long time.'

'I think most people did, but when he explained what his interest in the swaddling was, my heart warmed to him. Would you like you to be there when I meet them or have you got something planned for the near future?'

'I've cleared my diary. Ryland can look after the day-to-day operational matters. I'd love to spend more time with you. Can we have dinner tonight?'

'I cannot think of anything I'd like better. Afterwards, you can show me your grand apartment here at Sospitas. Everyone says how beautiful it is.'

* * *

Melody spent the rest of the morning showing Suzy around and was talking to Brodie when the receptionist entered the small conference room.

'Mr Bolt is here.'

Melody and Suzy exchanged glances.

'Thank you,' Stuart said. 'Please show him in.'

Bolt entered carrying his well-worn leather attaché case and Melody stepped forward to greet him.

'You know most of us, Mr Bolt, but this is Stuart Toulson,' she said. 'This is John Bolt, the renowned locksmith.' They shook hands, and Stuart gestured over to a side table containing the casket.

'I trust you had a pleasant stay in Oxford, Miss Thornton,' Bolt said whilst placing his case next to the casket.

'Uneventful,' she said. She could feel Suzy looking at her, but ignored it.

'Would you like me to open it or would you prefer to be the one to do it for the first time in two thousand years?' He held up two keys.

Suzy spoke first. 'Mel, it has to be you. After all you've been through, you must open it.'

'OK, though I admit I'm a little apprehensive.'

'This one is for the left and this is for the right,' Bolt said, presenting the keys. 'Turn the left one left and the right one right simultaneously.'

As she moved toward it, the room fell silent. The keys felt heavier than she expected. She inserted them and took a deep breath. Her heart was beating fast. Then she turned the keys. There was a pronounced click. She stepped back, her hands on her face, before she moved forward and opened the casket. The smell of lavender seemed to fill the room. She felt heady, almost euphoric. And yet a genuine sense of peace came over her as she stared into the empty casket.

No one spoke. Melody continued to stare. Stuart moved beside her and put a comforting arm around her shoulder as she picked up the small piece of parchment attached by wax and closed the lid.

'I don't understand. If it's not here, what produces the different fragrances? Just smell how strong the scent of lavender is,' Melody said, remembering the precious words spoken by the angel.

'Chosen, you are now the guardian of the swaddling. Peace be with you.' An angel could not lie or make a mistake. What am I missing?

'Perhaps it has just seeped into the lining,' Suzy said, breaking into her thoughts and squeezing her hand.

'What does the note say?' Stuart asked.

'It's in Avestan, almost all their writings were.' Melody read it, then re-read it, twice. Her face lit up, and she turned to face everyone, her hand over her mouth again. She was trembling.

'I know where the swaddling is. Stuart, we need to contact Anatoly Artamonovsky and Cardinal Poggi right away. The sooner the better.'

Tears began to flow down her cheeks.

Everyone else was confused.

Chapter Seventy-Four

Anatoly Artamonovsky was staying in Vatican City when the call came from Stuart Toulson. The conversation was brief and ended with Stuart saying, 'Let me know when your flight arrives in London and I'll get the helicopter to pick you up.'

Following the call, Anatoly did three things. First, he called Felix Breunig; 'We're leaving for London. Pack your things.'

Second, he called Cardinal Poggi. 'I don't know the full details yet, but Stuart Toulson, who is acting on behalf of Melody Thornton, wants to negotiate the ultimate resting place for the swaddling. Frankly, I didn't know they had recovered it. Can you have the plans for its secure storage delivered to my suite in the next hour?'

'I had given up hope,' Cardinal Poggi said. 'However, the plans are as complete as they are comprehensive. I'll have one of my staff walk them over now.'

Third, he arranged for his jet to take Felix Breunig and him to London.

Chapter Seventy-Five

Suzy held Melody's arm, preventing her from walking any further. 'First, tell me what the doctor said.'

'He said a traumatic event can have lasting effects, including flashbacks. He talked about Cognitive Behaviour Therapy. I'll let you know how I get on.'

'And second, it's been three days. Now I insist you tell me where the swaddling is. The suspense is killing me and I know you've already told your boyfriend. What did the message say? Stop teasing me.'

'Stop referring to him as my boyfriend, but he has asked me to go on holiday with him when this saga ends.'

Suzy tried a fresh approach. 'I missed you last night eating on my lonesome. What was his apartment like? Did you stay over?' she asked, feigning sadness.

'The apartment is to die for. You would love it, it could appear in the *Beautiful Homes Magazine* – four bedrooms and five bathrooms, it virtually takes up the top floor and no, I didn't stay over. I had the guest suite.' There was a long pause and then a sigh. 'I'm very fond of him, but I don't love him. It's complicated.'

Suzy sensed it was time to change the subject. 'Tell me about the swaddling. What did the message say, and where is it?'

'Well, roughly translated, the message said, "Gold does not require a silver lining". Which of course it doesn't, it sounds obvious. Why would gold have a silver lining? It wouldn't make sense to gild something with an inferior metal. They originally made the casket to carry the gold as a gift to the newborn king. They wouldn't have had a padded lining in it.'

'And?' Suzy said, holding her palms up.

'The lining is the swaddling; they hid it in the casket as a lining. That's the reason the fragrance is always present. It hadn't contaminated the lining; it is the lining.'

'Of course, it sounds obvious now, but how will you get it out without damaging it?'

'A specialist antique fabric restoration expert John Bolt knows is on her way here to remove it.'

'I understand Anatoly and Felix are also visiting.'

'They are already here. However, I insisted they settle in before we have dinner together and talk business.'

* * *

What concerned Anatoly about his visit was twofold. Would the plans the Vatican had drawn up be satisfactory to her? And what exactly had Melody meant in Italy when he last saw her and her parting words? 'I have something important to tell you, but not here, not now.'

Stuart, Melody and Ryland were waiting for them when the maître d' escorted Anatoly, Felix and Suzy to the table. 'Welcome everyone,' Stuart said, standing, as they took their seats.

Felix spoke. 'I was just saying to Suzy what a magnificent place you have here, Stuart.'

Melody replied. 'I'm glad you met up with her, but be careful. She's a reporter. Anything you say will be taken down in evidence, then appear in the newspaper.' Her humour settled the atmosphere.

'Cardinal Poggi sends his regards but is desperate to know the answer to the million-dollar question. How did you recover the swaddling?' Anatoly said.

'Let me put you out of your misery,' Melody said. 'The stolen casket was a decoy, a fake one. I had a replica made while I was in Turkmenbashi. I had the real one in my possession. You told me why you wanted it and what you subsequently intended to do, and I would like to honour your wishes if possible. The tip-off from the Cardinal and the early intervention of you and Felix was probably lifesaving.'

Stuart spoke next. 'Under normal circumstances, Melody would like to accommodate your wishes,' he said, elaborating. 'However, Russia is not a country to visit unannounced, least of all with an article they have shown a great deal of interest in. Many would regard Russia as corrupt, though I prefer to say perfidious, don't you agree?'

'I assume you require me to seek guarantees for the safety of all involved.'

'Naturally, but there is also a delicate matter I believe only the Russians can help us with, and at this stage of the negotiations I need someone on the inside, a son of the Mother Country, to oil the wheels, so to speak.'

'What is the delicate matter and what are you offering them?'

'An envoy of the Russian Ambassador here in England has informed us that a very high-ranking official at the Kremlin has a five-year-old child who is on life support and it's only a question of time before they switch it off. In addition, the Iranian Ayatollah Amini has a child also on life support who would be part of the overall deal.'

'And in return?'

'I have friends in Iran,' Melody said, 'who are in custody or under surveillance. The authorities must release them and allow them to come to England.'

'We also understand someone dear to you desperately needs healing,' Stuart said. 'And subsequently, Melody would like the home of the swaddling to be the British Museum, whereas the Vatican would like it to live there. The proposal she is offering would see it alternating bi-annually. There would, however, be certain provisos and a guarantee of its safekeeping.'

'I don't foresee a problem, and I have the Vatican proposals with me,' Anatoly said. 'The issue is – what are the certain provisos and what is the delicate matter you believe only the Russians can help you with?'

'Ah,' Stuart said, 'the zone of possible agreement. I would like to discuss this with you privately later, perhaps over a brandy. We have a Cognac Brugerolles 1795. It is said that a bottle accompanied Napoleon during his quest to conquer the world.'

Chapter Seventy-Six

Yevgeny Chuychenko, deputy head of the Russian Federal Security Service, put his hand on Stuart's shoulder. 'I'm so glad we met, at last, Stuart. So many times, our paths have crossed, how do you say, "like ships in the night" and now you are here in the flesh. Welcome to Russia. I was in London recently when you left us a gift at the gates of our embassy.' His voice went to a whisper. 'It saved a lot of embarrassment. You know how it is. Sometimes rogue elements surface from time to time.'

'Can I say, Yevgeny, how overjoyed Melody was when you arranged through your diplomatic channels to get Farrokh Mokri and his family out of Iran and, of course, her other friends, Dilshod and Soraya. Only you could have accomplished such a delicate issue.'

'It's true, though I had to lean on a few people and it was useful to have Anatoly greasing a few palms. But it was the least we could do. How is Farrokh settling in?'

'They have a house in Oxford and are enjoying life there. Farrokh lectures at Magdalen College. And now we have met formally, I hope we can open a more direct line of communication in the future. Calling one's friends for a favour occasionally can sometimes blow away the mists of subterfuge, don't you agree?'

'I couldn't agree more. Now, are you satisfied with the security arrangements for your visit later today?'

'Impressive. I always say the Russians do two things better than most nations. First, a military show of strength to discourage interlopers.'

'And the second?'

'Vodka.'

Yevgeny laughed. 'I would have put vodka first,' he said, lifting his shot glass of Beluga Noble Vodka. 'Cheers Stuart.'

'Ura, Yevgeny,'

The knock on the door interrupted them. 'Enter,' Yevgeny said.

'The cavalcade is ready when you are, comrade, and Miss Thornton is waiting,' he said, handing a note to Yevgeny.

'Thank you,' he said before turning to Stuart. 'He's old school.'

'Ah, the good old days, when one knew who one's enemies were?'

'Those were the days. But now, who knows, are we friends with Turkey, or are they our darkest enemy?'

'I couldn't possibly comment. I'd hate to poison your relationship.'

'You see,' Yevgeny said, laughing, 'that's what I love about the British, their sense of humour, "poison your relationship,"' he repeated. 'Come, let us join the cavalcade. Besides, we mustn't keep the lady waiting any longer.' He was speaking whilst reading the note as they walked. 'Oh, and just so you know, the Kremlin has announced the president's five-year-old daughter has fully recovered. Indeed, they may even give you a medal for this. I must admit, at first, I was sceptical.'

'Is the security convoy aware of the need for privacy during their next visit?' Stuart asked.

'They understand the need for discretion. A small detachment will take Melody and Anatoly closer to the house, but will remain concealed.'

'We appreciate your discretion.'

'I believe your party has one more visit here and is then leaving for the Vatican. We will miss you, Stuart. Our conversations have been illuminating. However, before you leave,' he stopped and held Stuart's arm. 'We seem to have a rogue operator in the UK. You may help us locate him. The Americans released him in a deal,' Yevgeny said, handing him a brown A4 envelope.

Stuart opened it whilst walking and withdrew a picture of Salvatore Lombardi. He slid it back and smiled.

The convoy of six vehicles was impressive and whisked them off to the rural area of Anatoly's childhood. Anatoly felt anxious as he approached the cottage with Melody. It had been several years since his last visit, but the memories flooded back. The cottage looked smaller, and the garden more overgrown, but the Virginia Creeper looked magnificent. Alana was at the door in her wheelchair, giddily waiting to greet them.

'Anatoly, I am so pleased to see you again. You must tell me the full story. Come in, leave nothing out, including this beautiful lady friend.' Alana was trying to sound upbeat, but it was a great effort. She looked pale, weak and chesty. They sat drinking tea and Anatoly told the entire story, starting with her father, Uncle Mikhail, reminding her of the Nativity story he told each Christmas regarding the Magi and the swaddling, his connection with Cardinal Poggi, and eventually the events in Italy, and Melody.

'I am disappointed, Anatoly. I thought this was your girlfriend. She's lovely,' Alana said.

'She is lovely, but she's spoken for. Anyway, enough about us. Now, do you understand what we are here for today?'

'Yes, but I'm extremely nervous,' Alana said.

Melody put a hand on Alana's arm. 'Are you afraid it will heal you or are you afraid it may not?'

'For the last two weeks, I have dreamt of what life would be like. I have had dreams of running freely, throwing this prison of a wheelchair away. But, at the back of my mind…' Alana's eyes filled up.

'Now here's an added incentive for you,' Melody said, putting the casket on Alana's lap. 'If you can guess the fragrance you will smell when I open this casket, Anatoly has promised to give you a hundred thousand roubles.'

Alana laughed a little as she wiped tears from her eyes using her sleeve. 'Any fragrance?' she asked, still wiping away the tears.

'Any, it's different every day and not one person has guessed it correctly so far. It can be anything from freshly cut hay to wildflowers, fruit, blossom, woodland, absolutely anything that smells wonderful to you or, more importantly, reminds you of something or someone special.'

'OK,' Alana said, sitting more upright. 'I'm going to say, I want it to smell like my father's study did.'

Now Anatoly's eyes filled up.

Melody turned the keys and opened the casket.

Alana closed her eyes and inhaled deeply. She was nodding and smiling; she opened her eyes, and her entire face lit up. 'It's exactly how I remember it – musty old books and a cardigan smelling of pipe tobacco.'

Melody looked at Anatoly. 'It does. I would never have believed it.' Anatoly said, leaning closer and sniffing. 'I remember the smell so well. Amazing.'

'I'm ready now,' Alana said.

'Now for the big prize,' Melody said, draping the swaddling around her neck. The two ends fell loosely over her folded arms.

As usual, nothing seemed to happen. Then it began. Alana rocked back and forth. After several minutes, the rocking stopped. Melody stepped back ten paces.

'What do I do now?'

'Stand up and walk to me,' Melody said.

Anatoly held out one hand to encourage her, but Alana shook her head. 'No. Not this time.' She put both hands on the arms of the wheelchair and, with a look of stubborn determination, began pushing herself up. Once upright on the carpet, she steadied her swaying body. Then, falteringly, at first, she walked towards Melody. By the time she reached her, all three were crying with the odd burst of laughter in between. They hugged for so long Melody's arms were aching, but she wouldn't let go. Alana insisted on walking as much as possible, but eventually she reluctantly agreed to sit down.

She was so tired. 'I don't want to sit down; I may not get up again,' she said, partly laughing and partly concerned.

'We have to go now, Alana,' Melody said. 'This has been one of the happiest days of my life. I'm so pleased to have met you. And not only are you completely healed, but you are also a hundred thousand rubles better off. Make sure he gives it to you.'

'Will you be healing others now?'

'I'm not healing them. Cardinal Poggi once told me only Jesus can miraculously heal, and the swaddling is simply a physical manifestation of his power. There's an example recorded in the bible in the book of Acts. Chapter nineteen says, "The Apostle Paul performed extraordinary miracles, curing illnesses and expelling evil spirits through handkerchiefs and aprons that had touched him."'

'Why won't you carry on helping to heal sick people?'

'Even if I lived to be a hundred, I could not heal everyone in need, not even in the United Kingdom, let alone the world. And anyway, how would I choose? Your healing and two others are part of a deal with Iran. Afterwards, there will be no more.'

'What if someone takes it from you?'

'The Lady Mary said you cannot take the swaddling; it has to be given, like a gift. Mary gave it to the Magi and their descendants as a blessing, not to save the world. She said that would take a far greater sacrifice.'

Chapter Seventy-Seven

~~~

It was so quiet in the private hospital suite in Moscow. 'She is beautiful and looks so angelic, but also so fragile. How long has she been on a ventilator?' Melody asked.

'It seems like forever. They wanted permission to switch it off,' Ayatollah Amina said, pulling his wife Jasmine closer, 'but we couldn't bring ourselves to do it. We were hoping for a miracle. When I discovered what you were attempting, it felt like our last hope.' He looked close to tears. A broken man. 'I have been a long-time admirer of your work, Miss Thornton,' he continued. 'Jasmine says I've watched far too many of your seminars on YouTube.' He smiled. 'In another life and under different circumstances, I would have loved to have joined you.' His face showed a mixture of regret and wistfulness.

'I didn't feel able to search through official channels,' Melody said. 'I thought I would lose control.'

'Yes, I understand. We need to be more transparent and co-operative in matters of international importance. When I realised you were looking for the swaddling, I tried to ensure we did not hinder you.'

'I am so pleased you now want me to lead an official expedition to the site. It's a fascinating place, with so many objects to study, you'll love it. The Ministry of Cultural Heritage has already been in touch, though they want to keep it secret for now, to avoid "Tomb Raiders". I look forward to you joining me there.'

'Believe me when I say I meant you no harm. My instructions were explicit: no harm should come to you. Some, however, became confused and over-zealous regarding their mission, and I apologise. It was always going to be a request – an act of free will. Even now, at this late stage, you are under no obligation. You are free to walk away.'

'I am more than happy to proceed,' Melody said, looking at baby Gulzaar and the attached monitoring equipment. The nurse attending her had smiled from the moment they arrived.

'There is always a fragrance when I open the casket and it is different on each occasion,' she said, turning the keys and lifting the lid. The smell of roses filled the room, bringing gasps of delight from Jasmine.

'The name Gulzaar is Persian for "a garden of roses". Surely it is a sign,' Jasmine said, turning to her husband. He smiled at her.

Melody placed the cloth over the baby's body and stood back. The only sound in the room now was the gentle hiss of the ventilator and the bleeps from the monitors.

As always, nothing happened at first. The nurse was alternately looking at the baby and the monitors. Ayatollah stepped forward. 'You can switch the machine off now,' he said to the nurse. His wife moved beside him and gripped his arm.

A complete silence enveloped them as the nurse removed all support, switched off the machines, and stood back, wringing her hands. They watched as the baby rolled from side to side. They held their breath when she stopped moving, stopped breathing, but moments later baby Gulzaar cried, a low grumbling plaintive cry at first, followed by a louder heartfelt cry, and then she sobbed. Her mum picked her up and cuddled her, and the baby's howling stopped. Melody watched as the child breathed comfortably against her mother's chest.

Now all the adults were crying.

There are always tears.

Chapter Seventy-Eight

~~~

Six Months Later

It was perfect weather for a wedding. There was a gentle breeze, and the sky was clear. 'How are the bridesmaids doing?' Suzy asked Melody.

'The two older ones, Laila and Brooke, look amazing. They've done this before, so they're more experienced than I am and the outfits are perfect. Blossom is more of a struggle, though. Her attention span is noticeably short, and she doesn't like her mum fussing with her hair, but she looks gorgeous.'

'Well, she is only four years old. How is her mum coping?'

'She's more stressed than I am! But at least baby River is content with Dad.' They both chuckled. 'I thought being Maid of Honour would freak me out, but I'm loving it. I'm so pleased for Dilshod and Soraya. They both helped me so much in Iran and to see them getting married is such a joy.'

'I'm not sure you told me the full story of how she got out of Iran?'

'Stuart put a deal together and Anatoly used his connection in the Kremlin to get it accepted. I had to use the swaddling to heal both the Russian president's baby and Ayatollah Amani's. In return, the Iranians let Farrokh Mokri, his family, and Soraya leave the country. They also permitted me to use the swaddling on Alana, the cousin of Anatoly. But not his friend Nikolai.'

'Was Soraya the woman he met in Iran?'

'Yes, she was the receptionist at the hospital. Her help saved me from capture.'

'Was this after the bear mauled you?'

'Yes, then after we parted in Azerbaijan, Dilshod went back for her, but her whole family was under surveillance. Although they were meeting in secret, they fell in love. As part of the deal, they allowed them to seek political asylum in the UK.'

'This story just gets better and better.'

'I know, incidentally, I've seated you next to Ryland at the reception. It's obvious you have a crush on him, I can tell.'

'I know. I think it must be Stockholm Syndrome.' They both started laughing again. 'I've missed you these last few months,' Suzy said.

'So have I,' Melody said, moving towards the Lychgate with the bridesmaids clutching their bowls of rose petals, nervously expecting the wedding car. The sun was shining, and the groomsmen were laughing and joking as they welcomed guests at the church entrance. Blossom was in her mum's arms, but getting grumpy at all the fuss people were making of her.

Anatoly strolled over to Melody. 'Will you cry today?'

'Probably, the story is about to end,' she said, then turned to the bridesmaids. 'Come on girls; get ready, the car's approaching.'

* * *

The sniper had settled down in the woodland overlooking the church. The camouflage outfit made it almost impossible to see him. He checked the wind speed again, then adjusted the sight for the light breeze and refocused. This time, Melody appeared perfect in his crosshairs. He smiled with satisfaction.

There was no noise; he just felt the metal of the pistol silencer on the back of his head, pushing it away from the sights.

'You are indeed a slippery character, Mr Lombardi. No wonder they call you the Viper. Put the rifle down,' Ryland said.

'Mr Carlisle, I expected you to be at the wedding.'

'I am. I'm a groomsman.'

'She killed my partner. You understand, don't you? Look, I have money. If you let me go, you won't see me again. We can call it quits. Quid pro quo.'

'You're fifty per cent right. Although you do not have enough money, you were correct in not seeing me again. I also have a message from Yevgeny Chuychenko.'

'What is it? What are you waiting for?' Lombardi asked as the wedding car pulled up and Soraya stepped out. The bridesmaids scattered rose petals, and the church bells chimed.

'Therefore, send not to know. For whom the bell tolls, it tolls for thee,' Ryland said as he pulled the trigger.

Chapter Seventy-Nine

~~~

Nikolai Levanevsky lay in his bed as his nurse Sasha entered. She glanced up at the wall clock and noticed it had stopped. The empty casket lay open on his bedside cabinet.

She checked his pulse, removed the cannula from his arm and closed his eyes. Then she pulled the bedsheet over his face, drew the curtains, closed the fake casket and left to inform Anatoly, who was in the relatives' waiting room, of his death.

Chapter Eighty

~~~

Perhaps it had been the excitement of the wedding so soon after all that had happened. 'Too many highs and not enough normal,' Suzy had told her. Whatever the reason, Melody felt low, unsettled, as if it wasn't over. Like leaving a cinema before the film had ended.

The visions have stopped. Still, something is missing, incomplete and unsatisfying. But what and why?

'Are you alright?' Stuart asked.

'Yes!' His words, though, were like an uninvited guest, bringing her back from a far-off place. 'I feel as though it hasn't ended, but I'm not sure why?'

'Looking back at your audience with the Cardinal, I seem to remember he made several points. His overarching comment was God plays the "long game" and we don't know what the end game looks like. He also pointed out this could simply be part one and others will take up the mantle.'

'I know, but I still have this feeling of unfinished business.'

'I believe his last observation was the most informative. A life you were involved in saving could be the one to accomplish his plan. Perhaps they'll become a world leader or discover a cure for cancer. Who knows? You have played your part, relax and accept all you've accomplished. The swaddling is being talked about all over the world. Your name is the top hit on Google. Also, I agree with the Cardinal when he said, two thousand years ago, God chose you. Remember, God plays the long game.'

She kissed him on the cheek. 'It's time for me to lie down and rest for a while. I feel tired. I'll be fine later,' she said, trying to smile but failing. Once she made it to the bedroom, her head had barely touched the pillow when an encounter started.

I don't want any more, surely it's over now. Leave me alone, I found it. She fought to stay conscious, but a sense of expectation had replaced the sense of despair, and it led her even deeper, as the darkness descended…

* * *

She was with Melker again, and still in Egypt. It was familiar. The market was busy as she walked with him towards the large imposing City Gate.

The background sounds are sharper and my sense of smell is keener. Something feels different. I want to stay and explore the market. Why? What's happening to me?

The men who were waiting at the gate spotted Melker and began cheering. Several ran to meet and hug him. She recognised many of them. A rag-a-muffin band of hardened soldiers, but as playful as children.

What is happening? The story is over; I found the swaddling. Let me go.

More loud cheering came as Lord Melchior and Captain Hormoz joined them. The relief on Lord Melchior's face was clear to see, and after a long embrace, the entire group headed out to their temporary camp.

'Let us eat together tonight, just you and me. You can update me on your exploits. All I know so far is you discovered them safe and well in Alexandria,' Melchior said to his son.

'It was the strangest of encounters. I look forward to retelling it. But not here and not now,' he paused. 'Strangely, father, Mary used the same phrase. There was something about her countenance that disarmed me, the words softly spoken, yet with such authority, a complete lack of fear, almost blind to the dangers of the present, and overwhelming and complete confidence in the future?'

'You must tell me all about it later.'

Supper was a quiet affair for Melker and his father, though occasionally interrupted by the sounds of the camp outside still celebrating their triumph and the prospect of rejoining the caravan and returning home.

Melker recounted the entire conversation with Mary, including how he sobbed when she gave him the blessing. 'It was as if her words burned deep into my soul.'

'I too had a similar experience in Bethlehem. Mine ended in laughter, yours in tears. She speaks to your heart, not to your head. I tell you, I could have remained in her presence, time without end. Now, listening to you recount her instructions,' he paused, 'what was it she said? "Your father has played his part. For him, the noble quest is over, and he must now return home". Remind me, Melker, what was the ending?'

'Knowing that his role was greater than he can ever imagine.'

'Yes, fine words.'

'You must write them down, father, lest you forget.'

'Yes, I will, and knowing the swaddling will be safe gives me a sense of closure and a feeling of peace. I'm sure Mary knew it would be in safe hands, even before handing it to you.'

'Do you have a secure place in mind?'

Melchior stood and looked directly at Melody, and smiled.

It shocked Melody. *He can see me; he has always seen me.*

'Indeed, I have,' he said, staring into Melody's eyes and nodding. 'Strange as it may sound, Melker. I believe I know who will discover it, and I am confident she will be an eminently suitable guardian. But now it is time for us all to go home.'

At last, it was over. Melody's tears fell unseen onto her pillow.

There's More to the Story

~

If you enjoyed Melody's story, look out for the first book in this trilogy.

The Swaddling

Making of the Magi
Coming soon

Everyone has heard the Nativity story, but this is the tale told from a spiritual perspective. A behind-the-scenes glimpse of what happened before and during the birth of Jesus.

Who were the Magi?

Characters in The Swaddling: Search for the Healing Cloth

~~

Melody Thornton – Main protagonist

Farrokh Mokri – Iranian friend from university

Prof. Broderick Kearney AKA Brodie – Family friend and past tutor at Magdalen College

John Bolt - Forensic locksmith

Sospitas

Stuart Toulson – Head of Cherished Anti-Surveillance (Sospitas)

Ryland Carlisle – Trainer and right-hand man to Stuart Toulson ex SAS

Tyke – Close protection officer

Gilford - Close protection officer

Sage – Tech Expert & covert surveillance

Landon Bailey – Freelance operative

Sharpe – Sospitas driver

Boston – Close protection officer

Gill - Close protection officer

Iran

IRCG Commander - Iranian Embassy in London

Zaynab Gilani – IRCG Commander in Tehran. Iran

Hossein – Gilani's assistant

The Regional Director of MOIS - Tehran. Iran.

Ayatollah Ahmad Amini - Iran

Farad El Sayed – Assassin, agent and spy for the Iranian Govt

Russian Billionaire Group

Nikolai Levanevsky – Russian Oligarch

Anatoly Artamonovsky – PA to Nikolai, also a billionaire

Ivan – Nikolai's Brother in law

Grigoriy - Nikolai's Brother in law

Vasily Valkov – AKA The Wolf. Assassin.

Sasha – Private nurse

Salvatore Lombardi – (Fake Priest) AKA the Viper. Assassin.

Maria Licciardi– (Fake Nun) AKA Praying Mantis. Assassin.

Milo – Getaway driver. Italian ex-Mafia.

Mikhail Artamonovsky – Uncle of Anatoly

Alana – Daughter of Mikhail and cousin of Anatoly, suffers from muscular dystrophy

Vatican

Cardinal Raffaele Poggi – Cardinal at the Vatican (relic hunter)

Erwin Friedrich Escher – Head of Vatican Bank

Father Elmer Janssen

Kremlin

Mikhail Gorbachev – President USSR

Boris Nikolayevich Yeltsin - First Secretary USSR.

Yevgeny Chuychenko – Deputy head of the Federal Security Service

Iran Camp Team

Amooz – Team Leader in Iran

Dilshod Karimova - Chief guide in Iran, Born in Uzbekistan. Worked in Azerbaijan.

Karus – Lead scout

Dawar- Lead scout

Zubeen – Head chef at camp in Iran.

Jadu – AKA Jad. Specialist in drone photography.

Nouri - Equipment, and communications

Farzad – Chief Archaeologist

Mechanic – not named

Melody's Visions & Magi Characters

Mary and Joseph

Melchior – Senior Magus. Gift of prophecy.

Balthazar – Magus. Gift of healing.

Caspar – Magus. Gift of seeing and talking to angels.

Melker – Melchior's son. Gifting Visions of past.

Troopers

Captain Hormoz

Joubin – Archer

Zhakfar – Chief Scout & Tracker

Musa – Swordsmanship

Roshan – Stable master & horsemanship

Faraj – Horsemanship

Bashkir – Scout

Hospital

Soraya – Hospital receptionist

Aytan Sharifi – Hospital Nurse

Airline and Hotels in Italy

Suzy Marash – Reporter Jewish Chronicle

Hannah Weil – Air Marshall /Cabin crew

Bill McGann - Air Marshall /Cabin crew

Rivka - Senior cabin crew member

Felix Breunig – Austrian American, ex NYPD homicide

Vasily Valkov – AKA The Wolf. Assassin

Oswald Cox – Working for Vatican

Commissario Renzo Ponti - Polizia di Stato

Marco Casale - Sostituto Commissario

Mossad

Fania Landver - Israeli Deputy Minister of Defence

Avraham Feinstein AKA Avi – Mossad Station Commander

Shayna - Avraham Feinstein Deputy

General Kadish Shamir - Israeli Air Force

Colonel Rafi Ginzburg - Israeli Air Force

Ezra - Local Mossad agent in Treviso

Additional Characters

Catherine Emerich – 16th Century Nun

King Herod

The King's Chamberlain

Melody's Journey

~~~

- Flight from the UK to Iran
- From Iran by road to Turkmenbashi in Turkmenistan
- Ferry from Turkmenbashi across the Caspian Sea to Baku in Azerbaijan
- Flight from Baku to Jordan
- Taxi from Jordan to Bethlehem in Israel
- Flight from Tel Aviv diverted to Treviso in Italy
- Flight from Italy to the UK

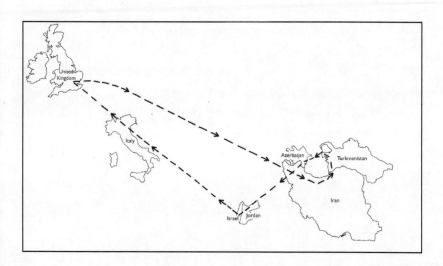

Acknowledgements

~~

I would like to give special thanks to Mark Stibbe for his developmental and structural editing. I appreciate his faith in me to complete this book, his wisdom in suggesting a trilogy, and his encouragement to enter the Page Turner Awards.

Thanks also for an early edit from my dear friend Pete Boydell, whose comments were encouraging and insightful.

Thank you to the later work of Andrew Chamberlain and his team at the British Christian Writers Conference. His editing was great and the workshops were so fruitful.

Also, a superb edit, feedback and encouragement from my friend and author Heather Cursham. I would also like to mention my friend Eden Devaney whose painstaking work was invaluable.

My final editor, Lydia Jenkins, for her much-needed detailed editing advice. Thank you for your patience. You are a star.

Finally, my loving wife Helen and the rest of my family, who have all encouraged me to complete the task.